The Romantic Tragedies of a DRAMA KING

Praise for

The Romantic Tragedies of a DRAMA KING

'*The Romantic Tragedies of a Drama King* is a spectacular and dazzling debut, filled with so much heart, humour and warmth, it is THE perfect teen romcom! A total delight to read.'
Beth Reekles, bestselling author of *The Kissing Booth*

'Funny, voicey and fresh. Patch makes Georgia Nicolson seem demure and composed'
Elle McNicoll, author of *Some Like it Cold*

'Funny and full of heart, Patch is up there with the great whingers Adrian Mole, Georgia Nicolson, and Bridget Jones'
Monica Heisey, bestselling author of *Really Good, Actually*

'A rarity of a novel that had me laughing out loud from the very first page. I loved it'
Tanya Reynolds

'*The Romantic Tragedies of a Drama King* is nothing short of perfect, a joy from start to finish. Patch is Gen Alpha's Adrian Mole'
Rebecca Humphries

The Romantic Tragedies of a DRAMA KING

HARRY
TREVALDWYN

FIRST INK

FIRST INK

Published 2025 by First Ink,
an imprint of Pan Macmillan
The Smithson, 6 Briset Street, London EC1M 5NR
EU representative: Macmillan Publishers Ireland Ltd, 1st Floor,
The Liffey Trust Centre, 117–126 Sheriff Street Upper
Dublin 1, D01 YC43
Associated companies throughout the world
www.panmacmillan.com

ISBN 978-1-0350-4920-2

1 3 5 7 9 8 6 4 2

A CIP catalogue record for this book is available from the British Library.

Printed and bound by CPI Group (UK) Ltd, Croydon CR0 4YY

To all the romances that couldn't happen,
and all the ones that still can.

Dear Jean-Pierre,

I regret to inform you that this will be the last letter you ever receive from me. You see, this year I have decided to get a boyfriend and unfortunately (for you) I simply don't have the time to both continue my pen-pal responsibilities and give this new task the focus it requires.

I don't want to lie to you and say that getting a boyfriend is the only reason I'm stopping my letters. I think, Jean-Pierre, you are partly to blame. We have been writing letters to each other for nearly two years now and there hasn't been the slightest hint that you'll invite me to France despite me having invited you to my house several times. Invitations which you have, rather rudely, ignored. There was also the issue last year when you addressed your letter to someone called 'Felix' and in the process made it abundantly clear that ours was not an exclusive writing relationship. Have you invited Felix to Normandy, Jean Pierre?? Don't even bother responding to that because I shan't reply. Lastly, and I don't quite know when this happened, but I've noticed that we now write all of our letters in English and because of this, my French has not improved <u>at all</u>. I wish you well and I hope that life is kind to you and despite all of this I genuinely hope that you get into the tennis team this year. I know how important that is to you.

But like I said, this is the last you will ever hear from me,

Kind regards, à bientôt,

Patrick Simmons (Patch)

PS In your first-ever letter, you attached a Milka chocolate bar (which was quite the incentive for keeping up our pen-pal relationship, and I wrongly assumed they would be a regular addition to your letters). I think it would be a really classy and symbolic move to send me one more as a final 'adieu' to our writing relationship. Also, they are really quite hard to find here. OK, now <u>that</u> is the last you'll ever hear from me, properly this time.

Au Revoir!

Patrick Simmons (Patch)

xxx

Chapter 1

I cross out the kisses at the end of my letter because I think it undermines the gravity of what I'm saying. My chair creaks as I lean back and hold the letter up for inspection. Faultless penmanship, as always.

I do feel a bit guilty for ending my pen-pal relationship with Jean-Pierre but 'in order to make room for new relationships in my life I have to de-weed the ones that aren't bearing fruit'. I learned that phrase from one of my mum's self-help books, which I've taken to borrowing on a semi-short-term basis. If you look past the tacky covers there are some real pearls of wisdom there. It's fascinating how much is applicable to both a divorcee in her mid-forties and a queer sixteen-year-old; especially as we're both desperately seeking a man. While, *of course*, seeming to be happy on our own in order to lure them in. Ah, Jean-Pierre, au revoir!

It's worth noting that I have been in love twice before. The first time was with Fred; very charming with neat blond hair and a penchant for accessories. The problem was that he was an animated character on *Scooby-Doo*. I appreciate that he was romantically linked with Daphne but I always felt their chemistry to be somewhat lacking. Fred took charge which I found very appealing (but now find a bit problematic) and he, alongside Velma, was a large factor of why the gang had such a high success rate when I don't think any of them were formally trained in detective work. The second time was with Josh, who was definitely a real person, but things turned sour when I discovered he was a paid babysitter rather than a seventeen-year-old genuinely interested in my origami and who weirdly enjoyed enforcing bedtimes.

You have to be *organized* in order to fall in love so I've given myself a 'boyfriend deadline'. The end of the school year feels much too far away; I'm ready to take the leap *now* and I'll get complacent if the deadline's too far in the future. Also I'm terrible at being patient. So, I've marked in my diary (with a big red heart) the perfect deadline: <u>Prom</u>. Our school doesn't do *actual* Prom, but my Drama Club puts on a party after the first big show which everyone calls 'Prom'. Apart from Ms Jenkins, who runs it, because she thinks that '*Americanisms* are melting our mind', which is ridiculous because America is responsible for such incredible things! Off the top of my head: Kelly Clarkson, the Hollywood sign and cereals so sweet they make your teeth shake. I even tried suggesting a big family holiday to America under the guise of 'political intrigue' but Mum quickly sniffed out it was for the cereals, so we went to Devon instead. Regardless, Prom is the *perfect* time to have a boyfriend:

Why Prom is the PERFECT time to have a boyfriend:

- Proms are romantic (ask any film).
- There's a photo element (it is so important to professionally document love).
- I won't have to spend an awkward amount of time pretending to browse the crisp selection when the slow songs come on.
- It's in December, so I'll probably receive a thoughtful and romantic Christmas present from him (jewellery seems a bit obvious, but also I want it).

Last year, our 'Prom' was tasteless and uninspired; the theme was 'party'. It was my mission to convince Ms Jenkins (partly through pretending to cry) that this year it was integral to have a legitimate planning committee. Luckily, as I'm the only person who volunteered to be on the committee, I can essentially organize my own perfect night!

'Patrick! We are leaving at 7.45 *on the dot*!'

I'm snapped out of my daydream of slow-dancing with a new boyfriend to the sound of my mum yelling at me from downstairs. Bugger. I spent too long trying to impress Jean-Pierre with my handwriting and now I have ruined my life.

I stand up from the little wooden desk in my room and go to the mirror on the wall, which is in the shape of a crescent moon, making it very difficult to see anything in. Today's the first day of school, so obviously I have to wear something that perfectly encapsulates the vibe of my upcoming year. Like a sociopath, I've left it until the morning to decide what that new look will be.

Looking at the moon mirror reminds me that I also need to redecorate my room to match my new vibe. I can't have my future boyfriend coming upstairs, obviously expecting to see the bedroom of a sophisticated adult with warm neutrals, wicker storage baskets and low lighting and instead entering the bedroom of a *child* – or more specifically a *child obsessed with space* because alongside the moon mirror are star curtains, an astronaut figurine, a giant poster of the moon landing and a hanging rotating model of the solar system. I don't even like space any more! I just so happened to be obsessed with it when I was last allowed to redesign my room. Luckily, over the last week I've managed to steal little touches that make my room seem more mature: a gingerbread-scented candle that my mum got for Christmas, one of the pillows from the sofa downstairs and a lamp I found in the shed which, unfortunately, gives me little electric shocks every time I turn it on, but it's worth it.

'Did you hear me, Patrick?!' Mum yells again.

Ugh. I lean my head out into the landing. 'It's *PATCH*!' I shout. Another part of my rebrand is shifting from Patrick to Patch to feel more characterful and mysterious. As if I just don't have *time* to say Patrick. 'Patrick' is the type of person to give his hand a hickey from practising kissing too hard (true story, unfortunately), while 'Patch' is the type of person to give other people tips on how to kiss while also smelling divine and having the perfect amount of rip on his ripped jeans.

'Also!' I continue over the sound of the coffee machine. 'You're stressing me out, and this is a really important day! You should be savouring this! Your child is going into lower sixth, a once-in-a-lifetime occasion!'

There is a pause while she waits for the coffee machine to stop whirring. 'Apart from when Kath did it last year. Forty-five minutes, *Patrick*!'

My older sister, Kath, is old for her year (a cruel, cold-hearted winter baby) and I'm young for my year (a joyful, warm-hearted summer baby) and because of that we're only one school year apart which Mum misguidedly hoped would make us close. She's also misguided in giving me forty-five minutes to get ready. You can't do anything momentous in forty-five minutes! I contort my body in an attempt to see as much of myself in the moon mirror as possible so I can figure out what will be the quickest route of personalization. All I see is slightly ginger hair – I've branded it as 'sunset blonde' – and arms that are too long. As always, I decide to FaceTime Jean.

'We can do this, we just need to streamline,' says Jean

calmly on loudspeaker while I sift through a box of slogan badges.

Jean is my best friend in the world. It's unfortunate that her name is Jean but it's not something I hold against her. She's *sensational* but also a bit of a nightmare. Recently, she's taken to wearing a different decorative hair clip every day and learning everything there is to know about queerness. At first this was largely to support me, but now it's gone too far and she just tells me off when I'm not being progressive enough. This is theoretically good but realistically very annoying because, sorry, *I am the queer one.*

'OK, so our main options are hair, shoes or accessories,' I remind her, as I empty out a box of loose crystals onto my bed. I'm not positive what I can do fashion-wise with loose crystals but I'm willing to get creative.

'This would be so much easier if we didn't have a school uniform,' she moans over the phone as she forces a cherry, her clip of the day, into her unruly hair.

'Ugh, I know.'

I'm lying. I would never admit this but I find it very helpful having a uniform because otherwise I would be overwhelmed with choice and nobody would understand my more abstract outfit aesthetics such as 'a chance encounter' or 'memories of bohemia'. Also, the green polo-shirt goes with my colouring.

'What shoes do you have?' asks Jean, but she's left the

screen so her voice sounds slightly echoey.

'Oooh, I don't think that's a route we want to go down because my shoes at the moment, while not super fashionable, have excellent arch—'

'—Arch support yes. You've actually mentioned that several times,' she says as she reappears onscreen with her school bag which, knowing Jean, has been packed ready for three days. 'Hair it is!'

I stick my fingers into the 'texture-enhancing putty wax' that I have received every Christmas for the past six years from my godmother Pamela. Her and my mum aren't even friends any more but she inexplicably still sends me hair wax every year with a flamingo-themed card. I'm following a hair tutorial called 'messy beach look' but after about ten minutes of twisting my ends in order 'to create effortless definition' the result is less 'beach look' and more 'recently died by electrocution'. I run my head under the tap to reset and borrow my sister's hairdryer. After another ten minutes, during which time Jean and I have two fights about whether it would be useful to invest in a hair diffuser (it definitely would) I inspect myself in the mirror and definitely have *volume.* I'm forced to lean quite far back in order to show Jean the full effect but we both decide that volume is something to celebrate so I hang up and proudly go downstairs to showcase my new look.

'Nice hair,' says Mum while grabbing her bag for what I

imagine is the eleventh time to look for her keys.

'Why do you never support my creative endeavours?' I snap, carefully tapping the top of my hair to make sure it hasn't lost any precious volume.

'By creative endeavours do you mean using a hairdryer?' she replies absentmindedly, barely looking up from her bag. 'Where are my flipping keys?'

'Caroline.' I address her by her first name so she knows I'm serious, and take in a slightly performative shaky breath. 'If you continue to stunt my personal growth by saying patronizing things like "nice hair" . . . then I'm not sure I can carry on living under this increasingly oppressive roof.'

Mum looks like she's about to snap something back but then furrows her brow in confusion. 'What?'

My mum used to be proud of my rapidly expanding vocabulary, but it appears she's no longer thrilled that her son is a word prodigy. In theory, I'm very impressed by my mother because she's a single mum raising two children (one of whom is an angel and one of whom is Kath) but in practice I find her to be increasingly annoying especially when she refuses to give me her unyielding support in my every endeavour, which surely is the whole point of being a parent?

'Alright, Patrick,' she continues, using the tone of voice I have learned to recognize as '*can this conversation be over?*'. 'Your hair is the best thing I've ever seen. It's close to godliness . . . and not just because of its height,' and proceeds to laugh at her own joke. 'Now where the eff are my effing keys!' she hisses into the butter dish.

I actually know where her keys are but in order to give myself time for Weetabix, and to punish her for both calling me Patrick and the hair joke, I withhold that piece of information. My trick with Weetabix is eating one at a time so you aren't left with the dreaded soggy mush. I crave texture both in life and in breakfast cereal.

As I move onto my second Weetabix, Kath trudges into the kitchen dragging her school bag behind her, not dissimilarly to how she sometimes drags me behind her. My sister has recently discovered eyeliner in an aggressive way, but won't let me show her how to do a 'flick' so instead just looks like she's making sure astronauts in space know exactly where her eyes are. Just before she crams whatever cured meat she can find in the fridge into her mouth she looks me up and down with unveiled contempt. 'What is going on with your hair?' she asks.

'What?' I self-consciously tap it. It's a bit crunchy.

'Looks weird,' she replies.

'"Weird" is just another word for unique. So *thank you*, Kath, for saying I look unique.'

'Whatever,' she says and fists a handful of salami in her mouth. There's been somewhat of a cold war between Kath and me over the last year or so because she refuses to admit that she broke my karaoke machine when the evidence is all there (aka, me just *knowing* it was her!). She mistakenly thinks I'll get over it eventually but she underestimates my skill in holding a grudge. It's actually one of my top five skills.

My Top Five Skills:

1. Acting.
2. Knowing what any TV advert is promoting within two seconds.
3. Being able to roll my r's.
4. Holding a grudge.
5. Triple jump (I'm weirdly good at triple jump but unfortunately it doesn't hold much weight nowadays).

'Alright, let's gooooo! We really are running late,' I say, swiping the keys off their spot and handing them to my puzzled mother who always thinks the key hook is 'too obvious' a place to look.

Just as Mum is about to lock the door, I stop her. It's funny how time-pressured situations always provide moments of clarity. I turn and sprint upstairs to grab the *one thing* that has the power to tie my entire look together and set the tone for the whole year.

Chapter 2

There are three schools in my humble town of Hiverhampton, and if awards were being given out, Hiverhampton High wouldn't win for 'most academic', 'most creative' or even 'most clean', but we would *definitely* win for 'most deceitful'. I'm almost deceived myself as Mum pulls up to a beautiful red-brick building with tall windows, genuine turrets and Latin writing carved above the door. The type of school you would see in a film where Colin Firth plays an inspiring but no-nonsense English teacher! But the building, though technically my school, is only the front of *one* of the buildings. That's where the deceit comes in. The rest of the school, which you can't see until it's too late and you're stuck inside, is what can only be described as three very beige rectangles that join together to make a square. If I were a school tour guide (a position I'm gunning for now that I'm in lower sixth), I would say: 'The school boasts a verdant communal outdoor space, state-of-the-art dining facilities and high-tech computer equipment.' But what I would *mean* is: 'There's a concrete outdoor space with two chained-down benches and one spindly tree, a cafeteria with an industrial-sized ketchup pump and a computer room with, at most, four computers that can confidently connect to the internet.'

It's only as Mum pulls away and I enter my deceitful school that I look down at my last-minute bolt of fashion inspiration and realize what a colossal mistake I've made. I'm wearing a giant wooden surfboard necklace. What was I thinking?! And my hair is a huge fluffy mess. This is the worst day of my life. The tone I've set for the upcoming year is 'utterly disastrous'.

'It's a statement piece,' says Jean, who can tell I'm spiralling. She inspects the bulky wooden necklace I bought in a gift shop in Devon years ago. 'And statement pieces are worn by bold people ready to take charge of their lives.'

Even though I know that it is a direct quote from one of my mum's self-help books that I leant her (*Owning Your Brand: How to Become a She-E-O*), it does soften the blow. Slightly. But when I look around the classroom it *feels* like everyone in our French class is staring at it. One person even comes up to me and asks if I like surfing?! Obviously I have no idea if I like surfing! Why must everyone take the necklace so *literally*; it's not about what necklace you're wearing, it's about being a necklace-wearer!

And just when things feel like they can't get any worse,

Jean elbows me and whispers, 'Incoming,' and in walks Tessa James; aka, my nemesis and sworn enemy (Jean and I swore it).

A bit of background on the 'Tessa Situation': Tessa joined our school two years ago and nobody would talk to her when she arrived because she wore vegan clogs. Jean and I, ever the humanitarians, spotted something fashion-forward in her Scandinavian and ecological approach to footwear, and took her under our wing. We thought it was very cool that she used to live near London but moved here because her mum was going through something personal (a divorce because she cheated on her husband). Tessa and I quickly bonded over both being children of divorce and also when I found out that she wants to be an actor like me. Jean isn't positive if she wants to be an actor herself, but I've repeatedly reassured her that she wouldn't be left out – she would be my publicist when the time comes.

For that first year, the three of us were inseparable. But then everything changed. Over the summer, Tessa had her hair highlighted and got tanned and all of a sudden the popular kids started asking her to hang out with *them* and by default she wanted nothing to do with us. By the end of the next term she was a firm member of the 'Lodge Crew' (that's what the cool group call themselves because they sometimes vape outside the Holiday Lodge in town). Since hanging around with that sort of clientele, Tessa has become a certified cow. Sometimes during lunch, I still catch her glaring at us from the cool table while Jean and I eat together or make mosaics out of the salt and pepper sachets.

Tessa struts in with her new cohort, including Callum Taylor, who immediately swipes the books off someone's desk as he passes. Callum Taylor is conventionally attractive, I suppose, but he is even more conventionally evil. It's as if he googled what a bully is supposed to do and perfectly executes it at every opportunity. While Callum guffaws, Tessa walks up to us, swishing her hair which is, predictably, perfectly highlighted and shiny and which matches Callum's pristinely white trainers which he replaces every month. It's too late to tuck my necklace into my shirt. She's spotted it like a shark smelling blood from miles away. Thank goodness I ran my disastrous hair under the tap as soon as I got into school so she doesn't have more ammo.

'Is that a necklace?' she drawls in her heavily contrived London accent, prompting a chorus of laughter from her drones.

'So it would seem,' I reply, trying to stop my face from turning red, even though I can feel my ears are ahead of the game and already crimson. I turn to Jean and roll my eyes. *If someone is trying something new you just have to compliment them, even if you hate it.*

‘I think it looks amazing, very chic,’ Jean says supportively, God bless her.

‘You’re into surfing now, Simmons?’ says Callum, placing his hands on our desk and leaning in to take a closer look. I can’t help but notice that he’s somehow become more muscular over summer and is trying to make that obvious with a shirt that’s far too small for him.

I shoot Tessa an annoyed look and I can see her dead eyes glinting, ready to go in for the kill.

‘Well if you must know, it’s my cousin’s necklace . . .’ The lie comes out before I can stop it. I lean in and take a shaky breath (my second of the day). ‘My cousin who is *incredibly ill* so I’m wearing it to support him?’ I don’t feel great about the harrowing lie, especially as Tessa knows my family, but it does its job to shut Tessa up. I can see her about to mouth a retort but she knows she can’t battle with an ill family member so swishes her hair again and goes to her desk.

Patch: 1, Tessa: 0.

Annoyingly, I now have to wear the necklace for ever. Or at least until I kill off my fictional cousin.

‘OK.’ I turn to Jean and whisper urgently, ‘You must never let me forget that I’ve said I have an ill cousin.’

‘I won’t. So, how are you getting on with your list?’

I pull out my notebook from my bag and go to the page titled ‘Boyfriend Checklist’. This was Jean’s brilliant idea and crucial in reminding me that I can have an *ideal* boyfriend rather than just any boyfriend which is what I was semi-willing to settle for.

Jean analyses the list, red pen in hand, like she's marking my actual homework. So far the list is as follows:

Boyfriend Checklist:

- Very, very hot (will make sure to tell people this doesn't matter, though).
- Has a healthy disregard for rules (but not belligerent of authority).
- Ambitious.
- Sporty (not in a regimented way; in a 'looks good in shorts' way).
- Good with adults and dogs.
- Famous relative (note – *relative*, not 'friend-of-a-friend').
- Willing to call me by my last name in a flirty sort of way (like in TV shows, not like Callum Taylor does).
- Speaks another language / open to learning another one / has Duolingo downloaded.
- Funny, but in a way where he appreciates *I'm* funny rather than funny himself.
- Kind, etc.

'OK, super doable. Although we might want to rethink "hot" being at the top and "kind" scribbled at the bottom . . . one thing I learned about being in a healthy, albeit heterosexual, relationship is that . . .'

I tune out because I know that Jean is about to go off on one of her '*this is what it's like to be in a relationship*' monologues.

Jean had a boyfriend over summer but they've since broken up. At first I was furious that she was the first one out of us to be in a long-term relationship (over a month) but now I'm happy for her (sort of) because she has become worldly about the mysterious and complicated world of dating. Her boyfriend was called Joe and things were pretty serious. Jean met him by the poolside after she decided to take swimming lessons. She had started having very vivid dreams about drowning in the *Titanic*, which I had made her watch a few times (eight). Jean, Joe and I hung out as a three a lot because she didn't want to put her romantic relationship over our friendship (which I think I will).

Even so, all I could figure out about him was that he wore a lot of khaki, had one filling and supported Tottenham Hotspur. Jean insisted that he was actually very poetic and deep and wrote beautiful lyrics, but I just can't believe a genuine creative would have a Billabong bag. Regardless, Jean said having a boyfriend was amazing and is completely on board with my goal for this year – perhaps a little *too* on board – while she takes the time to 're-learn how to be by herself'.

'. . . and I think that's integral for you to have in a relationship, Patch!'

I snap back into focus at the mention of my name.

'Completely,' I blindly agree. I'll work out what's integral for me in a relationship later.

'So . . .' says Jean, raising her eyebrow like she's the bawdy host of a dating show, 'anyone caught your eye today?'

Luckily, my answer is avoided with the late arrival of Madame Pattern, who immediately illustrates on the whiteboard how another car nearly hit her on the way to work and it was definitely *not* her fault.

While Madame Pattern erratically draws arrows, I think about Jean's question. I don't really know how to answer her. It's not that boys don't catch my eye. They very much do, almost constantly. The problem is I don't catch theirs.

The annoying thing is I had already *planned* in the back of my mind who my first boyfriend was going to be. It wasn't too hard a decision as there are only two other 'out' boys in my year: James and Ethan. Truth be told, I don't know or like either of them especially well, but I don't think that's reason enough to rule them out as a romantic partner. I couldn't work out whether to go for James or Ethan and flipping a coin felt insensitive. Luckily I found out last week that James's cousin was once an extra in *Doctor Who* so I decided to go for him as I can immediately tick 'famous relative' off my list. I was all ready to lay the groundwork with James through some flirtatious laughter and a gentle touch of the arm, but as soon as I got to school Jean told me that James and Ethan were now dating *each other*. This slightly scuppered my plans. I could wait for them to break up, but that feels unlikely considering after assembly I saw them writing each other's names on their arms in biro. Fortunately, a good boyfriend-finder always has a Plan B.

Mine is Drama Club . . .

Chapter 3

The rest of the school day passes me by in a flurry of 'How was your summer?', 'Can't believe school's started again' and 'I didn't realize you liked surfing?' The only thing of note was getting a nosebleed in Maths which was, as always, very exciting. I decided to take a quick picture of it in the bathroom in case I ever decided to do a gritty photography exhibition. Mostly I was waiting for the end of the day because Monday evenings are Drama Club – and tonight's is the first of the new school year.

Drama Club is a) my favourite thing in the world and b) one of the most likely spaces to get a new boyfriend because any teenager from the area can join! Although most choose not to. Regardless, Jean and I both agree that it's going to be an absolute hormone frenzy. And now that golden-boy Leo Stewart has left (his jawline helped him bag all the main parts) it's inevitable that I'm going to rule the drama scene.

'I bet it's going to be *Oliver!* again,' complains Jean as we walk towards the community theatre; a pointy stone building. She's looking down and carefully dividing a packet of Skittles so that I can have all the green and yellow ones. I don't so much *like* the green and yellow ones as I think they are a more interesting choice.

I steer Jean clear of an incoming lamppost. 'Don't worry, I texted Ms Jenkins a few of my suggestions last week.'

'What did she reply?' asks Jean, shaking a few more Skittles into her hand.

'She hasn't replied yet, but I think I've made it very clear that we should go in a darker direction this year. Art's got to *say* something, Jean.'

Jean looks a bit concerned as she plops another yellow Skittle into my open hand. 'Didn't Ms Jenkins tell you to stop texting her?'

This is true, technically. I'm the only person who has Ms Jenkins' personal number. She gave it to me when we went on a drama trip to see *The Taming of the Shrew* in London and I suggested we swap numbers in case of an emergency which she, somewhat reluctantly, agreed to.

'That's neither here nor there. Now, let's focus!' I push the doors open to the room that just might be holding my first-ever boyfriend.

The community theatre is made up of three main areas: the foyer where we do our rehearsals because it's got the most light and the fewest mice; backstage where everyone gets ready for the shows but is largely used for storage; and, of course, the theatre itself which, while slightly derelict, has a certain charm and a big red curtain in front of the stage which looks very glamorous as long as you don't look too closely. In the foyer, the unmistakable combination of dust, stale biscuit and mouse droppings fills the air as this year's Drama Club members assemble our chairs into a circle. Oh, it's good to be back.

Jean and I manage to secure the only two chairs with padded backs. We're sitting next to Flora and Rachel, twins who go to the all-girls school down the road. They aren't identical twins but (somewhat creepily) always wear matching colours in different tones. Today, Rachel has opted for bright poppy red while Flora is wearing crimson. Personality-wise, they couldn't be more different if they tried. Rachel is optimistic and sweet, whereas Flora is pessimistic and morbid. The only thing they share (aside from DNA) is a love of animals, but while Rachel dreams of becoming a vet, Flora wants to be a taxidermist. For me and Jean, the twins are 'Drama Club friends'; friends who exist strictly within the confines of the Drama Club bubble. It's an unspoken rule that it would be incredibly awkward to see them in any other context. One time Jean and I accidentally ran into Flora and Rachel at the cinema and it was unbelievably uncomfortable, but as soon as we see them in the context of the rehearsal room, we greet each other like we are long-lost family.

'It's been too long!'

'How was your summer?'

'I've missed you *SO MUCH*!'

'I've got a dead bug under my shoe.'

The last was Flora, who proceeds to stare wistfully at the bug while Jean and I quickly fill them both in on the boyfriend mission. Rachel squeals in excitement and Flora sighs in disappointment, muttering something about 'having another person in your life to disappoint you', but both agree to assist. The four of us sit in silence, scanning for potential candidates. There's about twenty to thirty people in Drama Club each year. Only about five of those people are *new*, and very rarely are they *boys*, so the odds aren't exactly in my favour. The only new person I can spot is a girl with pig-tails that are too long. I hear the door open and as I turn to see who's walked in my heart bobs. I'm greeted not with the love of my life, but with the very unwelcome appearance of *Tessa*. I can tell Jean's noticed her too because I hear her groan.

'What on *earth* is she doing here?' I hiss to Jean.

We introduced Tessa to Drama Club when she first started school and she loved it (and even got a special mention in the review of *Joseph and the Amazing Technicolor Dreamcoat* which I was mostly happy for her about). But just as she stopped talking to us at school, she stopped coming to Drama Club. I bet she hasn't told anyone in the Lodge Crew she's back because Callum Taylor once called plays 'long boring films with no explosions'.

Well, well, well, look who's come crawling back to the arts.

I briefly make eye contact with her and then immediately look away. I'm not going to let Tessa ruin Drama Club for me. I vow to ignore her and rise above it, but I am quietly thrilled when I see her sit next to Alexa Peters who I know for a fact has had nits at least three times.

Just as I'm about to give up hope and resort to Plan C (picketing for a boyfriend outside the town hall), Flora nudges me and gestures to the juice table in the corner where there are the unmistakable figures of two boys. Two boys I don't recognize.

I hold my breath, craning my neck and impatiently waiting for them to turn around. I try to make as many guesses as I can with their backs turned. One of them is wearing blue trousers and one of them is wearing bright red tracksuit bottoms. I can already tell they're *so* different. Trousers will be more artistic and tortured, while Tracksuits will be more sporty and casual. I think Trousers will probably write me letters and furrow his brows while I'm talking so I can tell that he's *really* listening. He'll be very good at drawing but won't show anyone, then one day I'll find that he's been sketching *me* when I haven't even been noticing and they will be *so good.* Whereas Tracksuits will fling his arm casually around me when we're having coffee and he'll have dimples, I'm sure of it. He'll get on really well with my sister and they'll both make fun of me but in a playful way that I'm on board with. Two very good options.

After what feels like an eternity, they finally turn around.

I can hear the collective exhale from Jean, Flora and Rachel as the two boys walk to the spare chairs in the corner. I'm so excited my vision goes blurry, but once my eyes refocus I take them in. Trousers has short, neat brown hair and sips carefully at his orange squash. What I wouldn't do to be that glass of squash. Tracksuits has floppy black hair and a quiet confidence as he lumbers over to some empty chairs. Tracksuits barges Trousers playfully, making him spill his squash down his front, and I can tell they have been friends for a while because Trousers just rolls his eyes. Should I offer to grab some napkins and dab his jumper? I wonder if they'll fight over me and it will ruin their friendship? I hope so.

'Right, everyone!' Ms Jenkins, our drama teacher, snaps me out of my fantasy with an authoritative clap as she strides into the centre of the room, her red and white polka-dot skirt swishing behind her. One day last year, about six months after her divorce, Ms Jenkins arrived at school as if she had been possessed by the spirit of someone from the fifties; hoop skirts, polka dots, pinned hair and red lipstick. My mum said that it sometimes happens to people going through a crisis.

'Welcome back, welcome back,' she calls as she turns around the circle. 'And for those of you that are new here, *welcome.* Drama is life. Life is *drama,*' and I nod in agreement, life *is* drama.

'Every term we put on a musical! This might seem ludicrous to you but the old hands here can confirm that with determination, creativity and generous cuts to the original material, we manage to pull it together in time. Apart from our production of *Cats.* But I think we can blame that on the nasty stomach bug that went around. Now, let's get straight to it! I'm sure you're all eager to know what our play is going to be this year . . .'

Ms Jenkins knows that she has us in the palm of her hand. You could hear a pin drop. I actually do hear a pin drop, but it turns out to be Jean's cherry hair clip that's fallen out.

'After much deliberation and several trips to *London* over the summer . . .' she leaves a dramatic pause to allow room for us to be impressed, 'and, despite several people trying to influence my decision . . .' she throws me a quick glare, 'I have decided that this year we shall be doing . . . *Sweeney Todd*!'

There's an excited bubbling of conversation and chatter. I look at Flora (who looks uninterested) and Rachel (who looks excited) and give them both a knowing nod to make them think that I was somewhat involved in the decision.

I can't actually quite remember anything about *Sweeney Todd*, but what I do know is that if the name of the musical is a person's name, then that means there's a *main part.* The way it works in Drama Club is that, the older you are, the bigger the parts you get. I didn't used to think it was fair but I do now, and not *just* because I'm one of the older ones. My hands are almost not my own as I get out my phone and start googling the play.

'Auditions will be next Monday. I want you to prepare a short,' she looks at me again, '*short* monologue and song of your choice. Now, let's loosen up and play some games!'

'Patch, you are definitely *definitely* going to get the part of Sweeney Todd!' whispers Rachel excitedly as we start moving the chairs to the side of the room.

'Of course he is!' confirms Jean, patting my arm as if I have already.

'I will not,' I protest. 'Honestly, I would be so happy getting any part. The part of Anthony would be great, and actually Judge Turpin is a really interesting role,' I say as I scroll down the character list. But in reality I'm already preparing my graciously surprised face for when I am offered the role of Sweeney.

We're semi-efficiently assembled into yet another circle to play an introduction game for the new members of Drama Club. Through force of will, and a fair bit of elbowing, Jean and I manage to get ourselves right next to Trousers and

Tracksuits. I'm standing next to Trousers and I can tell that he uses a peppermint body wash which already feels *so him*.

'Let's start by going around the circle, telling everyone our name and one interesting fact about ourselves!'

There is a collective groan as everyone's mind races to find a single unique quality about their existence, which is impossible as soon as you're in a pressured setting.

'Patrick, why don't we start with you!' smiles Ms Jenkins.

Damn. Why do I have to be this year's Queen Bee of Drama Club? Heavy is the head that wears the crown. I clear my throat.

'Hello! I'm Patrick but everyone calls me . . . Patch.' There is a look of confusion among the returning Drama Club members who have only ever known me as Patrick. 'Or, if you don't call me Patch yet, now you should,' I backtrack nervously, glancing at Trousers and Tracksuits who aren't even looking at me but whispering to each other. My God, what if they're whispering about me? OK, focus, Patrick. Patch, I mean! Focus, *Patch*.

'And an interesting fact about me is that . . .' my brain is working incredibly fast but doing absolutely nothing. It's flicking erratically through a completely empty book. What is interesting about me? I *know* I'm interesting! I'm incredibly interesting! But what on God's green earth is interesting about me?!

'And an interesting fact about meeee . . .' I repeat with

a different inflection to buy me some time, 'is that I . . . am . . . gay.'

Silence.

Oh my God.

Why on earth did I say that?!

What is the matter with me?!

That cannot be my most interesting fact . . . *TWO YEARS IN A ROW.*

I hear a snicker of laughter coming from Tessa's direction and feel my face burning up. My eyes flick nervously to Trousers and Tracksuits. They are both looking at me now, but they both just . . . smile. Not in a mean way, but in a . . . well, I don't know . . .

'Well, *Patch*, thank you! That's not exactly a new fact, but it's very exciting nonetheless!' tries Ms Jenkins.

'Love is love!' yells Jean from my right, and clutches my hand in solidarity.

Ms Jenkins looks at us blankly before smiling and clapping her hands together. 'That it is, Jean . . . OK, why don't you go next!'

I don't really hear the rest of the circle's interesting facts as I'm too humiliated, but I do hear Tessa say that her interesting fact is that 'she grew up in London', so at least I'm not the only one rehashing old answers. And also, for the record, she grew up at least forty minutes from London, so at least mine's true! I snap out of my lamenting when it gets to the end of the circle. Trousers and Tracksuits are coming up and it's important I know their actual names. Tracksuits goes first.

'Uh, hey, my name's Peter.' Oh my goodness, curve-ball! He's *American*! 'And an interesting fact about me is that I just moved here from New York.'

I have never heard a more glamorous sentence IN MY LIFE. Apparently I'm not alone in thinking this as there is a chorus of 'Ooohs' from Drama Club, including Ms Jenkins. I need to separate myself from the rest of the group to seem worldly and travelled, so I lean over to Tracksuits, who I now know is called Peter, and whisper, 'New York is where the Empire State Building is!'

'Totally,' he replies, looking a bit confused. I nod sagely, lean back, and make a mental note to learn more about New York's lesser-known landmarks. 'Have you been?' he asks.

Damn. I wasn't expecting follow-up questions. 'Have I been?' I stammer. 'Have I been . . . well, not technically . . . Or physically, actually.'

He furrows his brows at me, but nods politely, smiling. I might not have nailed my very first 'back and forth' with Peter, but there will be time for that! Luckily, it's Trousers' turn to speak now. He looks a bit more nervous than Peter and is chewing the inside of his cheek.

'Helloooo, I'm Sam,' he murmurs so quietly I'm pretty sure only Peter, Jean and I can hear. 'And an interesting fact about me is . . . that I've never done acting before.' He smiles tightly, eyes firmly planted on the ground. I slowly shift my foot into what I hope is his field of vision. It's basically eye contact. My head is already swimming with possibility and I can feel my stomach doing excited flips like when I find out we're having scampi for dinner, but *even more.*

Sam and Peter. Peter and Sam. Two boys who *might* just change my life.

Chapter 4

'Right, let's have a recap. What do we *know*?' says Jean while she decides which cup is the most conventionally sized for a 'cup of rice'. We're having dinner together because that's tradition after Monday Drama Club. Or at least it *will* be a tradition once we've done it a second time. Over the last year or so, to prove how close we are, Jean and I have started implementing as many 'traditions' into our friendship as possible. Today we are attempting to cook rice which we've both been a bit wary about. Jean pulls out a perfectly regular green cup from near the back of the cupboard while I recite the information we've gathered about Sam and Peter.

Thus far, I've categorized them in my head as:

Peter: American + confident

Sam: English + quiet

It's not a detailed categorization but it's a start.

'So Peter and Sam are family friends, and went to nursery together.'

'Correct,' confirms Jean. 'But then Peter's mother, or "mom", got a job in New York so he moved there when he was young.'

'Right, and *then* something happened with Peter's family . . . which neither of them seemed super keen on sharing, but for whatever reason Peter is now living with Sam's family for the rest of the school year?'

We both look at each other and nod, having successfully concentrated fifteen minutes' worth of small-talk during various drama games into a few concise sentences.

'What I need to do,' I explain, 'is decide which one to pursue first. Instinctively, I feel like Peter is more confident so might be the easier route. But might that be *too* much confidence in one relationship . . . ? Maybe Sam would balance things out a bit more.'

I turn to Jean hoping she'll give me the answer, but instead she looks at me with a patronizing expression.

'At the moment we don't know if either of them is attracted to men, *or* attracted to you.'

'Jean!'

'Not that you're *not* a man,' she quickly clarifies, 'but you need to remember that they have to be attracted to both men *and* you in order for them to qualify. One thing that I discovered through my relationship with Joe was that it's super important that you both like each other. Also, never go to bed angry.'

Annoyingly, Jean has a point. I was so excited about there being two new boys that it didn't cross my mind that they were not falling in love with me this very second. Or even worse . . . straight. I *hate* it when reality gets in the way of life. I rack my brain for signs that Sam and Peter might be queer.

'Well,' I say, 'Peter was wearing colourful trousers and that could very easily be seen as a nod to the pride flag—'

Jean throws me a pointed look. 'Boys can wear whatever they like, Patch, and using clothing as a reason they are into men isn't very progressive of you.'

I roll my eyes, but quickly, so that she doesn't see.

'What we should do,' she says, pacing with a wooden spoon in her hand, 'is ask leading questions and work it out from there.' Jean nods to herself and I can tell that she's already coming up with questions in her head. 'Also, obviously you need to get to know them first because *you* might not even fancy *them*!'

'Jean.' I spin around and place my hands firmly on her shoulders, looking deep into her eyes to show her *how* serious I am. 'I definitely, definitely, *definitely* fancy them . . . *a lot*. I can seriously imagine building a life with them.'

Jean looks unconvinced. 'Which one?'

I think for a moment.

'Whichever.'

Even though I'm keen to write an exhaustive pros and cons list about each boy to see which would be more suitable, Jean insists we concentrate on the meal at hand. Scanning the spice rack, we finally settle on 'Ground

Nutmeg' as our spice of choice, mainly because nutmeg is satisfying to say. Nutmeg. *Gorgeous.* One of the best things about Jean's house is that they have tons of spices, whereas my mum thinks that we need to 'finish off the spices we already have before buying new ones'. Because of this, everything we eat at home tastes of 'Italian seasoning'. Part of the reason that Jean and I started learning to cook was because we want to host soirées where people dress up fancy and come over to tell anecdotes and glamorous stories. *Also,* one of my mum's self-help books very clearly states that the quickest way to a man's heart is through his stomach (it wasn't a medical book), so I'm now on my own private mission to create a meal that will make Peter or Sam fall in love with me. We are trying to create a completely new recipe and we list our attempted recipes in three sections: 'Culinary Excellence', 'Requires Work' and 'Avoid'. So far it goes:

<u>Culinary Excellence:</u>

- Mushroom, olive and Rice-Krispies blitzed on a bed of baby gem lettuce
- Branston pickle on five-seed granary with a pinch of za'atar
- Scrambled eggs with oregano and curry-powder breadcrumbs and chilli jam

Requires Work:
- Dijon mustard on spinach with candied almonds
- Mashed potato sandwich with balsamic vinegar

Avoid:
- Spicy spaghetti with cucumber and capers
- Noodles with rosemary and coconut oil
- Marinated tuna with honey, yoghurt and dark chocolate glaze

Forty minutes of stirring, prodding, garnishing and apologizing to Jean's mum for setting off the fire alarm later, Jean and I stare at each other from opposite ends of the table with our meal laid out before us. After taking a look, the rest of Jean's family decided to opt for oven pizza in front of the TV instead of tucking into our creation, even though there was plenty to spare. Granted, it requires a bit of work visually. I prod it with my fork but the rice doesn't give way, which I don't think is a great sign. It's darker than rice is traditionally served because we burnt it on the bottom of the pan but we brand it as 'charred rice', which makes it sound more gourmet. Jean and I take a sip of our red wine which is actually undiluted blackcurrant squash (unpleasantly sweet but looks the part) and dive in.

One mouthful in and . . . hmmm. It's not great. Quite hard to chew actually, and somehow both bitter and sweet.

'So,' murmurs Jean, trying very hard to swallow. 'Requires Work?'

I nod in agreement while the shards of rice inch down my throat. It turns out that risotto rice is not interchangeable for regular rice and because of this we have managed to both overcook and undercook it which I believe, in time, we will appreciate to be quite interesting from a scientific standpoint. Also nutmeg, while a fun word to say, is quite an overwhelming flavour.

We both agree to have very very little portions because it's quite French to do that (probably) and thoughtfully put the rest in a selection of Tupperware for Jean's mum to take to work for the next few days. We then head into the living room to demand a slice of pizza from each of Jean's family members. Although I want to carry on talking about the Peter and Sam dilemma (I think the situation warrants the word dilemma), Jean gets a message from Joe asking if he left a hoodie at her house and doesn't use any kisses at the end of the text so we need to dissect that for the rest of the evening. But all the while I'm thinking about Peter and Sam. And the upcoming play. There's simply too much to think about and I come to the conclusion I need professional help.

Chapter 5

'I'm just feeling very torn at the moment.' I shift on my plastic chair to see if I can balance on just two legs at a time. 'Do I follow my career or my heart? On the one hand, I have this amazing creative opportunity to be the main part in a play, but now I've found myself in a position where I could finally fall in love!'

I sense an interruption so I hold up my hand. 'I know what you're going to say. I should put my career first. But I suppose I'm worried that if I do that then I might close myself off from love at this crucial stage in my romantic development. Especially when the whole point of this year was getting a boyfriend! And doing well in my exams, obviously.'

'That's actually not what I was going to say, Patch . . .' replies my ex-English teacher and reluctant life coach Ms Beckett. 'I was going to say that if you carry on leaning on your chair like that you're going to break your neck.'

I don't know why teachers are so *obsessed* with us breaking our necks, but I suppose it is something worth avoiding so I quickly rebalance and ground myself.

When I grow up I want to be *exactly* like Ms Beckett (except not an English teacher). Even though she's not my actual teacher any more, I find she is an endless fountain of knowledge and sometimes says things that are even more poignant than the professionals in my mum's books. I always make time to go to her classroom for a biscuit (bourbon for me, ginger snap for her) and some enforced life advice.

For example, at one point last year, Jean had asked me to make her a cake for her charity bake sale and the one I decided to make was way too ambitious (gluten-free Black Forest gâteau). It looked horrid, tasted awful and I knew deep down that all Jean wanted from me was a simple coffee and walnut cake. Instead I was using her charity function in yet another attempt to try and impress everyone and was ultimately a horrible human being. I was having a baking-related existential crisis (not my first). At that point, I ran into Ms Beckett's classroom on the cusp of tears, and she told me to take a breath and said something I will never forget: 'Patrick, it's only bloody cake.' Inspired! Now, whenever I find myself getting worked up about something small I try to say to myself, 'It's only bloody cake' and I immediately either feel much better or very hungry. But today's issue is one of the rare situations that can't be helped with that phrase.

'I'm serious, Jo, what should I do?'

'Don't call me Jo, it's completely inappropriate,' says Ms

Beckett with a smile as she finally looks up from her laptop. 'I'm very busy and important, as you know.'

'Oh, I know,' I reply. 'And by the way, I think you should absolutely buy it. A real capsule item.'

She looks confused so I point to her glasses where I can see the reflection of the shopping site she's on. She snaps the laptop shut and takes off her glasses.

'Don't be a prick.'

'Ms Beckett!' I open my mouth in faux-shock, even though I *love* that she said it because it means we're confidants and she sees me as a grown-up. Which I am.

'Patch, I have my Year 9s coming in five minutes – what *exactly* are you asking?'

To the point. So her.

'Well, truth be told, this was my way of telling you that my love life is coming along *very well* and at this rate I should definitely have a boyfriend by Prom.'

'Thrilled to hear it,' she replies dryly.

'But I guess I just wanted some advice on whether I should be focusing on the boyz,' I add the 'z' to seem casual, 'or the audition.'

'Well, it's not really a question, is it?' she says as she cracks the spine of an untouched poetry book. 'Obviously focus on the audition. You've barely spoken to these boys. And if they've chosen to be in Drama Club they are obviously into acting, so getting a good part in the play is surely a good move that will impress them?'

I let this sit for a second, digesting both her advice and my third bourbon.

'Honestly, Ms Beckett, you need to write a book. How did you get to be so wise and clever?'

'Years of mistakes. Years of them. Now bugger off.'

I grab another biscuit from the desk and shove it in my mouth.

'Fank oou! Shee you later!' I mumble, proving once and for all that you *can* talk with your mouth full. As I walk down the corridor I make a promise to myself that for the rest of this week I will *only* focus on the audition and nothing else, not even my Physics lesson which is where I'm currently heading. My problem with Physics is that I'm naturally trusting of how the world works when it comes to gravity and things like that. I don't know why we have to analyse everything to death, leaving no room for mystery. Science can be so repressive.

When I finally get home, I plant myself down on the kitchen table and open my mum's computer. I begin working on my process for the audition. I do have my own laptop but it's old and clunky and not very 'me', but I reckon if I carry on using Mum's lovely sleek one, she'll eventually just give it to me. My mission this evening is to find all the barbers in our area to see if I can get some last-minute work experience with them. The story of *Sweeney Todd* is basically about a barber who starts killing people and then gives the bodies to his landlord (Mrs Lovett) who bakes them into pies. Not a particularly cheery story but I just feel that I can't head into an audition to play Sweeney Todd when I don't have the professional experience to draw from; to know the feel of the cold steely blade in my hand and deftly swipe!

To be super clear, I want to get experience to cut hair and not start a killing spree, I'm not going down Sweeney's *exact* path. My draft email to the local barbers currently reads:

To whom may be concerned,

Hello!

My name is Patch Simmons and to CUT a long story short (excuse the pun!), I'm OBSESSED with your establishment! The noble art of haircutting, according to the internet, started around 1200 BC when iron was discovered and it just goes to show that if something works, it really stands the test of time. I bet when the first barber turned that iron into scissors and gave one of their friends a short back and sides, they would have been so pleased to know that they started a long line of barbers that continues today at [INSERT BARBERSHOP NAME] on [INSERT STREET NAME] near the [INSERT LANDMARK].

At this point in the email, you might be wondering why I'm contacting you and that is a very pertinent question. Well done! The reason is that I would love nothing more than to shadow you after school one day this week and learn more about your esteemed industry. I appreciate I'm not ready to give anyone a full haircut (?) but I would be more than happy covering the front desk or even tidying up someone's fringe. I can't reveal too much right now for PR reasons (annoying, I know!), but if you allow me to do this it could really help with a pretty exciting project I have coming up . . .

Please do let me know ASAP because I will need to factor it into my already bustling professional and social calendar.

Kind regards, and happy chopping!

Patrick (Patch) Simmons

I'm trying to personalize each email so the barbers don't think I've just copied and pasted and get offended. I've also attached a lookbook of my favourite hairstyles (which is quite Tracee Ellis Ross- and Blake Lively-heavy). After spell-checking for the third time (as expected, faultless) I hit send on my first email to 'Prestige Trims' and begin working my way down the list.

I wait semi-patiently for nearly a full day, but as good as I am at games I've never been good at life's most tricky one: the waiting game. By Wednesday I haven't got a single reply from a barber. Not one! I'm getting desperate and decide I have to try something else. This unfortunately involves pimping out my mother.

Chapter 6

Now, my mum has sworn off men since she broke up with her last boyfriend, Ralph, who was an *utter prat.* Her words not mine. He wore so much aftershave you could smell him coming from a mile off and had a 'car salesman' energy when in fact he worked as a computer salesman. They met when my mum was getting a new laptop (the one I use) and Ralph was trying to prove how strong the screen was by repeatedly punching it. Somehow this act of primitive strength (a sort of man vs. machine where both ended up losing) worked on my mum and resulted in her getting both the computer and a boyfriend for free. Bargain! Things ended when she found something on his phone, she won't tell me what, but my connection with him had ended far before that point when he started calling me 'darling' in a theatrical sort of way that made me think he was secretly a homophobe.

The one good thing I will say about Ralph, he sure knows his computers. I've dropped that laptop upwards of six times now and it's never so much as scratched. My plan today is quite simple: get my mum to drop me off at the barbers after school while she runs errands in the hope that one of the barbers becomes so infatuated by her (hopefully their type is 'mother of two who never knows where their phone is') that they agree to show me the ropes while she goes to the big Tesco.

The bell chimes with a satisfying confidence as we enter 'A Cutting Above', which is very nearly wordplay and therefore very nearly promising. I've never had my hair cut here as it's more of a 'salt of the earth' establishment and I *love* to have my hair washed for me. But I thought this place had an eighteenth-century London vibe which would be good for character work. Annoyingly, my mum is wearing a very old shirt and shapeless jeans, but I cleverly asked to borrow her hairband in the car so it wasn't all piled up on her head like a bad imitation of Helena Bonham Carter.

'You really want to get your hair cut here?' asks my mum quietly as she looks around the aggressively lit shop. Inside there are three barbers but only one customer. Not an amazing ratio.

'Oh, do not worry, I'm not getting my haircut *here*,' I reply dismissively.

'Then why are we—'

'Helloooo!' I call to the barbers, interrupting my mum before she can scupper my plans.

The slightly shorter barber looks up from his phone. 'Haircut?'

'Not right now, no. I just wanted to say *this* is my

mother, Caroline.' I gesture to her even though it's pretty obvious who I'm talking about. 'I emailed the other day about maybe shadowing you? Oh, and she's single by the way!'

My mum quickly takes my arm. 'Patrick what on *earth* are you doing?'

I scurry my mum away from the barbers so as not to embarrass myself in front of my potential colleagues and come clean.

'I need to see what it's like working in a barbershop!' I whisper urgently.

'Why? I mean, God, I know you're always saying that a fringe can change *everything,* but you're still in school.'

'Oh, not as a career! It's for research!'

'Research?' she asks, and then I see the penny drop. 'Patrick, please tell me this is not about the play?'

I try to give her a winning smile, but she stares at me blankly.

'Listen, if you just go along with this then you won't have me pestering you around Tesco about treating ourselves, and the planet, with higher-quality produce,' I reason.

She thinks for a second.

'Oh, bloody fine,' she says, realizing this is definitely the lesser of two evils. I'm a nightmare to shop with.

'OK, now just go up and ask them if I can stay here for thirty minutes or so while you do the shopping because I'm very interested in the trade.'

Mum hesitates for a second, rolls her eyes and turns to go.

'Oh,' I quickly add, 'and don't be afraid to twirl your hair, you know, if it helps.'

She gives me a glare.

'What? Their business is hair! They're clearly very interested in it!'

She mutters something under her breath and walks up to the barbers. I can't quite make out what they're saying but they seem suspicious. I wonder if they think that maybe I am an undercover scout for hairdressing talent and, with the right cut, could call them up to the big leagues. That would make a great TV show.

I hear my mum doing that fake laugh she sometimes does on the phone and although she doesn't *twirl* her hair she's certainly shimmying it about more than usual. I see the taller barber give a curt nod to the other, my mum turns around and gives me the thumbs up. I'm in.

'I'll be back in half an hour!' calls my mum, the bell chiming as she heads off to do the shopping.

'No rush!' I call after her. 'And remember, if the sauerkraut isn't in the fridge section then it's not going to have the good bacteria!'

Mum makes no indication that she's heard me so I turn around and size up what's going to be my new workplace for the next thirty minutes.

Maroon must have featured heavily when they did the mood board for the interior design. They also inexplicably have pictures of scissors, clippers and stock images of people having their hair cut all over the walls which feels a bit obvious. The one customer who was here is finishing up and being shown the back of his neck with a mirror. The man barely looks, but does a small nod of acknowledgement for a job well done, whereas I can tell you: if the back of my neck looked like that . . . I would *certainly* have something to say.

'So,' I say, walking up to the two barbers by the till and smiling broadly, 'I'm Patch. What are your names?'

The taller one points to himself, 'Vince', and points to the smaller one, 'Jimmy', and then points to the barber finishing up with his customer, 'Joseph'.

'Lovely to meet you, Vincent and Jimmy . . . of course.' Not knowing quite what to do next, I decide to shake both their hands to buy me some time.

The bell chimes again and in marches a man in his forties, staring down at his phone and looking like he's just got out of work. He tears his eyes away from his screen for a second to look at Vince. They seem to have a completely silent male communication which says:

Hey mate.

Hey.

You free now?

Sure.

Haircut.

Grab a seat.

Thank you.

Perhaps this is why I don't have a natural rapport with adult men, because I have never once in my life, given the option, said nothing.

As Vince leaves to continue his telepathic conversation with the businessman and Joseph handles a crisp ten-pound note at the till, I turn to Jimmy.

'So, Jimmy, what I was hoping for was simply to watch you guys do what you do, ask some questions and then, depending on how things go, maybe I could help out on a haircut or a . . . shave. Whatever works for you.'

Jimmy looks at me a bit like I'm an alien, but also a bit intrigued as to what this alien wants to know about the art of cutting hair.

Twenty minutes later I'm sitting on the surprisingly comfy padded maroon bench which serves as the waiting space. There are a pile of magazines on the glass table that look like they haven't been replaced since before I was born. At first, Vinny asked me to help sweep up the hair, but that made me feel so queasy I had to request a peppermint tea, so I decided to sit down and flick through some of the magazines instead and soak up the atmosphere. Most of the magazines are largely car-, football- or motorbike-focused, but there's a couple of good ones underneath, even if a lot of the headlines are trying to make me decide between 'Team Angelina' or 'Team Jennifer'. I found one very interesting article that I quietly ripped out to show Jean later, which was '*Nine Ways to Get Him to Commit*'.

I look up at the clock, which has scissor blades instead of hands, and see I'm running out of time to find the spirit of what it is to be a barber. I clear my throat and take a sip of my peppermint tea before standing.

'So, gentlemen.' I tentatively approach them. 'Do you like being barbers?'

They make noises I take to mean '*it's alright*' in response, but don't give me much more than that.

'I think it's quite beautiful. I mean, you might think you're just in charge of hair, but you're actually in charge of someone's self-esteem and that's incredibly powerful. Let's take you, Jimmy.' Jimmy looks up nervously. 'Do you find it humbling knowing that with the right snips of hair, you can completely change someone's day?'

'I s'pose,' mumbles Jimmy, as he gently lifts the chin of his customer. 'I mean . . .' he begins, but then stops.

'Go on,' I encourage, frightened he might shut up like a clam.

Jimmy doesn't look up. 'Well, usually they ask for short back and sides and you don't really get, I dunno . . .'

'The opportunity to be creative?' I suggest.

'Yeah, exactly,' Jimmy agrees. 'But then, once in a while, someone will come in asking for something completely different. That's always a bit mental.'

'Mental how?'

'Remember when that man with the long ponytail came and asked us to give him a buzz cut?' Jimmy says to the other two, and they all grin at the memory.

'We all wanted to be the ones to snip off the ponytail so we ended up doing a third of it each.'

They all chuckle, suitably warmed up. I decide to take my chance and ask the question that will really help me get into the mind of Sweeney Todd.

'Sounds amazing,' I laugh. 'And do you ever find that it's quite an intimidating position? You have these men, necks exposed, at your mercy. Have you ever felt the desire to just let your razor . . . slip?'

The snipping stops. Silence.

Not even the gentle snipping of hair.

The man sitting next to me inches slowly away and I see the three barbers giving each other very worried looks. Ah, bugger. Upon immediate reflection, I perhaps should have said that I was researching a character who goes on a murderous barbering spree rather than casually incorporating murder into chit-chat. But I wanted an instinctive response from them!

'Oooh, bit quiet in here,' says my mum, as the chime of the bell marks her entrance: the perfect escape route saving me from having to explain that I'm actually not a murderous psychopathic sixteen-year-old.

'OK! Well, this was amazing, thank you so, so much,' I say quickly, grabbing my things. 'Vincent, Jimmy, Joseph, you've all been so helpful. Thanks again!' And I push my mum out of the silent shop.

'That was weird,' says my mum as she waits for a very slow woman carrying a very large plant to move out of her way so she can pull out of the parking spot.

'What's weird,' I say as I rummage through the bags she's left in the front of the car, 'is that I see no sauerkraut in here when I explicitly mentioned it upwards of three times?'

'Good lord, it's in the back of the car. Less of that attitude, please.'

'Sorry.'

'So, did you get everything you needed from . . . whatever it was that that was?'

I think about it.

'On the whole it was useful. I now sort of get what it's like to be inside a run-of-the-mill barber.' Then I add: 'Not that I *ever* want to get my hair cut in one.'

There's a nice quiet as we drive along. It's a lovely cold clear day and the air smells smoky and spicy. I would never admit it to her because she would tell all her friends and I would sound like a loser, but I do quite like driving when it's just Mum and me in the car (unless she's being a nightmare or has done something I deem as unjust). Sometimes we'll sing country music because she's obsessed with it and though I *really* like it I don't want to become obsessed with it just yet because I'm too young to be into country music. She once tried to bring her love of country music into her wardrobe and that resulted in quite a difficult conversation I didn't want to have but equally felt compelled to. Tasselled suede shirts have no place in our home.

'I think the barbers fancied you,' I said.

'Oh, they did not,' she replies, physically batting away the comment.

'No, they definitely, definitely did. I'm amazing at reading body language. Would you be interested in going out with one of the barbers?' I ask in the full knowledge that I can never return there. 'I'd give Jimmy a glowing review.'

'No.' She shakes her head. 'I don't like hair all over the place. That's why we don't have a dog.'

'Don't deflect with humour, Mother. It was my round-about way of asking if you're open to dating at the moment?'

My mum drums her hand on the wheel. 'Not at the moment.' She pauses. I can tell she's thinking about Ralph and my dad and all the other useless men she's had in her life. 'I'm really busy and it's, you know, ugh, it's a scary thing to put yourself out there.'

'God, don't I know it.' I nod in agreement. 'But you know *struggle is good, scary is good.*'

I see my mum's brow furrow. 'Is that from . . .'

'*Tough Mama: A Mother's Guide to Resilience*? Yes, yes it is.'

'Stop taking my books,' Mum snaps, indicating her car off the road and out of the conversation.

Chapter 7

It's finally the day of the audition. As we pull into the community theatre, I grab Jean's hand and take a deep breath. It tastes a bit sweet and minty because I've taken several lozenges to keep my throat relaxed. I'm worried I've taken too many, but a quick google says it's impossible to overdose on lozenges.

I've done everything I can to prepare for the audition even though my vocal warm-ups were cut short this morning by Kath coming into my room, telling me to shut up, and giving me a dead arm (I've hidden her eyeliner as punishment). For breakfast I wanted a typical eighteenth-century breakfast to help me get into character but, upon investigation, it turns out that would have been something called 'offal' which is made of kidney and cold meats. Vile. Mum made the very good point that people in the eighteenth century probably *would* have eaten cereal if it had been invented, so I opted for Weetabix instead. Also I'm currently vegan-adjacent or 'vegan-xious', which means that I still eat meat and cheese and everything, but I do feel guilty about it and 'offal' sounds decidedly *not* vegan.

⋆

There's an *oomph* of air as I push open the heavy doors to the theatre and walk into a flurry of activity. People running lines, pacing up and down and, in at least three cases, crying; trust the drama kids to make this overly dramatic. Tessa is stretching obnoxiously in the middle of the room, demonstrating to the world that she can touch her toes. Well done, Tessa. Rachel has brought flapjacks and is handing them out to everyone, encouraging us to keep our blood sugar up. Meanwhile, I spot Flora, stony-faced, listening to someone tell her about a dream they had. She shakes her head and walks away in the middle of their story.

'Oh my God, was the audition *today*?' I call loudly once I'm sure everyone has clocked us entering the auditorium. 'I completely forgot!'

'Oh no! How could we possibly have forgotten?!' cries Jean as she puts her hands to her head. We planned this entrance in the car with the following reasoning: if we didn't get big parts then we could blame it on not having had time to prepare and if we *did* get big parts then we would seem naturally gifted. As Jean gives a melodramatic sigh, I can't help but think that with a hammy performance like this she will never get a main part. I'm not worried about myself, of course. Rachel darts towards us and hands us each a sticky flapjack. I do a very casual scan for Peter and Sam even though today is *not about them.* They aren't here yet which just reminds me that I find tardiness weirdly attractive as long as it's not over ten minutes. We push our way to the board where the audition timings are laid out, but Tessa's glossy blonde hair is obstructing our view.

'Can you let someone else have a look at the list, please?' I say tetchily.

Tessa turns around, glares and pushes past us.

'I still can't believe she's joined again,' I say to Jean. 'This is meant to be *our* place.'

'I know,' Jean replies. 'But remember our plan.'

I nod, our plan being the simple act of not letting her get to us. I trace my finger down the list of auditions to find that Tessa is up first, followed by Jean right after, and . . . I'm almost right at the end:

- Peter Fincham
- Patrick Simmons
- Sam Gatehouse

Peter is right before me and Sam is right after me. I'm literally *between them*! I know I'm not supposed to be focusing on boys but I can't help but notice that fate has given me a giant sign.

'Ugh, it's so good that you're early on because Ms Jenkins will still have energy and excitement and she'll be really *present*,' I sigh pointedly to Jean.

'No way,' replies Jean, shaking her head, which makes her ice-cream hair clip glint in the overhead light. 'It's so much better to be later on because that way you'll be fresh in her mind when she has to decide who gets which part.'

I don't admit to Jean that I completely agree. We grab a free bench and heave out a sigh, both wanting to seem like the unlucky party.

Fifteen minutes later and I am tapping my foot impatiently on the synthetic blue ridged carpet. I discovered last year that if you rub your hand on the carpet very quickly, it will make your hand feel fizzy.

'She's only gon' 'n' been in there for a blinkin' age!' I whisper to Jean in my cockney accent which I'm not going to drop until after the audition.

'I know, darlin',' replies Jean, who's doing the same thing. 'Alas, if Tessa spends too much time in there with ol' Ms Jenkins it just means there's gonna be less time for us sorry souls!'

Just at that moment (her timing is annoyingly impeccable), Tessa comes through the door to the theatre and is suddenly surrounded by a group. I don't know how but she has already managed to get a gaggle of loyal followers despite only having *just* rejoined Drama Club. Perhaps they are drawn to her blonde highlights like moths to a flame.

'How did it go? How did it go?' one of them asks.

'I don't really want to say because I don't want to throw anyone else off,' she says so loudly that I'm actually impressed by her projection. 'But Ms Jenkins said I did a really, really, *really* good job!'

I shake my head while Jean whispers, 'There ain't no way Ms Jenkins said "really" that many times!'

'And,' continues Tessa, 'it actually looked like she was tearing up by the end of my song!'

'What an absolute rotter,' I say.

'The devil cut himself a copy when he made 'er,' nods Jean.

We roll our eyes at each other, but because we're doing this we don't notice Tessa walking up to us.

'Hey.'

Jean and I look up. 'Hey' may be the nicest thing Tessa has said to us in months.

'Hey,' we reply in unison, having both simultaneously dropped our accents to avoid humiliation. My brain is working overdrive thinking about several comebacks for whatever insult she's about to fling our way. If she says '*You'll never get the main part*', then I'll say '*What? The main part of being a cow? No, because that part has already been cast . . . by you!*' A bit wordy, perhaps.

'Nice hair clip,' she drawls. Jean's hand shoots up to her ice-cream hair clip protectively.

'Are you being sarcastic?' I ask.

'No, I *really* like it,' Tessa responds sarcastically, which just makes the interaction even more confusing; she's like a conversational matador and Jean and I are the bulls, blindly looking for red flags.

'Anyway,' she continues, crossing her arms, 'Ms Jenkins asked me to call the next person in and that's you, Jean . . . Good luck.'

'You don't have to be so mean, Tessa,' I venture.

'I'm not being . . . ugh,' she shakes her head and storms away.

I turn to Jean and re-engage my cockney accent. 'Listen, love, *you* are a bloomin' diamond in this world of stones, you are perfect 'n' talented and 'n' otherworldly star, you *absolutely have this.*'

Jean nods, takes a deep breath, and heads in.

I look over my lines for my monologue even though I know them off by heart. I have decided to do Julia Roberts' speech from the film *Erin Brockovich.* Technically, I haven't seen the film but I used my mum's Facebook account to find Ms Jenkins' profile and I saw 'Erin Brockovich' was listed as an interest of hers so I watched a scene from the film on YouTube and it looks *amazing.* It includes a few swear words but I wanted to show Ms Jenkins that I'm not afraid of getting *real.*

I hear the *oomph* of air from the door again and look up to see Peter and Sam rushing in, pulling the universal apology face of *I know we're late.* Although they are over my usual limit of ten minutes, I've decided to forgive them because they do look very sorry about it. Plus, Peter's not from England so you've got to factor time-difference into it. He's wearing something which feels very American which helps that point; a short T-shirt over a long T-shirt, while Sam looks a bit like he's heading into work experience at a law firm, wearing an ironed shirt under a grey knit jumper. They walk up to the board with the audition times and then scan the room for a place to sit. Luckily, Tessa's back is turned, no doubt describing for the seventh time how close Ms Jenkins was to crying at her song. Otherwise I just know she would beckon them over like a siren luring sailors to their death. I very subtly slide myself over to the far end of my bench to make it seem like the most obvious option. They take the bait and walk up towards me.

'Hey, Patch, do you mind if we sit here?' asks Peter with a confidence that can only come with an American accent, while Sam lingers behind him.

I'm so pleased that he remembers my name that I completely forget to drop my cockney accent. 'Plen'y of room at the inn!'

'Excuse me?' Sam asks, looking genuinely concerned.

'Oh, nothing,' I say back in my normal accent. 'Yeah, absolutely, grab some bench!' I'm not positive if '*grab some bench*' is a saying but neither of them seems particularly fazed by it. Sam quickly sits on the opposite end of the bench, forcing Peter to sit in between us.

Now, I know that I promised Jean, Ms Beckett, the

delivery man *and myself* that I would focus on the audition and not Peter and Sam, but this opportunity was literally handed to me on a platter! On a bench! Plus, being a good actor is about getting life experiences and this is definitely a life experience waiting to happen.

I realize that while I've been having this internal monologue I've just been smiling at them, so I desperately grasp for something to say.

'Why were you late?' I ask, unfortunately adopting the tone of a disappointed teacher.

'Oh,' Peter replies, 'I was just on the phone to my parents in New York and we . . . um . . .'

'We lost track of time,' says Sam firmly and Peter smiles thankfully at him.

'For over twenty minutes?' I say with a tilt of my head before I can stop myself. I must stop acting so sternly or they will never see me as a romantic free spirit!

'Kidding!' I add, somewhat unconvincingly.

Out of the corner of my eye I see Jean leave the audition room looking both flustered and relieved. She begins to head back to where we're sitting, but I widen my eyes at her in warning. She seamlessly nods and changes direction to Rachel and Flora who are either doing 'the mirror exercise' or just both scratching their knees. She's so amazing at picking up cues! I need to remember to thank her.

'So, I was just wond—'

'Do you know what—'

Peter and I say at the same time. We laugh a bit and I can't help but notice he has very straight teeth. I pull my lips down over my teeth, suddenly conscious of the fact that I have one tooth (left incisor) that refuses to stand with the rest of its comrades. Peter gestures for me to go ahead.

'Well,' I say, 'speaking of New York, I was just wondering what you thought about the City Reliquary Museum in Brooklyn?'

OK, so although I would say I was 99.9% focused on the audition, I may have also spent one evening googling obscure places in New York to impress Peter.

'Oh, I dunno, I haven't been,' he replies. 'Is it any good?'

'It's OK actually . . .' I nod.

'I thought you hadn't been to New York?' asks Sam from the other side of the bench.

I flush red, annoyed at him for calling me out.

'Well no, but according to Google reviews it's a solid three-star.'

'Solid three-star,' Peter says, nodding. 'Well, I'll make sure I check it out when the four-star stuff gets too overwhelming.'

'Just make sure you don't go to the five-star stuff or your head will explode,' I add, doing a little mime of my head exploding and he laughs.

Is this flirting?! Is that what we're doing right now? I think it is.

Flirting feels a bit like playing tennis with sexy tennis rackets, but neither of us really want to win. Instead, we want to carry on playing but look like we're still being professional athletes; we're just like Roger Federer and Rafael Nadal, but *somehow* with even more sexual chemistry. I refocus and see Peter looking at me expectantly. Oh crap, did he say something? Did I just say the tennis simile out loud? No. Oh God, I'm overthinking flirting. I've got carried away and I've lost the rally. I can save this. I just need to not say anything stupid.

'It's scary how so many Americans have guns,' I say, gravely.

Both their faces drop. Nice one, Patch, what a monumental mood killer.

'Anyway,' I say chirpily, 'I'm just going to . . .' and gesture down to my printed and laminated monologue.

I stare down at my monologue. I'm not clocking any of the words, but instead I'm grimacing, going over the two-minute conversation I've just had with Peter, over and over again until he's eventually called in for his audition.

'Good luck!' I say to him and he smiles back in response. OK, this means that I'm next. I start running my tongue over each of my (imperfect) teeth to start warming up my mouth. I can feel Sam looking at me, so I turn to him but he immediately looks down at his feet. I decide to use this opportunity of Peter not being here to try and crack Sam open a bit more.

'Are you nervous?' I ask him.

'A bit,' he replies tightly, continuing to stare down at his shoes which are the type of shoes an old man would wear rather than a teenager; shiny brown leather slip-ons.

There's an uncomfortable silence which I mostly blame on Sam, as he could have very easily asked me a question back. I'm coming to the realization that Peter might be the stronger candidate to hold the position of my 'first love'.

'I'm a bit nervous too,' I continue gibbering away. 'I mean I'm quite used to the audition process at this point but when I was younger I used to get really nervous about going up escalators and getting shredded at the top if I didn't get off quickly enough. Anyway, I read about this breathing tip if you want to try it?'

Sam shrugs his shoulders. 'Sure.'

'OK,' I say, turning further towards him. 'So you breathe in through your nose.'

He does.

'Hold it for a second.'

He does.

'And out through your mouth.'

He does.

'In through your nose,' I repeat.

He does.

'Hold,' I say, sounding a bit like one of the meditation gurus I listen to on YouTube. I notice that Sam has *such long eyelashes*, a bit like a cow. And actually at first I thought his eyes were just brown – I suppose technically they are but they also have little flecks of gold and green in there. Another thing is that his cheeks are a lot rosier than I thought, *a lot* rosier. Also he sort of gets veins around his eyes that sort of bulge and – *oh my God I haven't let him breathe out!*

'Crap, sorry, and breathe out!' I blurt and Sam sputters out an exhale and gasps for air.

'I'm so sorry, I'm so sorry, I got distracted!' I apologize as Sam tries to catch his breath.

'It's OK, it's OK,' he says between breaths. 'Less nervous about the audition and more about the lack of oxygen to my brain, so in a way it worked.'

I don't laugh because he doesn't say it like a joke, just goes back to staring at his stupid brogues and panting.

I cross my arms and face away. I've decided that I think Sam is quite rude. He isn't making any effort to chat to me and seems generally quite annoyed by my presence. I can't work out what he's thinking and I consider myself amazing at reading people. He just feels very 'on purpose', like he's already lived a full life and doesn't have time for my silly childish antics.

I nod to myself, resolved that Peter is definitely the boy I will choose. If I'm honest, I've always imagined myself with an American. Also, I can see the relief on Sam's face when Peter lollops up to us after his audition as it means he's not stuck alone with me.

'You're up!' Peter says, unaware that he has just been promoted to the object of my affection. Congratulations, Peter!

Oh my God, it's actually time to audition. It's *time.*

I pull a face to Peter to show that I'm both nervous and excited while trying to put matters of the heart to the back of my mind. At least for now.

I get up and walk purposefully towards the audition room door, taking some steadying breaths as I get into character. I see Jean, Flora and Rachel in my peripherals giving me the thumbs up. I imagine myself walking through the cobbled streets and foggy spires of London and I am not being dramatic when I say I start to cough a little bit due to the pretend smog, such is the power of my imagination.

Five minutes later and I've finished my monologue, slightly out of breath from the emotional intensity I gave it.

'Thank you, Patch,' says Ms Jenkins as she writes down some notes. 'I love *Erin Brockovich.*'

'One of my absolute favourite films,' I reply earnestly, silently hoping she doesn't ask any follow-up questions about the film.

'OK, and your song?'

'Well ma'am,' I say, dropping seamlessly into my cockney

accent, 'it might seem a bit naff but I've decided to go for "The Ballad of Sweeney Todd".'

Ms Jenkins smiles and leans back in her chair, very much adopting the body language of one of the *X-Factor* judges.

There's a bit of an awkward pause as we both stare at each other, smiling.

'Whenever you're ready,' she says gently.

'Have you not hired a pianist to accompany?' I ask, genuinely confused. I've been practising with a piano karaoke version I found on YouTube.

'Not this time, Patrick, no,' she replies.

'No worries!' I chirp. 'One of the exciting challenges of live theatre is that you have to be prepared for anything. Let's just do it a cappella! Why not?'

I take a deep breath and begin. My song is just over three minutes long, which allows me to show off the strength of my vocals. I start out a bit shaky but after the first couple of lines I really get into the swing of it. In fact I would go as far as to say I'm utterly *nailing it.*

By the time I get to the chorus I'm certain I'll not only get this role but surely a role in the West End can't be far off.

'Swing your razor wide, Sweeney, hold it to the sky!' I sing.

I'm dancing around the stage, pulling faces and completely enraptured by my own performance. In fact . . . yes.

I've given myself goosebumps.

I steal a glance at Ms Jenkins who looks like she's enjoying it, though not quite as much as my performance deserves.

I'm getting to the end of the song, and in order to bag the main part I need to make it memorable. I slowly reach into my pocket for my final trick to really seal the deal.

'*The demon barber of Fleet . . .*' I pull out the Gillette razor that I found in the bottom of one of our bathroom cupboards that I think must have belonged to Ralph and hold it high in the air. I look Ms Jenkins dead in the eye and slash it down in the air in front of me, 'Street!'

Panting, I take a deep bow before lifting my head to look up at Ms Jenkins. I expect a look of excited shock closely followed by a slow clap. Instead, I am greeted by a look of out-and-out disapproval.

'Patrick, it is not appropriate to bring a blade into the audition room,' she says sternly.

'No, no, no, but look,' I say holding up the blade again. 'It's got the safety guard on!'

'Well, I'm willing to let it go on this occasion because that was . . .' she gives a pregnant pause, 'a great audition!' and gives me a double thumbs up.

'Thank you so much, Ms Jenkins,' I gush. 'And I just want to say thank you for the opportunity, it's truly been an honour to live inside the world of Sweeney Todd this last week.' I go to leave before turning back and quickly adding, 'Also, I want you to know that I take knife crime incredibly seriously and I would never trivialize it to add shock value to an already very polished audition.'

'Noted,' says Ms Jenkins. 'If you could call Sam in for his audition?'

'Yes, of course,' I say. 'Do you want a few minutes to emotionally recover before I do?'

'I think I'll be alright,' says Ms Jenkins, holding it together remarkably well as I do a stage run off the stage. A stage run is what I've seen actors do when they come on for an encore after a musical, so it's a little visual cue to Ms Jenkins that I'm very familiar with the dark and dastardly world of theatre.

I try to contain my smile, which I know looks incredibly smug as I continue my stage-run to Peter and Sam who are chatting animatedly. Clearly Sam's got a lot to say to Peter, which makes it clearer to me that he was *choosing* not to chat to me earlier.

'Sam,' I say slightly coldly, 'your turn.'

'Ahh, OK,' he replies nervously, smiling tightly at Peter before heading into the audition room.

I'm standing awkwardly in front of Peter, but decide to use this powerful and elated feeling of the post-audition high to take a chance because *you will never experience personal growth if you fear taking chances* and I would go as far as to list personal growth as one of my hobbies.

'I was wondering if you wanted to meet up over the weekend in town!' I shout.

God, I really am amped post-audition. Did that sound too keen? I quickly tone myself down both in terms of volume and commitment.

'With Jean, obviously,' I add in a casual way. 'And Sam, if you want. I'm *completely* unbothered either way.'

I feel the blood rushing to my head and my legs go wobbly in fear of him saying no. Why have I put myself on the line like this? I hate being on the line!

'Sure,' Peter grins.

I love being on the line!

'Cool!' I reply, trying to contain my elation.

Thank GOD. I really don't know what I would have done if he had said no . . . I mean I would definitely have to move or frame him for something criminal so that *he* would have to move back to America . . . I wonder what crime I could conceivably frame him for—

Doesn't matter, it hasn't come to that!

I exchange numbers with Peter – which feels very vintage but also glamorous because Peter has an *American number* – and then head straight over to Jean.

'OK, I've got two incredible bits of news,' I tell her excitedly in a quiet enough voice that nobody can overhear, especially Tessa who is nearby.

'Firstly, I've decided it's Peter!'

'What's Peter?' she replies confused.

'Peter will be my first boyfriend!'

'Oh!' I see Jean try and look enthusiastic. 'Patch, that's great . . . . Did you ask him if he's—'

'No,' I say emphatically, 'I don't know if he's queer or likes me blah-blah-blah, but that brings me to point number two: do you have any plans for Saturday?'

'Yeah, it's my parents' anniversary, remember? So we have to all go out for dinner, so annoy—'

'Not any more you don't,' I interrupt excitedly. 'I've got us a double date with Peter and Sam!'

'Patch—'

'OK, fine, you can go to your parents' anniversary dinner but Saturday *daytime* you're coming with me into town.'

Jean still looks concerned. 'Yeah, but Patch, I'm meant to be celebrating *myself* right now? I can't go on a date with Sam.' She leans in close and whispers, 'That's cheating on myself.'

'Oh, it's not actually a double date!' I explain. 'It's just a very casual hang that you happen to be there for, but what will quickly turn into a double date or at least a single date after I've sussed out what Peter's deal is!'

'So it's a sort of pre-date?'

'Exactly,' I nod. 'And you, my sweet, sweet Jean,' I take her hand, 'will be the platonic friend who is there solely to big me up and make me look amazing. So make sure you don't wear purple because it suits you too much.'

Jean beams. 'Sold!'

Everybody needs a Jean in their life.

Chapter 8

If planning for a date is tiring (which it probably is) then planning for a pre-date is exhausting. At least with a date you know what the vibe is so you can dress romantically (I imagine it's a lot more ruffles than one would usually wear). With a pre-date there are so many possibilities that it's almost impossible to choose a direction. You can't dress too romantically because it'll be humiliating if it's not a romantic vibe, but you need to be open to the possibility of romance so you can't dress completely platonically. After several back and forths, one meltdown (mine) and one very heated argument with Mum who told me off for cutting the sleeves off a jumper she *never wore*, I've finally settled on an outfit, and that outfit is sitting on the bus next to Jean on the way to my first-ever pre-date. I've decided to go down the something-very-casual-but-with-a-flourish route: cargo trousers to show that I'm spontaneous and always willing to do an activity (which I'm not, but Peter won't figure that out until further down the line), a pair of white trainers, a white shirt (classic, understated, chic) and the jumper I took the sleeves off (which is red, the colour of passion). I'm slightly worried I put a bit too much texturizing putty in my hair again, though, because I tried to pat it down and it basically fought back and won.

Jean and I managed to nab the best seats on the bus: top floor, right at the front, no contest. I watch our town whizz past. Hiverhampton town centre isn't exactly the glitz and glamour of London or New York, but it does have a Costa, Superdrug and a River Island which I think covers the fundamentals of metropolitan life. There was a rumour a while ago that they were going to open a bubble tea shop but this has yet to materialize.

The bus soon jolts to a stop and Jean and I both lean forward in our seats and crane our necks to get a glimpse of 'the fancy square'. That's what we call the square of houses not too far away from the theatre. They are, without a doubt, the most beautiful houses in Hiverhampton. It's like this little square has been picked up from a film set and dropped right into our town. All the houses are different colours and have beautiful flowers and plants outside the windows. They form a square around a private gated garden that Jean and I are obsessed with, but terrified of going too near in case we get told off. I love exclusive things even when I myself am excluded from them, and that private garden is top of the list. The bus moves off again and Jean and I reluctantly turn back to the very ordinary road.

★

Jean and I used to go to town practically every Saturday. This was partly due to the deep and passionate desire Jean and I had to be scouted as models; I had googled and we both reached the height requirements needed to be models (basically) so we used to dress up in all black and hang outside River Island. There was a girl four years above us who had been scouted when she went to a music festival last year and people are still talking about it (by which I mean me and Jean). Although Jean and I have never *technically* been scouted, we were once asked if we were interested in volunteering for the local charity shop. That was quite cool because it's still the world of fashion!

We get off the bus and make our way down the high street towards Costa. Even though we are no longer actively looking to get scouted, because we're more than just our very good looks, I can't help but notice that we are both clenching our jaws and elongating our necks as we go.

For us, 'getting coffee' has always been the mark of maturity and sophistication and I still feel a little (un-caffeinated) buzz every time we walk in. We tried desperately to get a regular table that the staff would hold for us, but apparently saving a table for two teenagers who, at most, get two drinks a week isn't 'financially viable'. Ugh, capitalism! (Maybe? Need to double-check what capitalism is.)

'The usual, please,' I say loudly. 'Honestly I'm barely functioning, I *need* some caffeine.'

‘So what will it be?’ asks the barista, who has the longest ponytail I’ve ever seen.

‘Just the usual,’ repeats Jean, slinging her arm on the counter. ‘*Please*, we’re desperate!’

The barista looks at us blankly, ‘Which is . . . ?’

Humiliating. Jean lowers her voice and leans in. ‘Two coffee frappes with extra hazelnut syrup, please.’

We’re slowly working our way towards liking black coffee (the chicest of drinks) but aren’t quite there yet. I casually turn around and scan the coffee shop while the barista passive-aggressively pumps out the hazelnut syrup.

As expected, Sam and Peter aren’t here yet. I expected that. In fact, we’re twenty minutes early so that we can stage the perfect tableau as they walk in and see us. And considering their track record with tardiness, we have a lot of time to play with. Jean and I collect our coffees and find a table that’s visible as soon as you walk in. We place our bags down and get to work setting the scene. Essentially, I want to appear smart and interesting but also cool and funny and definitely not *try-hard.* I asked Jean to bring ‘conversation starters’ to avoid there being any awkward silences. As Jean opens up her iridescent tote bag, I can see we’ve slightly got our wires crossed as she brings out an A4 printed picture of some modern art.

‘Jean, what on earth is that?’ I demand.

‘What? It’s a conversation starter. We can talk about *art*!’

she replies tartly, placing it in the middle of the table.

'I wanted *natural* conversation starters. Like this!' I say and pull out my keys and hold up my aquarium keychain. 'They might spot it and be like, "Hey, what's your favourite fish?"'

'I see.' Jean falters and bites her lip. 'So I probably shouldn't bring out these either?' and takes out a selection of DVDs.

'Absolutely not.'

'Out of curiosity, what *is* your favourite fish?'

'Red-lipped batfish,' I reply without hesitation. 'Reminds me of my gran.'

Jean and I sit down and take out the final piece of the puzzle: our books. I told Jean to make sure to bring one with her because, firstly, it's a good conversation topic, and secondly you seem interesting and smart if someone catches you completely lost in your own world reading (and in a coffee shop of all places). Very adult. I've brought a copy of *Sense and Sensibility* by Jane Austen which I've never read, but I found in a charity shop so it looks like I've read it tons. Jean has brought a copy of *Twilight: Breaking Dawn* which would be absolutely fine if not for the movie poster as the front cover which, I'm sorry, is tacky.

'Ready?' I ask Jean.

'Ready.'

We nod to each other and lock our eyes down on our

books, making sure not to look up every time someone comes in or the illusion will be shattered.

'Hey, guys.'

It's been about fifteen minutes of pretending to read when I look up from my book to find Peter and Sam standing in front of us.

'Are you two . . . OK?' Peter asks.

I turn to Jean as it suddenly dawns on me that being sat down staring at our books in complete silence might imply quite a hostile environment.

'Yeah, yeah, totally fine! Just completely *engrossed* in our books,' I say, putting my book down.

'Engrossed,' parrots Jean.

'Cool. We're going to get a drink, do you guys want anything?' Peter asks.

'Gosh, I could *really do* with another coffee, but,' I look at Jean, 'we've probably had enough caffeine for one day, haven't we? Absolute coffee addicts, we are!'

'Addicts,' Jean nods with such severity that it actually looks like we are suffering from a life-affecting addiction.

As the boys go to the counter I elbow Jean *very* gently.

'Ow!' she yelps. 'What?'

'You're going to have to take the reins here and work out if Peter's single and if he likes men,' I quickly explain, keeping an eye on Peter and Sam to make sure they aren't heading back.

'Why do I have to do it?'

'Well, I can't do it, can I? I need to remain aloof! *Asking too many questions will make you seem overly interested and you'll lose the upper hand*,' I quote to her.

'You know,' says Jean earnestly, 'I'm not sure how helpful your mum's self-help books actually are.'

I'm shocked at her allegation. 'They're written by *doctors*, Jean!'

'The "Doctor of Love" is not an official title,' she retorts. 'Anyway, *I've* been in an actual committed relationship and I think you should just be honest. Joe and I were always honest with each other. He once admitted he thought that the past was actually in black and white, like in old films,' she says wistfully.

'We don't have time to discuss this! They're coming back,' I say through the corner of my mouth.

Sam and Peter place their drinks down on the table and sit down.

'What's ya poison?' I ask in what I suppose you could call, at a stretch, a southern-American accent.

'Poison?' inquires Sam.

'I mean *order*. What did you order? What did you *get*? What hot drink did you get? Or cold drink—'

Thankfully Peter interrupts live footage of my brain melting by laughing and saying, 'Oh, I got a latte and Sam got a hot chocolate.'

Sam coughs stiffly. 'I just don't really enjoy the taste of coffee.'

I nod understandingly, even though liking the taste has nothing to do with getting a coffee.

'Apparently,' says Jean, 'if you put a tiny bit of salt in hot chocolate it tastes even better.'

Sam looks unconvinced as he sits down. 'Salt? Really?'

'Try it!' urges Peter, handing him one of the salt packets that's on the table.

Sam apprehensively tears open the brown paper packet and shakes some of the salt in. He takes a sip while we watch expectantly. His face cracks open with delight. 'Oh wow!' he exclaims before getting embarrassed at his reaction and mumbling, 'It's not bad.'

He puts the cup down and nudges it towards Peter. 'Try.'

Peter takes a gulp. 'Oh, yeah.' He grins and passes the cup to me to take a sip (which, I'm sorry, is very erotic and basically kissing).

'Mmm,' I confirm slightly robotically, as I'm still flustered about sharing a cup with not one but two boys.

We pass it around the table and each take a sip, thrilled with our new discovery.

'My ex-boyfriend Joe told me that,' says Jean before leaning towards Peter and Sam. 'Have your partners ever taught *you* anything?'

It wasn't the smoothest of questions but it served its

purpose. Subtlety has never been Jean's strong suit; she owns two separate 'event capes' for crying out loud.

'Oh, I'm – I'm not . . . well, I mean,' stammers Sam, 'I'm not seeing anyone.'

Sam clearly isn't comfortable talking about feelings.

Peter throws an arm around an awkward Sam and playfully jibes, 'Nobody's ever good enough for my Samuel.'

'Oh, that's cool, I think it's actually very important to be single when you're you—' begins Jean before I kick her under the table, '. . . but also keep a tab on that,' she quickly adds.

'And what about you, Peter?' I ask in a casual way.

Peter looks at me and then breaks eye contact as his eyebrows furrow. He stares down into his latte, stirring it around with the little wooden stick, suddenly looking incredibly emotionally tortured. It suits him.

'It's a bit complicated,' he admits, not looking up.

'Oh, OK, well we don't have to talk about it,' says Jean gently. I give her another instructive kick.

'But also,' she grimaces, 'I think we should . . . actually.'

Sam looks supportively over to Peter. I can tell they've chatted this through before.

'Well, basically I was seeing someone in New York,' he begins hesitantly, 'and we decided to do long-distance when I came here, but it's . . .'

'A woman?' I ask, positive I was completing his sentence and he was just nervous about breaking the news of his heterosexuality.

'Uh, no, I was going to say it's difficult.'

'Of course.' I nod. '*So* difficult.'

I don't let the ball drop on this one, which is ironic considering my sporting history. But when mine and Peter's future literally hangs in the balance I *have* to push a little further.

'Difficult with . . . a woman?' I'm suddenly aware I haven't blinked in quite some time.

Peter looks a little taken aback, but he answers, 'Yeah.'

I can feel my stomach drop like I've swallowed an encyclopaedia and I want to let out a very loud 'ugggghhhhh', but I just about suppress it. Suddenly my dreams are flying away; him doing a bad English accent and me slapping his arm playfully, us laughing while I do an American accent which is, obviously, pitch perfect, before Peter kisses me because he's just so dazzled by my talent.

I tilt my head to the side because that's what you do when you look concerned. I can feel Jean push her leg into mine in support.

'Well, I'm sure you'll work it out,' I say tightly.

Maybe one day Peter will kiss me out of pity? No. Must aim higher.

'I dunno,' says Peter and wrinkles his nose. 'I was once

seeing a guy who only moved to New Jersey but that fell apart pretty quickly. I just don't think I'm good at long-distance.'

It takes a couple of seconds for my brain to compute what Peter just said and in the meantime I just stare slack-jawed at him.

'*A guy?*'

Jean and I say at the same time.

'Uh, yeah,' says Peter a bit nervously. 'Why? Are you not . . . is that—'

Oh God, he thinks we're homophobes.

Jean immediately backtracks, realizing her 'ally' status is on razor-thin ice.

'Oh my God, no, of course that's amazing! I actually love that so much. Not that you guys broke up, but what I love is non-normative couples . . . I mean, not that same-sex couples isn't the norm, of course, just . . . well – *love is love*!' she exclaims.

I can see Sam suck in his cheeks, trying to hide a smirk, while Peter raises his eyebrows and grins.

'Glad to hear it!' he says.

I feel like I could sing and whoop and dance (and I can actually do two of those things to a graded level). Instead I lean forward and ask, 'So you're . . . bi?'

Peter thinks for a moment, then shrugs. 'I haven't fully worked it out yet and I don't love labels.'

'Oh God, me neither,' I quickly agree. 'I once had a label maker and I just . . . threw it away. Although if I *had* to have a label it would be just . . . gay, I think. Just your bog-standard homosexual.'

Not one of my top-tier anecdotes, but I'm too excited to care! The only obstacle in my way now is this broad in New York. I bet her name is Ashley or something like that. And I bet she has dyed her hair tons of interesting colours and probably has a nose ring or something.

We spend the rest of the morning slowly nursing our drinks so the barista can't ask for the table back. We talk about all the normal things: siblings, holidays, school and whether we think our birth stones accurately represent us. But all the while I am slowly hatching a plan.

I don't feel good about this plan (and I can already hear Jean telling me that 'as a gay man I should *always* support women'), but Ashley, who's name it turns out is actually Maddison (basically the same thing), needs to be *destroyed.* To be perfectly clear, I'm not going to murder Maddison, but I do need to make Peter realize that I'm the one for him.

As we part ways to go to different bus stops (we all hugged goodbye apart from Sam who gave us both a formal handshake like a teacher giving out a prize), I'm poised to tell Jean about my plan when I realize I can set things in motion immediately.

'I'll be one second,' I say to Jean and chase down the boys to let Peter know that I'm *always* here if he wants to talk about relationship difficulties with Maddison or anything, thus becoming his confidant. Just as I'm reaching out to tap Peter on the back, I hear the end of whatever Sam is saying to Peter,

'—didn't have a *single* interesting thing to say.'

Sam clearly senses someone behind him and turns around. His bright red face and rabbit-in-headlights expression confirm that he *was* talking about me.

What on earth is Sam's problem? Did I accidentally say something to annoy him? Can't he just not like me in silence like a normal person? I swallow the reply that I want to say which is, *'I might not have anything interesting to say but at least I have SOMETHING to say!'* But I have to keep Sam on side if I'm to get Peter to fall in love with me in time for Prom. Sam is the dry bun I have to deal with to get through to the delicious burger. Gosh, I really need to start thinking of some more vegan-friendly metaphors. I suppose the burger could be made of black beans? Progress!

'Everything OK?' asks Peter.

'Oh, yes!' I reply in a high pitch, trying to act as if I hadn't overheard them. 'I was just wondering if you guys knew the time?'

Brilliant.

Chapter 9

'What exactly do you mean when you say "mind games"?' asks Jean nervously as we sit in the audience of the theatre awaiting our fate (aka, finding out what parts in the play we have got).

I've enlisted the help of Jean in my plan for what I've coined 'Operation Free America'. 'America' being Peter and 'Free' being out of Maddison's (potentially) vice-like grip.

I've thought about it long and hard (almost all weekend) and it really feels like the only option.

My plan is pretty simple: I need to gain Peter's trust and then he'll realize for himself that I am the one for him. I think the rehearsal process will be the best time to do that. I am aware that this might make me the baddie in Maddison's version of this story, but Maddison is all the way in America so I'm trying not to concern myself too much with that; you have to be cruel to be kind, and so I've decided to be cruel to *her* in order to be kind to *me*.

'OK maybe *mind games* is the wrong phrase,' I explain to Jean. 'What we need to do is just subtly, but persistently, make it clear that Maddison is bad news and that I am hot property.'

'Hot property?'

'*Smoking* hot property,' I confirm, while rubbing in Jean's hand sanitizer, sort of making me look like a cartoon villain.

The rest of our conversation is cut short by Ms Jenkins arriving and causing everyone to fall silent. Today she is wearing an electric blue skirt and matching kitten heels. She walks slowly to the front of the stage like she's the lady in *The Hunger Games* who has to announce who is about to be picked to fight for their life.

'OK, everyone, before I read the cast list I just want to say that I was *blown away* by the quality of last week's audition. It's incredibly exciting to know that Hiverhampton has such talent!' She grins manically at us all, semi-expecting, I think, to get a small round of applause. 'Now, I want to remind you that there are no "main parts", because we are a company of artists, and in a company, there isn't a *boss*.'

I'm not sure this is technically true from a business or economic standpoint because companies famously *do* have bosses, but I'm willing to let her get away with it in the pursuit of getting to the point. I've been trying my best not to think too much about the play and for the most part I've done an excellent job. Apart from the two times I ran into Ms Beckett's office threatening to give up acting and become a corporate stooge (which she didn't seem too affected by).

I settle into the faded red faux-velvet spring-up seat of the auditorium and imagine myself up on stage as Sweeney Todd, slashing away at people's necks and tugging at people's heartstrings. I've already decided I'll try and show the humanity in Sweeney; how *circumstance* made him the monster he is today.

'Without further ado, the part of Sweeney Todd will be played by . . .' continues Ms Jenkins.

This is it! The moment I've been waiting for my whole life. Jean clutches my hand, and Rachel and Flora, who are sitting in front of us, turn around and give me a thumbs up. I very subtly practise my surprised face for when everyone turns around. Would it be too much to cry? I decide not to blink in preparation *just in case.*

But in the end, I don't have to do a fake surprise face for long, as a much more authentic one takes its place when Ms Jenkins calls out a name that is decidedly *not mine.*

Not even a little bit.

I suppose maybe if you were mumbling and substituted all of the letters . . . ? No it's just not my name. I'm not playing Sweeney Todd.

It's Sam.

I can hear my heart throbbing in my ears.

'Sam Gatehouse, where are you?' calls Ms Jenkins again, scouring the audience for him.

In my peripheries I see a tentative hand go up. I follow

the hand down and see that Sam's face has gone a violent shade of red.

'There you are!' says Ms Jenkins, beaming at him while there's a small patter of applause.

'Yes, SAM!' Peter whoops, grinning from ear to ear and holding up Sam's hand like a coach does after a wrestler has just won a match. Ms Jenkins goes on to say something else but I don't hear it over that throbbing. I feel the blood rushing up to my face in a desperate attempt to out-red Sam, who looks like he wants the ground to swallow him. I also want the ground to swallow him up because the main part should be *mine.* I can feel my eyes prickle and a molten-hot tear slips down my face. Rachel and Flora awkwardly turn away from me. *How humiliating.*

'Patch.'

I can't believe this.

'Patch.'

What am I going to do?

'*PATCH!*' I'm snapped out of my downward spiral as Jean elbows me and gestures to the stage (my fickle friend). I turn back to where Ms Jenkins is standing with her vile piece of paper and see her smiling at me. Sadistic cow.

'Patch, I was just saying you will be playing the part of Judge Turpin! Congratulations!' she says, followed by an even smaller patter of applause. I can feel Jean eyeing me nervously, unsure of how I'm going to react. She has good reason to be concerned; when I wasn't chosen to play the Angel in the nativity (you got to wear an amazing silk robe which I now believe to be Ms Jenkins' dressing gown), I tore the arm off Baby Jesus. The son of God was played by a doll, it's important to add.

Part of me definitely wants to cause a scene, run away backstage and spend many years in the rafters haunting people like the Phantom of the Opera. But that was the old Patch. That was *Patrick*. What new Patch does is act with grace and decorum *always*; like Julie Andrews in nearly everything that she does. Even if Julie Andrews was arrested for public urination, I think she would do it in such a way that would be excused. I force my numb face into a smile and look to Jean.

'I'm fine!' I try to reassure her.

'Are you sure?' she whispers. 'Because that vein across your nose is bright blue.'

Damn that vein! It's constantly undermining me; I wear my heart on my sleeve and my anger on my nose.

'It's ridiculous that you aren't playing Sweeney,' she continues, squeezing me closer. 'And you did better than me anyway! Did you hear? I'm a *chorus member*.'

I take a deep breath and rest my head on Jean's shoulder because I hate to admit it but that did make me feel loads better.

*

I somehow manage to hold it together throughout the remainder of Drama Club but as soon as I'm home I fully embrace the turmoil of what's happened, made even more bitter by the fact that Tessa got the part of Mrs Lovett. She even came up to me at the end and said, 'I knew you would get Turpin.' The sadist; she might as well have said, *you don't have the gravitas to be the lead of this show.*

And Sam, the traitor! I think it's completely unacceptable for a Drama Club newcomer to get the lead! Especially one who doesn't look like he even wants to be there. What happened to good old-fashioned favouritism?

Jean gave me permission to cancel our new tradition of having dinner together so I can fully sit in my feelings, and sometimes you *have* to sit in your feelings solo. Also her mum used up all the orzo which scuppered our dinner plans.

I'm in the bathroom sitting on the closed toilet lid and picking at the faded cartoon fish sticker from when I decided to personalize everything. I let the injustice of what's happened to me rise up. As soon as I feel myself start to cry I rush to the mirror to watch the process in real time but, as per usual, the excitement of seeing myself cry immediately stops it from happening. I always love watching myself cry, firstly because I need to work out if I'm a good-looking crier (which I'm not because I'm always blotchy and my nose gets wet) and so that I can recreate it when I'm asked to cry on demand.

I stare at my now non-crying face and decide two things: I've actually got quite nice eyebrows and also that I want some pity. I know people always say that they don't want pity (me included) but sometimes it's the nicest thing in the world and I want validation that I have been wronged and am the faultless party. Mum's downstairs making lasagne (which isn't vegan, but I'll make sure I get a slice that is more pasta than mince, for the planet) so I decide to make wailing noises until she comes up and checks that I'm OK.

'Agggghh,' I cry half-heartedly.

Nothing. I decide to bang the sink alongside my cry for good measure.

'Uggghhh,' I wail and slap the sink followed by some heavy sniffs.

Still nothing! I'm about to write my mother off as a sociopath and begin another email to my gran begging to live with her, when I hear the unmistakable tones of Robbie Williams from downstairs. She's listening to music!

I take a big breath in, very certain of the fact that I can match Robbie in terms of vocal power, when the door crashes open and I'm face to face with my raccoon-eyed sister.

'Whaddyadoingcanyoushutthehellup,' she grunts, staring at me like a bull that's about to charge. I hurry to wipe the single tear that I had left as evidence of *how* upset I was to my mother, and Kath's face softens.

'Oh, nothing, I was just . . . practising,' I mumble, suddenly embarrassed. Kath isn't exactly someone who you want to share feelings with because she has the emotional capacity of the hand soap she is currently staring at because she doesn't want to see me cry.

'Are there . . .' she attempts. 'Are kids being mean to you?'

'What? No,' I say sharply. I don't love the fact that Kath always assumes I'm being bullied.

'Good,' she nods. 'Because if they are, I'll break their legs.'

'Kath!' I cry, shocked at her violence but secretly very pleased. 'I was just upset because I didn't get the main part in the play.'

Kath furrows her brows. 'Good, plays are embarrassing.'

I make a noise to show that I strongly disagree, but I don't want to get into an argument with her again about how theatre is the lifeblood of society. Kath plays with the sleeve of her jacket and I notice she's wearing her favourite one (faux leather with the slogan 'No Mercy' on the back).

'Are you heading out to the park?' I ask.

Kath's main hobby is going to the park with a group of her friends and looking vaguely menacing while they share a single cigarette.

'Yeah,' she grunts, looking like she's desperate to both say something and to leave this conversation.

'Before you go . . .' I venture, 'can I *please* fix your

eyeliner?'

I can't decide if she's about to punch me or not, but in a very uncharacteristic move, Kath shrugs her shoulders and steps in.

I get almost light-headed with excitement and go about getting the necessary tools: micellar water, a Q-tip, eyeliner and some cream blush (if she'll let me).

Kath sits down on the toilet and acts as if this whole thing is below her, which it probably is. I immediately adopt the tone of a chatty make-up artist as I get to work removing the inch-thick eyeliner she's etched around her eyes, which are the exact same colour as mine, which unfortunately is an ordinary brown colour I sometimes try to brand as 'hazel'.

'So, who are you meeting at the park?'

'Some mates.'

'Cool, cool.'

I try not to press too hard both with the Q-Tip nor the questions, but I notice Kath keeps stealing glances in the mirror. Kath never cares about what she looks like (I assume) so it can't just be pity that is letting me do her make-up . . .

'Anyone new on the scene?' I ask casually.

'Uh . . . yeah. No. I mean. Sort of.'

I try to conceal my glee as I carefully elongate Kath's eyes with a subtle wing.

'Cool. Cool, cool, cool. I think that's cool.'

'Stop saying cool.'

'Cool.' I carefully grab the cream blush and dispense a tiny amount on my fingers. It's very strange to be having such a long conversation with Kath. I know this isn't really a *long* conversation but over the last two years the bar has been pretty low. The last time it was just the two of us talking this long was when Mum left us in the car for two hours because she fell asleep testing out mattresses.

'Someone you like?' I ask, as I begin patting the coral hue onto her cheeks.

Kath bats my hand away like I had suddenly splashed toilet water on her.

'Whaddyadoing?' she yells, getting up to look in the mirror and wiping away the blush with the heel of her hand.

'I just think a tiny bit of blush will liven up your face – and the coral colour *really* goes with your skin tone, Kath!' I hurry to explain. I once colour-matched her while she was sleeping.

'Uggh,' growls Kath, but I notice she stops rubbing the blush off quite so hard.

Kath, having reached her conversational capacity, turns to leave, but I decide to nobly extend an olive branch with the hopes we could be like the siblings in books, always *having* each other's backs rather than having to *watch* our backs. We could be the types of siblings who go on *japes* together and roll our eyes when Mum does something that's *so Mum.*

We could have a podcast!

'Kath, wait,' I plead and she turns around looking frankly dazzling.

'I just want to say I know we fight sometimes but . . . I do love you.' Kath stares at me like I'm speaking a different language, but I see her features soften slightly. 'And if you just admit that you broke my karaoke machine then I really think we can move forward as siblings.' I extend my arm to cement this new relationship with a symbolic handshake. After the handshake I think she'll pull me into a hug and it will be incredibly cinematic and moving and maybe music will start to—

Smack.

'Ow, Kath!'

Kath has instead given me a dead arm.

She turns around and stomps down the stairs. I rub where she hit and realize that I asked for too much; I flew too close to the sun and the sun gave me a dead arm (which is a stupid name for it because if it was dead it wouldn't hurt so much).

'*I know you broke it, Kath!!! MUUUUUM!*' I scream down the stairs. I suppose there's comfort in the natural order of things returning so quickly.

I close the bathroom door and continue wallowing on my own. That night, I leaf through one of my mum's books that I haven't revisited in ages – *Live, Laugh, Loving Yourself:*

How to Think Yourself Happy! – just to give my life some much-needed guidance, and rather helpfully, I come across some mind-blowing advice.

Chapter 10

It's a new day and I have a fresh take on life. The skies are clear (or they would be if the clouds weren't in the way) and *anything is possible.*

Anything is possible. That's my mantra for the day. I basically skip down the corridor at school in break. *Live, Laugh, Loving Yourself* had proved particularly insightful and even *moving* in parts. It talks about how if you put positivity out into the world, good things will come back to you (sort of like ordering something online). The book also talks about how *integral* it is to treat yourself with kindness. Upon reading that, I realized I haven't been *nearly* as kind to myself as I could be. So one thing I'm going to do is give myself a little treat every single day. For example, yesterday's treat was helping myself to one of Mum's special birthday chocolates for a snack, and I've already ordered a pair of sewing scissors on Mum's card that I've been coveting for tomorrow's treat! It's so important to have something to look forward to.

I bounce into Ms Beckett's office to give her the run-down on my new zest for life and how I'm being kind to myself. Although I'm sure this is the right course of action,

I do want to double-check with her.

'Well, yeah, obviously it's good to be kind to yourself . . . What about this?' she asks and I shake my head politely. I'm helping her pick a dress for her ex's wedding, but I don't know how many different ways I can tell her that cap-sleeves are not the way to go.

'But yes,' she continues, 'you should absolutely be kind to yourself. But that's not *just* about giving yourself little presents.'

'No, of course I *know* . . .' I quickly agree, despite that being exactly what I thought it was. 'So what would you say it was? I mean I know, but how would *you* phrase it?'

I think Ms Beckett sees right through this but kindly doesn't call me out.

'Well it's about *being* kind to yourself and not giving yourself a hard time . . . Like, OK, I could be very upset that I'm going to an ex's wedding and tell myself that I'll be single for ever and I've ruined my one shot at happiness, *but*,' she takes a deep breath through her nose, 'instead I'm thinking of all the things I'm proud of and how it will be a good chance to see people I haven't seen in ages . . . like that little snake Sophie,' she quietly adds.

From what I've gathered, Ms Beckett was going out with someone and then her best friend (Sophie) started going out with him when they broke up.

'What about this one?' asks Ms Beckett as she zooms in on a purple dress which looks like a hammock having a fight with a fishing net.

'If *you* want to be kind to yourself,' I gently say, 'don't put that in your basket.'

Ms Beckett barks out a laugh and pops a ginger snap in her mouth.

'So being kind to yourself is about doing nice things for yourself rather than just buying nice things?' I ask, realizing I probably should have read the whole chapter of the book rather than just the opening paragraph.

Ms Beckett shrugs. 'I mean, what do I know, but it's about doing things like . . . practising gratitude and treating yourself how you would like others to treat you.'

I nod.

'Can you give me an example?'

Ms Beckett stops scrolling and spins to face me. 'For example, I am grateful that I don't have to share my bathroom with someone, because I live alone, so I can have all the things I want by the sink. I'm grateful that . . . I know how to make a pretty good puttanesca. I'm grateful that I . . . don't have any fillings – well, apart from one. I'm grateful that I'm not with *Ian* any more. I'm grateful that Sophie has to deal with Ian constantly forgetting what plans we had that week, even though *we literally shared a Google calendar*!'

I'm not quite sure what's happening, but it seems that whatever Ms Beckett is grateful for has made her quite red in the face. She takes in a sharp breath and stands up.

'I'm just going to pop to the loo,' she says tightly.

'But I don't know how to be kind to myself yet!' I complain.

'I tell you what, just . . .' she grabs a piece of paper and pen from her desk and puts it in front of me, 'write a letter to yourself as if you were your best friend. A therapist told me to do that once. I'll be back in two minutes!' and she hurries out of the classroom, sniffing as she goes.

I look at the piece of paper in front of me. I suppose this exercise is sort of like writing a letter to Jean-Pierre, except it's to myself and I don't have to worry about *myself* fancying my sister because that would be . . . well, gross and illegal. How do I start? '*To whom it may concern*'? Too formal. '*To Me*'? No. '*Dear Patch*'? OK.

Dear Patch,

Firstly, your hair looks amazing today. I've got no idea how you manage to get such effortless tousled waves. I think you should be in a V05 commercial. Seriously!

I know you had a rough day yesterday and you didn't get everything that you wanted (a boyfriend and the main part in the play) but if you got everything that you wanted constantly then you would get too used to it and it wouldn't feel special, like if it was sunny every day then a sunny day wouldn't be a treat . . .

that being said, you normally like to wear layers because it provides more options fashion-wise and prefer long-sleeve T-shirts, so actually I don't think sunny days are all they're cracked up to be. A sunny autumn day, however, that's the stuff!

We've gone off track. So: you can't have everything you want all the time . . . but you definitely deserved the part of Sweeney Todd and you can absolutely mention that Ms Jenkins didn't give you the main part in the school play when you are one day telling anecdotes on Graham Norton's chair. 'Hahahaha,' Graham will chuckle warmly while Emily Blunt will playfully elbow me and say, 'I bet Ms Jenkins is pinching herself now!' Oh, Emily! You mustn't!

Anyway, let's get real, what you need to remember is that you are yourself and even though not everyone quite 'gets you', it doesn't really matter. Because you get yourself and Jean gets you and Peter seems to get you and Mum sometimes gets you, so if you add all those people up that's quite a few people who have got you if you stumble (which you sometimes do, but only because you've got such lovely slender ankles).

So. Just to recap, I love you so much and I think you can definitely tell that you've been doing press-ups sometimes.
Definitely!
I love you!
Patch xxx

As soon as I've finished I do actually feel great. A bit like when Jean and I play 'compliment tennis' which is where we take it in turns complimenting each other. I look up at the clock and realize that Ms Beckett has been gone for fifteen minutes and I'm about to be late for Maths and I'm already in trouble with Mr Clarke because I claimed I didn't need long division because I would have an accountant when I'm older.

Before I leave, I quickly write a note for Ms Beckett:

You are brilliant. Ian is an idiot + Sophie is trash.
But mostly, you are brilliant!

I purposefully don't sign it so technically she can't tell me off for calling her oldest friend trash. But I also make a silent wish that nothing ever happens to make it so Jean and I hate each other, but I can't think of anything that will drive us apart. I wiggle the touchpad on Ms Beckett's laptop to make it wake up and scroll for a second before seeing a very fun green dress that she would look amazing in. I click on it so she can see it when she comes back, but also add it to her basket. I fold up my letter before rushing out the door to pretend to care about long division. And I'm very thankful that I also remember to put some bourbons in my pocket for later. Here's to gratitude! I think gratitude might be one of those practices that really sticks.

Chapter 11

I learn pretty quickly that 'gratitude' isn't for me. It turns out to be very tiring work. How can you be expected to be grateful when *all* you ask is for scallops because you're curious about what they taste like and your mother point-blank refuses because they're too expensive and, to make matters worse, calls you *ungrateful* when you say that the scampi she gets as a compromise are 'pedestrian scallops'?

Also, Prom is fast approaching and I couldn't be *further* from getting a boyfriend (or doing any sort of planning for the Prom, come to think of it).

The one thing I've kept from my 'gratitude era' (can it be an era if it lasts two days?) is the letter I wrote to myself which I keep in my pocket to try and remember to be kind to myself. It serves as a little confidence boost because whenever I pat my pocket I hear the paper crinkle in response, almost saying, 'You've got this, Patch!' I give it a little tap as Jean and I step into the theatre for Drama Club and immediately stand up a little straighter (also because I want to improve my posture).

⋆

'Alright everyone,' trills Ms Jenkins as we are 'balancing the space'. 'Today is about *finding our character* – yes, Miles?'

'But I'm a stagehand?' he asks.

'Well . . . find him, then!' continues Ms Jenkins. 'Now, I'm going to be spending a bit of time with Sam and Tessa today to talk through their roles and for the rest of you . . . I want you to . . . think of . . . an *object* that you think best describes your character!' Sometimes I wonder if Ms Jenkins is making this up as she goes along.

Before any of us can argue, she ushers an obnoxious Tessa and nervous Sam into the corner to talk about whatever the *main characters* need to talk about. Probably how amazing and talented and full of themselves they are. Not that I'm bitter.

'Now, pair up and talk with your partner about what your object is going to be and *why*,' calls Ms Jenkins from the exclusive little trio-corner she has created.

I see Jean instinctively walk towards me as soon as she hears our prompt of 'pair up', but I communicate with my eyes that she can't pair up with me today. I *have* to pair up with Peter. Jean doesn't read my eye communication so I have to resort to good old-fashioned mouth communication, formally known as talking.

'Jean,' I hiss, 'I can't pair up with you!'

'Why?' she exclaims. 'Is this because I told you that you couldn't pull off the name Igor? Patch, that's a *good thing*!'

'No, no, no.' I look around at Peter who looks a bit lost. 'Listen, I have to pair up with Peter to carry on my mission.'

'Right . . .' nods Jean. 'But who do I pair up with, then?'

'Umm . . .' I scout around the room of people awkwardly pairing up like Ms Jenkins is hosting a very inappropriate sort of speed-dating mixer. I spot Miles standing alone and push Jean in his direction. 'Miles, go for Miles!'

'No, Patch, he—'

'MILES!' I yell over what I'm sure was Jean's incredibly justified objection. 'Jean wants to pair up with you!' and all but propel her into his field of vision. I'll make it up to her later, but for now I spin on my heel and storm towards Peter. Out of the corner of my eye I spot Alexa Peters edging towards Peter. *Not on my watch, Alexa.*

I try to keep the top of my body still and casual while I speedily walk to Peter. Alexa catches me doing this and ups her pace, so I up mine in return, landing somewhere between a trot and a sprint. My focus is so zeroed in on Alexa that I completely misjudge how far away I am from Peter and find myself crashing into him and knocking him to the floor.

'Sorry, Peter, sorry!' I say, extending my hand to help him up. I wonder if I can play it off as boyish japes, but look down at what I have called my 'rehearsal loafers' and decide probably not.

'My depth perception is all over the place, but seeing as

I'm here . . . do you want to pair up?'

Peter looks a bit dazed but grabs my hand and grins. 'Uh, yeah, sure!'

'Great!' I smile back before sliding my eye contact over to Alexa to make sure she knows that I am the victor in this battle. But, it turns out, she was just rushing to go to the loo. Apologies, Alexa.

I hold Peter's hands a moment too long after helping him up but I can't help myself. I can tell that he doesn't have a specific hand moisturizer (I have three), but he manages to pull it off.

'So,' says Peter, brushing himself down, 'any idea what your object is?'

I pretend to mull over what Judge Turpin's object is even though I immediately know. 'Umm, maybe a quill? By which I mean a pen from the olden-times because while Sweeney is dangerous with weapons, Turpin uses language and the law to be the *real* villain.'

Peter nods his head. 'Woah, yeah. Did you just think of that now?'

I shrug. 'What about you? What's your object?'

'As chorus member number four, you mean?' he says, grinning and pushing his hands into his pockets.

'Well, if you were chorus member number six I don't think you would need an object, but chorus member number four . . . it's really the heart of the musical,' I say and Peter laughs, which makes me fizz with happiness. 'But seriously,' I continue, 'you've got no idea how much you'll be in the musical. And there are no small parts so you have to think of *something*.'

Peter pouts as he thinks of an object in a genuine way like that's what he actually looks like when he thinks. If I looked like that when I thought I would think *all the time*.

'A spoon,' Peter says decidedly. He looks so confident in his decision I can't help but laugh.

'Why's that so funny?'

'I'm sorry. I didn't mean to laugh, but a spoon?! Why a spoon?!'

'Well,' explains Peter very seriously, 'as I understand it, there wasn't a lot of food around then, at least not for everybody, so if you found food you'd want to be prepared to eat it. And I think a spoon is the most useful eating utensil.'

'What about a fork?'

'Ah, well, I thought about a fork, but what about soup?'

'Or stew. Amazing point,' I concede.

'So, a quill and a spoon?' Peter asks.

'A quill and a spoon,' I confirm.

'Well, Quill, what do we do now?'

'I don't know, Spoon. We've got through our task in record time.'

I can't believe that we have so effortlessly given ourselves our own private nicknames when I spent a large part of

Year 4 trying to make the nickname 'Pat-Attack' stick. The closest I got was somebody calling me 'Patrick the loser', which wasn't close at all, come to think of it.

'We could do truth or dare?' suggests Peter, shrugging.

'Truth or dare? That's very American. Do people do that outside of films?'

'Well, if it's good enough for films . . .'

'True.'

'So,' Peter says, raising his eyebrows, 'truth or dare?'

I rapidly think through my choices and all the terrible things that could happen. If I pick *dare* then I will likely be forced to do something humiliating like lick the floor and it will then be hard to be seen as a potential suitor but if I pick *truth* and he asks me, 'Who do I fancy?' I wouldn't want to lie because, as my mum's book says, '*if you start the foundations of your relationship house with lies then the building will soon come crumbling down*'.

'Dare,' I say confidently.

Peter smiles mischievously and my stomach does a little flip like the last spin of the washing machine before it beeps to tell you your clothes are ready.

'OK . . . I dare you to take an ugly photo of yourself and then I get to send it to anyone on your phone.'

'And by anyone you mean . . .'

'Anyone.'

I have to do the dare because otherwise I'll seem not fun,

so I take out my phone and turn away from Peter so he can't see me contort my face. I decide to go for a low shot where I can generate as many chins as possible. I take the photo and have a quick check. The result is . . . alarming. Before I can take a more appealing 'ugly' photo, Peter grabs my phone.

'No, let me take another!' I cry in protest, trying to take the phone back.

Peter looks at the phone and his face turns quite severe. 'I really didn't think you would be able to take an ugly photo, but . . . wow. This is something.'

I hit his arm playfully, thrilled that he didn't think I could take a bad photo!!! Reminder to myself to never let him see the acting headshots that Jean and I took in the woods, which look like an advert to join a cult.

'OK, now who am I going to send it to . . .' he says to himself as he scrolls down my (quite short) list of contacts. 'How about "Valerie Tesco"?'

'No!' I yelp.

'Ooooh, who is *Valerie Tesco*?'

'No, she's no one, she's—'

'Sent!'

The little swoosh sound confirms that.

'Oh God, she's the woman who saw someone knock into my mum's car at Tesco and so I had to take her number as a witness!'

Peter covers his mouth.

'No, Peter, it's not funny, *look*!' I snatch my phone back and show my chat history with Valerie Tesco, which consists of reams of unanswered gifs.

'All she does is send me religious gifs and she only bloody gave up a few months ago, look!'

I show him the most recent message which is an image of a rather large boy with a giant pie in front of him with the text above saying, *Save room for Jesus!*

Peter launches into a bout of roaring laughter, and other pairs start to look over to us. Jean gives me a thumbs up as she has long maintained that 'comedy is king' when it comes to flirtation. The twins haven't noticed, but I overhear Rachel telling Flora, 'You can't pick a haunted raven as your object, Flora!' and it's with no small amount of satisfaction that I note that both Tessa and Sam are glowering at us, clearly jealous of all the fun we are having.

I adopt the stance of a TV sitcom 'mom' with my hands on my hips looking down at Peter with exaggerated annoyance.

'I'm sorry, I'm sorry!' gasps Peter as he finally recovers, wiping actual tears from his eyes.

'You are not forgiven and it's *my turn now.* Truth . . . or dare?' I whisper ominously.

'Oh God. Truth, only because I'm scared about what you will make me do if I say dare.'

I look into Peter's eyes which are still crinkled with

laughter and think of all the things I want to ask him.

Tell me the truth, do you want to break up with Maddison?

Tell me the truth, if you break up with Maddison, how long before you're ready for a new boyfriend?

Tell me the truth, am I a bad person for wanting you to break up with Maddison (bearing in mind that I donated to Children in Need last year on my mum's phone)?

Tell me the truth, do you fancy me?

Tell me the truth, do you use a tinted lip balm or are your lips really that rosy?

But I can't be that obvious. My mouth is so dry already, I can't go for anything *romance*-led or I'm worried my voice will break halfway through saying it, which will be impossible to recover from. I look over to Sam and Tessa, where Sam is staring stony-faced at a sheet of music Ms Jenkins is showing him.

'Tell me the truth . . . Sam doesn't like me at all, does he?'

Peter's eyebrows rise, surprised by the question. 'Why do you say that?' he asks.

I raise my eyebrows in return and give him a look as I think it's pretty obvious.

'Seriously, why do you think he doesn't like you?' he repeats.

'I don't know, he gives off that vibe, I think. And especially when we went for coffee. You're just very easy to chat to and he . . . I mean, he's constantly looking at me like I'm speaking another language,' I explain quietly before quickly adding, 'Which I can, by the way, I'm pretty good at French and I know enough Spanish to get by, if people *only* ask me what my favourite colour is.'

'Good to know.' Peter smiles. 'What is your favourite colour by the way?'

'Burnt orange, but you're avoiding the question and you *have* to tell the truth. Those are the rules.'

'Sam does like you, he does! He just . . . I don't think he's ever met anyone like you and he's also quite hard to read sometimes. He thinks too much, I reckon. But he's like that with everyone, trust me.'

'He's not like that with you,' I say.

'Well, that's different. I've known him *for ever*, we're basically brothers.'

I want to correct him that if they were actual siblings they wouldn't laugh nearly as much together and one of them would nearly always have a dead arm.

Peter glances over to Sam who is now nodding, listening intently to Ms Jenkins with his hands behind his back before looking back at me. 'Would it bother you, if he didn't?' Peter asks.

'Well, yeah,' I say, and Peter does a little nod which I can't quite read. 'But it would bother me if *anyone* didn't like me. Even now, I'm worried Valerie Tesco won't like me if I don't reply to her text.'

Peter chuckles. 'OK, I think you get another truth or dare because technically I also found out the truth that your favourite colour was orange.'

'Burnt orange,' I correct him. 'But OK, *truth* . . . who in this room would you most like to kiss?'

I almost can't believe I've asked the question. My mouth tricked me by not letting my brain think about it too much before it came out.

Peter looks taken aback, but after a beat he answers, 'Ms Jenkins.'

'You *have* to tell the truth,' I reprimand him, hopefully playfully.

Peter grins and I feel my face go hot at even asking such a direct question. Peter looks down at the carpet and then back up at me and opens his mouth to answer, but just as he's about to say a name, maybe even *my name.*

'OK, everyone! Gather round!' calls out Ms Jenkins.

'Ooh, saved by Ms Jenkins!' smiles Peter and walks away before I can force him to tell me.

Damn you, Ms Jenkins.

At the end of Drama Club, Jean and I are outside waiting for her mum to pick us up and while Jean is explaining to me that Miles needs to invest in some prescription strength deodorant, Peter jogs up to us. For a second I imagine the scene . . .

Peter stops in front of me and says, 'Patch, I didn't get to finish what I was saying earlier. If I could pick anyone in the room to kiss it would have been you.' He smiles as a cinematic swell of music begins. 'It's always been you, if I could pick anyone in any room . . . it's you!'

And then we kiss and everyone around us starts clapping while Jean playfully says, 'Get a room!' and we all laugh. But then, we actually DO get a room and before I know it we're—

Jean elbows me out of my imaginary sequence.

'Sorry, what did you say?' I ask Peter.

'Oh, I was just saying it's my birthday—'

'HAPPY BIRTHDAY!' I interrupt, already furious with myself that I didn't know my future boyfriend's *birthday.*

Peter smiles. 'Friday. It's my birthday on Friday and Sam's family are sort of forcing me to do a birthday celebration thing because I can't go home to see my parents. It's going to be at Sam's house this Saturday and I'm inviting some of the drama gang, so . . . yeah, if you can make it – I'll text you the details!'

'Definitely!' says Jean.

'Definitely!' I repeat.

'We'll be there!' says Jean.

'We'll *be there*!' I repeat again because I am too excited to think of anything original to say.

'Great!' says Peter and he jogs off to tell someone else. Annoyingly, I see that that person is Tessa, who smiles at him and subtly takes her ponytail out. Well played.

I spin around and clutch Jean's hands.

'Jean, a birthday party, did you hear?!'

'Yes, Patch, I was right there.'

'Of course, but *good lord* this is huge. You know eighty-three per cent of couples meet at birthday parties?' I tell her.

'You aren't *meeting* at a birthday party, you're just going to one,' Jean reminds me. 'And are you sure that statistic is true?'

'Jean, we can't get constantly bogged down with what's true and what isn't, it completely gets in the way.'

'Of what?'

'Of *life,* Jean!'

'I'm not sure that makes sense.' Jean smiles and then her face drops.

'What?' I ask.

'I think life is about to get in the way again . . .' says Jean gingerly. 'Aren't you meant to be going to your gran's this weekend?'

My stomach drops. How had I completely forgotten that?!

'Nooo,' I groan. 'Why do I have to have stupid family that want to see me? You are *so* lucky your grandparents are dead.'

Jean stares at me with an open mouth.

'Sorry, *sorry*. I didn't mean that, I just—' I stammer.

'It was a Patch exaggeration. Luckily I'm familiar with them. What are you going to do?'

I think for a second.

'I don't know, but I'll think of something. Jean, there is no way on earth that I'm missing this party.'

Chapter 12

It's Saturday morning. I'm sitting in the back of the car. I'm on my way to my gran's house.

I'm missing the party.

I really tried everything I could to get out of this weekend. Every weapon at my disposal: intellectual manipulation and pity. My first mode of attack was pointing out a gang of deplorable teenagers loitering around our house to my mum and expressing they had the *look* of people who would break into your house and take your most sentimental possessions. That plan was thwarted when Kath brought that same gang inside the house for pizza because they were her close group of friends.

Next, I said that I was super behind on planning for the after-show Prom, but that resulted in a lecture about my 'poor time management'. After that, I said that I couldn't go to Gran's house because she might have changed her mind about supporting me in my LGBTQ+ journey, to which Mum responded by pulling up a picture of Gran at pride last year with a group of drag queens who had the same necklace as her. After that I went for the fact that Jean was having a *really hard* time at school and I really should stay here to support her, but I forgot to prep Jean on the backstory. When Jean came over to watch a movie, Mum asked her what was wrong at school, I elbowed her and she panickedly blurted out 'School uniforms' like it was a French GCSE answer, so that argument unravelled as well.

So here I am. Sitting in the back of the car halfway through a three-hour journey, having finished all my car snacks before we even left the driveway, and looking forlornly out of the rain-streaked window. I need to ensure I remain mournful for the entire journey in case Mum looks at me in the rear-view mirror.

Being grateful really is just a waste of my time. I will be grateful when life gives me a *reason* to be grateful. A good opportunity for life to prove itself would have been life letting me sit in the front seat, but here I am suffering in the back seat even though it's definitely my turn. Kath and I technically have a rota of who sits where on long car journeys, but this rota is given the same reverence as a substitute teacher meekly saying 'shhh' as their classroom descends into chaos. I dig my knee into the back of Kath's seat which she then pushes back on with her back and we have a small battle between my knee and her back. Kath breaks the rules of this pressure battle by swinging her arm behind the seat to whack me in the leg.

'Ow, Mum!' I cry.

'He's digging his leg into my seat!' yells Kath.

'I am *not*!'

'You are!'

'Well, only because it's my turn to be in the front seat!'

'It's not!'

'It *is*!'

'Stop it *both of you*! You're both nearly adults, will you *stop bickering*!' screams Mum and the car is returned to stony silence with only the cheery sound of ABBA playing on the radio. The car radio broke a few years ago so it's stuck on a regional station that exclusively plays ABBA and Johnny Cash. After another chorus of 'Fernando' I let out an audible inhale of breath.

'What now, Patch?' says my mum witheringly.

'Oh no!' I slap my head, relying on sound effects, while Mum is looking at the road. 'I think I left the oven on! We really should go back and check.'

I can see my mum eyeing me in the mirror. 'What did you make in the oven?'

I pause for a little bit too long. 'Cornish . . . fajitas.'

Dammit. I started saying Cornish pasties and then second-guessed if pasties are made in the oven.

'Cornish fajitas?' scoffs Kath.

'They're a thing!' I retort.

'And who did you make these *Cornish fajitas* for?' enquires Mum.

'Well, obviously I made it for someone who is from Cornwall but enjoys Mexican food.'

'Uh-huh, and who is this?'

'Mum! That's neither here nor there, the issue is that our house could be set ablaze any second and instead you two are interrogating me about my Cornish fajitas, which I *definitely made*!'

'Well, luckily for you,' says Mum, 'I made sure the oven was off before we set off.'

'Oh,' I reply. 'Sorry, I meant the microwave.'

'Well, then I'm afraid your Cornish fajitas might be cold. Apart from that, I'm not too worried.'

I see Mum and Kath exchange a knowing smile in the front seat and there's nothing I hate more than not being involved in a knowing smile.

'Well, I'm *so sorry* that I care about the safety of our home!' I bark. 'But I'm just saying that there have been a lot of signs that we should *not* be going to Gran's house this weekend and sometimes you have got to listen to the universe!'

Mum turns down the volume on the radio. 'Patrick, if we didn't go to Gran's house it wouldn't be listening to the universe it would be listening to *you*. You have been trying to get out of this trip all week. What is going on? You normally love going to Gran's.'

I start running my fingers up and down the length of the seat belt and decide to come clean. While honesty may be heralded as the 'best policy', it really is my last resort and I hate that it's come to this.

'OK, the thing is,' I begin and quickly spill it out, 'there's a birthday party this weekend that I *really* want to go to because if I don't go then I'm worried that the boy I like will decide that he doesn't actually like me and stay with his stupid girlfriend from America!'

I stare down at my lap to avoid the looks I'm sure Kath and Mum are giving each other.

'Patch,' says my mum gently. 'There's a boy you like?'

'Yes,' I grumble reluctantly.

'Well, if this boy doesn't like you just because you're not *directly* in front of him, then he's not really the right boy, is he?'

I think about this. I suppose technically she's right even if I don't love what she said. I think it's a bit of a grey area because one of her self-help books claims that *absence makes the heart grow fonder*, while another says *out of sight, out of mind.*

'Now,' she continues, 'if you really want, we can turn this car around and you can go to the party.'

I look up, sure this is some sort of test.

'*But*, I know that your gran will be really upset that she won't see you.'

'I'd like to go to the party,' I reply immediately.

'OK, if you *really, really* want to let your gran down just to go to a party. Then we can absolutely do that, if you really want to upset Gran.'

'I'd like to go to the party,' I repeat confidently. 'Actually, since we're in the car can we stop off somewhere so I can get a present for—'

'*Patrick*, we're not going to the bloody party!' Mum snaps.

'Then why did you give me the option?!' I shout.

'Because you were supposed to do the right thing and come to that decision by yourself!'

'So we're not going to the birthday party?'

'*No!* We're going to your gran's and we're going to have a *lovely time*.'

With that, she cranks the volume up and Johnny Cash is suddenly doing his best to sing over the increasingly frosty atmosphere in the car.

Chapter 13

My goal is to spend the whole weekend sulking, but as soon as I walk into Gran's house it feels like a giant hug. Mostly because Gran envelops me into a giant hug. If I could sum up my gran in two objects they would be red lipstick and creamy mashed potato. The red lipstick is always Chanel and the creamy mashed potato, I assume, is just made with a lot of butter, which Gran claims makes everything taste good. She has never fully got on board with what she calls 'new wave fats', by which she means olive oil and vegetable oil.

The first thing Gran does as soon as we arrive is fuss over us, and there's something very lovely about being fussed over. Within ten minutes of arriving, I'm sitting down on the sofa in front of the TV, tucked under a blanket, given a plate of bourbons because I am a 'growing boy', a handful of cod-liver oil tablets because she saw an advert about how important they are, and a mug of nettle tea to help my digestion which tastes bad but feels a bit like I'm an ancient druid or a witch, so I allow it.

My phone pings in my pocket and I try to check it but

I'm pinned in by Gran's military-grade blanket-tucking. With some difficulty, I manage to shimmy my phone out of my pocket to see a series of texts from Jean, two religious gifs from 'Valerie Tesco' and one from an unknown number. I very rarely get texts from unknown numbers so read that one first.

Hi Patch, Peter says you can't come to his party. That's a shame, it would have been good to see you. Sam Gatehouse (from Drama Club).

I blink at the text and re-read it. Why does Sam message like a dad and why is he messaging me at all? Unless . . . Peter must have *told* Sam I thought he didn't like me and so encouraged him to extend an olive branch! That knowledge (combined with the nettle tea) puts a warm feeling in my belly. Surely that means Peter cares about me a *bit* in order to do that. I then go to my messages from Jean. First, she wishes me luck in my sulking plan, then she reminds me that she is definitely not going to go to Peter's party out of solidarity, and then she sends me a link to a video saying 'love this!!!'. The video is of two apparently queer hamsters running around on a hamster wheel together. I'm not sure what the process was for identifying the sexuality of the hamsters, but they both seem happy, so that's good.

★

Time always moves differently at Gran's house. It could be the familiar routine (marmalade on toast in bed in the morning, short walk, big lunch, film, big dinner, sleep), the overpowering smell of 'jasmine' air freshener, being busy helping Gran sort through old clothes to see if any of Grandpa's old jackets fit me (they never do), fighting Kath about who gets the remote or simply the sheer amount of mashed potato I've consumed. Whatever it is, I'm lulled into a sort of happy waking coma and forget all about the party I'm missing and before I know it, the weekend's nearly over.

It's the night before we leave and I can't sleep. Not because my mind is racing, but because I'm sharing a room with Kath who refuses to wear headphones when she watches TV on her phone. After several passive-aggressive sighs and tuts, I eventually give up and go downstairs to get some water. The carpet on the stairs is faded and not particularly soft but feels nice and worn by all the steps my family have taken on them. I know that the third step on the way down creaks loudly, and I step on it heavily as I'm going down. I've done this since I was young because I was constantly worried about burglars (even in the daytime) so it was my way of alerting anyone that I was coming downstairs so they could scarper in time.

As I purposefully make the *creak* with the ball of my foot, my gran calls from downstairs.

'Patrick?'

I trot down the rest of the stairs and into the kitchen where Gran is sitting at the little table with the rest of the jackets we haven't tried on piled up.

'How did you know it was me?' I ask her as I pull out the chair and take a seat.

'Ah, grans just know,' she replies sagely. 'Now, while you're down here let's try on the last of these jackets so it's out the way and I'll make you another nettle tea.'

'Can I have coffee instead?'

'Since when do you like coffee?'

'Well, I don't yet but I'm working on it.'

'You can't have coffee just before bed, but how about a hot chocolate?'

'Deal.' I think about Sam adding the salt to his drink. 'Hot chocolate does taste better.'

'Agreed,' says Gran and she stands up and opens up the fridge to warm up some milk in a pan. I asked her if she had any oat milk yesterday and she looked at my mum like I had asked her for dodo milk.

'Don't be a spare part, try on some of those jackets.'

I stand up and pull on a wool jacket that is somewhere between brown and green and nearly comes down to my knees. This 'trying on jackets' is an endless cycle. Every time I visit Gran she asks me to try them on and says she'll throw away the ones that don't fit, but never does.

'Yes or no,' she calls from the hob.

'Nope.'

'OK, put it on the green chair,' and I do.

I pull on the next jacket which is double-breasted and navy blue. The inside is silky and cold and feels like I'm dipping my hand in cold water as I push my arms through. It would actually be very nice if it weren't *so giant* on me, my hands don't even come out the bottom. I look in the mirror on the wall and look a bit like a scrawny child poking his head out of a navy-blue box.

I stick my hands in the pockets to make sure it's definitely not a cool oversized boxy jacket and as I do my fingers fumble around a piece of card inside. I pull it out. It looks like an old ticket.

'Gran,' I call out. 'What's this?'

'What's what?' she asks from the stove.

'This,' I say and turn around to give it to her.

Gran wipes her hands on her trousers and peers very closely at it. As she does her eyes crinkle in recognition.

'Where did you get this?' she asks.

'It was in the jacket pocket.'

She looks at me and the jacket and smiles. 'Oh, yes.'

She sits down at the table. 'This is the ticket from the day your grandpa asked me to marry him.'

'Really?' I scoot to sit next to her. 'Can I have a look?'

Gran doesn't really talk about *my* grandpa that much. I say *my* grandpa because Gran has been married four times, which I think is amazing because she wears all the engagement rings on her right hand like medals of honour but glitzy. She's hoping to wrack it up to five times by the time she turns eighty, and told us this weekend that she's started seeing the optician down the road who keeps giving her free eyedrops, so it's looking likely.

'Careful,' she instructs as she slides it back over to me. The ticket is in pretty good condition. It shows a journey from Newcastle to London.

'I had only gone on one date with your grandpa,' she said. 'And it was a *fabulous* date, but I had already decided I was going to move to London and I didn't want to stay in Newcastle which is where we were both living at the time. He asked if he could drop me off at the train station, which he did. And then I started on the long journey to London, worried I had missed out on one of the loves of my life. And it was a different time then, I couldn't just email him. Anyway, I finally arrived in London and I was pulling my bags through the station when someone tapped me on the shoulder and asked if they could help with my bags. Guess who that was?'

'My grandpa?'

'*Your* grandpa. He had bought a ticket without me knowing and managed to hide himself in a different carriage so he could surprise me when I got there. "I can carry my own bags *thank you very much*," I said to him because I was a stubborn old mare, and he said, "Of course you can, but I'd like to be with you while you carry your bags, for as long as you'll have me," and he knelt down and gave me *this* ring,' and Gran dangles her middle finger in front of me.

'Wow,' I say, as I inspect the thin gold band which has a little emerald on the top.

'Big gestures, Patrick, they are the ones to go for. No point being shy in love,' she winks, in a way that makes me suspect Mum has told her about Peter.

I smile back at her but then wrinkle my nose as a horrid smell suddenly takes over the entire room.

'What *is that*?' I grimace.

Gran sniffs the air before running to the stove. The milk has burnt.

Big gestures. I think to myself.

Chapter 14

I'm hopping from foot to foot in the car park of the theatre to keep warm as Jean gets the final supplies from the back of her car. It's so cold that I can see my breath plume out in front of me and I decide to rub my hands together for good measure.

'Sorry, I forgot how *heavy* this thing is,' grunts Jean as she hauls a giant black suitcase. The suitcase is paramount to my big romantic gesture, which I've been thinking about non-stop since Gran mentioned it. I hurry inside while Jean lumbers behind me, thankfully we are the only ones here (we told Jean's mum that they had cancelled the last school lesson of the day so that we could get in early). We quickly go about setting up. I've watched enough rom-coms to know what makes a big romantic gesture and I strongly believe that the perfect gesture must consist of three things:

The perfect big romantic gesture:

1. Doing it *publicly*, i.e. in front of a lot of people.
2. Giving a list of all the things you like about someone

(these are often things that you also find annoying but you still like it somehow).

3. A brass band suddenly playing something as you are speaking.

Jean unclasps the giant suitcase, swings it open and, with some effort, lugs out a trombone. It might not quite be the 'brass band' I had envisioned but Jean got a Grade 2 in trombone (with a merit) before giving it up because it was too heavy to carry around and that's better than nothing.

'Are you sure about this?' she grunts as she carries it towards me.

'Positive,' I reply as I go through my list of things I like about Peter:

Things I like about Peter:

1. He is American.
2. The way he says my name (in an American accent).
3. The way he rolls his sleeves up and down throughout the day.
4. His smile (again, his teeth = v. American).
5. His laugh which is a bit like a lawnmower, but nicer.
6. Our secret names for each other (Quill and Spoon).
7. That he loves to wear red.

I can feel Jean sceptically reading the list over my shoulder.

'What?' I snap.

'Nothing,' Jean says in a way that basically means the *opposite* of nothing.

'Whaaat?' I repeat.

'Well,' says Jean carefully, avoiding my eyes as she checks over her trombone. 'It just seems that most of your reasons for liking Peter are that he's American.'

I am about to disagree when Jean presses on. 'Plus, you've seen him wear like three outfits so how can you be sure he likes to wear red . . . I'm not saying that it isn't good to make a big gesture and be brave with love, *especially* LGBTQ+ love, but I just don't know if you know him well enough yet.'

Jean finally looks up at me and I notice she's got a trumpet hair clip in, which I think is a nice touch.

'Jean, I know I don't know him *super* well, but Romeo and Juliet only knew each other for like an evening when they decided to be together for ever.'

Jean gives me a concerned look. 'I'm not sure Romeo and Juliet are a good model to base your relationship off. They both die.'

'Jean, trust me, this is going to work. Have I ever made a bad decision before in my life?'

She goes to reply, but I say 'Exactly' before she has the chance.

Jean relents and smiles. 'OK, well if we're going to do this let's get ready, people will be getting here soon.'

I stick up a sign on the main door that says SPECIAL ANNOUNCEMENT TO BE MADE IN THE THEATRE FIRST THING!! and rush to the stage.

From the wings, Jean and I can hear the thrum of people arriving, murmuring about what this 'special announcement' might be. The lights on the stage are incredibly bright because Jean and I couldn't figure out how to get a single spotlight so we just turned them all on instead. Because of this, I can't really see anything when I look out. After another minute or so, Jean whispers in my ear, 'OK, I reckon that must be everyone, show time!'

I take in a deep breath and step out into the lights.

'Hello, everyone!' I call as I stride in. 'I'm sure you're all wondering what this announcement is all about . . .' I blink a few times to try and get used to the lights, but the blaze of the bulbs are there even when I blink, essentially blinding me.

'Now, I can't really see anything so I'm going to need an oral cue that you're all here!'

There's a lacklustre sort of cheer and suddenly I feel like I'm giving a school assembly on how smoking cigarettes is *not groovy.*

Thankfully, Jean comes in at that point with a sonorous note from the trombone. The note isn't quite right though so she tries it again and then begins playing. We hadn't discussed what song she was going to play, but after a few notes I realize that she has gone for the one that earned her her merit in Grade 2. I am now accompanied by the unmistakable notes from the *Pink Panther* theme tune.

'I am on stage right now with a singular aim, and that aim is love. Because if you're not aiming for love you're probably just aiming at, well, something that *isn't love*, aren't you?' I realize now I could have spent a little bit more time fine-tuning the script but we're too deep into it now for re-drafts. 'So I have something pretty huge to say. Are you ready? OK, I—'

Just at that moment the lights switch off. I blink a few times with the ghosts of the shine still in my eyes. Then I hear Ms Jenkins clacking down the stairs calling, 'Patch, what on earth are you doing?'

My eyes finally get used to the dark and I can make out everyone in their seats staring at me with a heady combination of confusion, amusement and boredom (rather than the heady combo of respect, awe and admiration that I was hoping for). My eyes search the crowd for Peter. I find Flora, Rachel, Tessa, Sam and then . . .

What?

My eyes dart back and my heart plummets past my stomach and straight into the core of the earth, only to bounce back up again and whack me over the head. Because there's Peter, staring up at me with his arms wrapped around . . . Tessa.

A million questions charge through my mind as my breathing gets shallow.

When did this happen? What is he thinking? Oh my God, what do I do?

'Patch . . .' repeats Ms Jenkins, who has now got to the bottom of the stage. 'What is this?'

I feel my mouth desperately trying to make the shape of words, but nothing is coming out. I imagine I look a bit like a fish. I desperately turn to Jean, but she is also staring at Peter and Tessa in shock, I look at them again to make sure they are definitely not canoodling *platonically* but no, she's even got her creepy little hands playing with his hair.

'He was just going to say something pretty huge?' calls Tessa and I'm positive I see a cruel glint in her eye from all the way up here. 'Something about love?' she says.

Ms Jenkins turns to me inquisitively. 'Patch?'

'Yeah,' I stutter, 'well . . . I was just going to say something pretty huge . . . . about . . . yeah, love.'

'Alright. Can you hurry it up because we need to start our warm-up, there is *nothing* more dangerous than a voice that hasn't been warmed up properly, Patch, you know that,' says Ms Jenkins with the utmost severity.

'Yes, of course. So what I was going to say about love is that I . . .' I turn to Jean to save me from this car crash, but she looks equally panicked. I can feel the next words making their way out and there's nothing I can do to stop them. 'I . . . am gay.'

There is a stony silence and I can see several people covering their mouths to hide their smiles, Tessa very much included.

This has got to be the worst day, the worst moment, of my humiliating life.

I have never been so embarrassed and so heartbroken. In fact, *nobody* has ever been as heartbroken on stage as I am at this moment. Honestly, even Romeo and Juliet would stop their silly little laments and come over to me and be like, 'Gosh, Patch, that was harsh, art thou OK?'

Before I can hear the humiliation of Ms Jenkins reminding me that this is now the *third* time I have come out in Drama Club, I run off the stage and into the wings. Exit pursued by *anguish* (and Jean).

I pace around backstage trying to process what has just happened. 'Tessa?' I hiss to Jean as she warily approaches me like I'm a frenzied badger she's found in the kitchen. 'Tessa?!' I repeat, asking a question but having no idea what that question really is.

'I know, I know,' she coos as she wraps me in a conciliatory hug. 'It's *incredibly* heteronormative of him!'

'And what about Maddison? Doesn't Peter already have a girlfriend? So, what? He just has *two* now?'

'I don't know.' She strokes my back.

'It's not very bi of him to have *two* girlfriends.'

'Patch, remember, being bi isn't a statistical game. You can identify as bi and never have a same-sex relationship . . .' she gently reminds me and I don't have the energy to be annoyed that, once again, Jean is proving herself a better queer ally than I am a queer person.

'I just . . . I can't believe he's not in love with me,' I muffle into the stiff wool of Jean's school blazer.

'He might be! He might just not *know* that he's in love with you!'

'Oh come on, you saw them, Jean! They're all over each other,' I sniffle.

'But love can come slowly. I didn't realize that I was madly in love with Joe until I saw him *really* concentrate to tie his laces and I suddenly realized, I love this idiot!'

Jean sees that this isn't as helpful as she thought it was, so she puts her hands on either side of my head and looks me dead in the eyes. 'He's an idiot and he's made a huge mistake and *she* . . .' I can see Jean trying to conjure up the most despicable thing that she can say about Tessa while still being a feminist. 'She used to think that banoffee pie was the best pudding in the world.'

I can't help but smile a bit.

'I mean it's a *fine* pudding,' she continues, leaning in conspiratorially. 'If it was put in front of me when I was hungry, would I eat it? Of course I would! But it's not the best pudding in the world, is it?'

'No,' I chuckle and shake my head.

From outside I can hear the beginnings of a game of Zip, Zap, Boing.

Jean grabs hold of my shoulders and looks at me sternly. 'Now, we're going to go out there and you are going to hold your head high because you've done nothing embarrassing—'

'Apart from just coming out for the third time,' I interrupt.

'Well, yes, apart from that. But I think queer visibility is always a good thing. So we are going to *stride* out there and we are going to *destroy* at Zip, Zap, Boing! OK?'

'OK,' I sniffle, stopping my tears with the heel of my hand and stepping out onto the stage again. Once more unto the breach! Thank goodness I have Jean as the constant co-star in my life.

Chapter 15

Getting over someone is hard. Especially when you were never even together, because then you have the added struggle of getting over a *potential* relationship which is even more perfect than the actual relationship you were going to have. I decided, as per usual, to make a list. This list is of all the things Peter and I *might* have done that I will miss (or *would* miss, should they have happened, which they haven't, but could have).

Things Peter and I might have done if we had been in a relationship:

- The way Peter would always open the car door for me when stepping into taxis (specifically London black cabs when we would take day trips to London because we are both 'culture vultures').
- The way Peter, when we were at events and galas, would squeeze my hand under the table when I was talking to the movers and shakers of the fashion world because he knew that I would be nervous.
- The way he would surprise me every single day with a

baked treat and I would be like, 'Peter, I can't have a baked treat *every day*!' and he would be like, 'Of course you can, because I get a treat every day too . . .' And I would say, 'Oh really? What?' and then he would wrap me in his arms and say, 'My treat is that I get to be with you!' and we would kiss ferociously for hours.

- The way, when we were ancient (in our forties), we would be the last to leave a restaurant because we were just talking and laughing so much. A waiter would come up to us and say, 'You know what, I have to close up shop, but I just want to say that you two make me believe in real love. Here are the keys, you guys lock up when you're done!' and we would play music on the vinyl player and dance with red wine that costs more than £25 per bottle in the empty restaurant.

I am aware that my list is perhaps a *little* optimistic and when I show it to Jean as we're queuing up for lunch she replies, 'Honestly, Patch, what's more likely is that you would have got to second base in the park after a tin of "winterberry" flavoured cider.'

Romance is alive and well.

We got the 'full story' of what happened from Rachel and Flora who had gone to the party (traitors). Apparently Maddison and Peter had got into a fight because she had forgotten his birthday and it resulted in her breaking up with him. Flora thinks that Maddison was cheating on him the whole time, but Rachel thinks it's just that Americans are bad at remembering the dates of things because they put the month and the day the wrong way around. It was too late to call off the party so it went ahead, but apparently it was a bit awkward. At some point Tessa and Peter went for a 'DMC' (Deep, Meaningful Conversation) in the garden and came back holding hands and were basically a couple after that. I did try to explain to Flora and Rachel that we're not really getting the 'full story' if most of the juicy details happened while they were in the garden.

'You know what the *worst* thing is?' I ask Jean, who is lingering in front of the lunch lady, signalling that she would like another spoonful of pasta salad.

'There's another worst thing?' she asks wearily.

'The *very* worst thing is that everyone will start calling them the "power couple" of Drama Club. That's a title that Peter and I were meant to have! God, Tessa is the worst.'

Jean purses her lips and I can tell she wants to say something.

'What?' I demand.

'OK, yes, Tessa is the worst . . . but I don't think you can blame her for this.'

Why must Jean *always* be my moral compass? I wish that just once she was the unreasonable one that I had to talk down.

'No, I know,' I admit, grabbing a bowl of sponge and custard, 'but I can't just *let it go.* It's not in my nature! I have so much snap in me and I just need to snap at someone.'

We sit down opposite each other and I pull out two little jars of home-made dressing to spice up the wet leaves at the side of our pasta salad and hand one over to Jean.

'Why don't you try snapping at me? To get it out of your system?' Jean suggests.

I put down my fork and look her up and down trying to find something.

'I can't. You're literally perfect,' I sigh, 'Have you been using a new conditioner? Your hair looks *so* soft.'

'Patch, focus!'

'Ugh, OK . . . I suppose, I don't *love* today's hair clip as much?'

Jean's voice immediately crumbles. 'Patch!'

'You just told me to snap at you!'

'Yeah, *snap* at me, not eviscerate me!' she hisses, tearing her tomato hair clip out of her hair.

That went about as well as can be expected. I think part of the reason Jean is so saintly is *because* she doesn't deal with criticism at all well.

At that moment, I see Tessa's hair glint in the overhead light as she swishes it behind her shoulder to sit down with her lunch. She is, uncharacteristically, sitting alone. I probably have a maximum of five minutes to talk to her before her cronies join. I *need* to find out what happened in the garden.

I stand up.

'Where are you going?' asks Jean.

'Look, I'm sorry about the hair clip.'

I can hear Jean explaining why she felt particularly connected to the tomato hair clip, but I can't help glaring at Tessa. She has everything I want. She has Peter. She has a main part in the school play. She has perfect hair *and* a cinema room! As I'm staring, Tessa's phone goes off and she whips it out and smiles down at it. I wonder if it's a message from Peter and I immediately see red.

'I'm just going to quickly talk to Tessa,' I say decisively.

'Patch, no!'

Jean looks incredibly panicked, but before she can convince me that this is an unquestionably horrid idea I storm across the cafeteria. I don't quite have a gameplan and before I can think of one I'm sitting opposite Tessa, who looks up from her phone startled.

'Hi?' she says.

'So?'

'So what?'

'You and Peter?'

'Yeah, what about it?'

'You *know*.'

I look into the eyes of the girl who used to be one of

my best friends, and she stares back. I remember us saying that we wished we could swap eyes for a day to see if we saw colour completely differently. Like, maybe my version of green was actually purple and her version of red was my version of blue. My fiery wall of rage is doused somewhat.

Tessa breaks eye contact first and looks down at her phone, but I can tell she's not *really* looking at it.

'What do you want, Patrick?'

'What happened between us?' I ask quietly.

Tessa's eyes move back up to me, wary. I think she's trying to work out if I'm being serious or not and even I'm not really sure at that moment.

'What do you mean?'

'We used to be really close and then we weren't. How come?'

Tessa stares at me and looks around, clearly wanting her friends to arrive and liberate her from this awkward conversation.

'I don't know.' She shrugs. 'I guess we just outgrew each other?'

'Outgrew each other?' I scoff. 'More like we weren't cool enough for you any more.'

'That wasn't it,' she mutters quietly but forcefully.

'What was it then?'

Tessa chews the inside of her cheek and doesn't answer. It's weird seeing her not looking so . . . smug.

'Well, whatever it *was*,' I continue, 'are you going to do the same thing with Peter? Just "outgrow" him when he doesn't make you look cool any more?'

'Why do you care so much about Peter and I?' she asks.

Peter and I. Who does she think she is? But I falter at the question and try to think of something to say.

'I don't care,' I say. 'I just – I don't want you to like . . . he's really great, you know?'

'Oh my God,' she says, leaning forwards, 'I know you fancy Peter.'

Crap. Crap, crap, crap.

'What?! No I don't!' I say in a very high-pitched tone, perhaps my least convincing performance to date. I hear Callum Taylor's loud obnoxious voice booming towards us, so before Tessa can say anything else or I can blab any other secret, I spin away from her table and march back to Jean with my head down. This is why you should always plan a conversation with a nemesis in advance.

What have I done?

Chapter 16

I am now in a near-constant state of fear that my crush on Peter is going to be revealed by Tessa, if she hasn't revealed it already. How did she know I liked him? Even if she wasn't positive I liked him and was just testing the waters, the way I reacted certainly made it crystal clear. I don't know what I was thinking. It's like giving a shark a taste of my blood and then splashing slowly away crying, 'Please, don't chase me!'

But running alongside that constant fear of humiliation is a thought that keeps niggling at the back of my head. Tessa said that Jean and me not being cool enough *wasn't* the reason we stopped hanging out. But if that's true, then what was it? I go through all the other possibilities:

Possible reasons Tessa ditched us:

1. She was forced to stop being friends with us by an authority figure (Her mum? A teacher? God??).
2. She is allergic to Jean's 'tropical paradise' body spray and kept breaking out in hives but was too embarrassed to say anything.
3. She has fallen deeply in love with me. Or Jean.

(Probably me.) Because of this she can't spend time with us as friends because it's just too painful.

4. Callum Taylor is brainwashing her and promising her a lifetime supply of new trainers if she carries on being a cow.
5. She's actually a forty-year-old woman pretending to be a sixteen-year-old girl and has been hired by the FBI to find out state secrets. At first, she thought Jean and I might be involved, but she's since given up on that hypothesis.

None of the possibilities quite ring true apart from the last one about her being a forty-year-old woman because she always *claimed* she was an old soul in a young body, but perhaps that was simply to throw us off the scent and she's actually just a regular soul and *is* an old woman?

One of my mum's books once said that you can will things into action with your mind (it was called *Manifesting with Angela*, which I don't love as a title). In theory this sounds like a good thing; you could will your hair to always sit right or to win the lottery, but as I walk into Drama Club the next Monday I see that it can also be a terrible thing. My mind has been constantly worrying about Tessa spilling my secret about liking Peter and I think I've accidentally willed it into action.

★

As Jean and I walk in, everyone turns towards us and stops talking. I look to Jean to see if I'm just being paranoid but she's grimacing as well. She squeezes my hand and we march with our heads down to a spot in the corner just like celebrities trying not to get spotted at the airport.

As soon as we've sat down, Rachel and Flora, who are wearing lavender and deep purple, rush up to us and whisper at the same time.

'I promise it wasn't me.'

'What wasn't you?' I ask, even though I know what the answer is.

'About you . . .' begins Rachel.

'Liking Peter,' finishes Flora.

I train my eyes down on the floor.

'Does everyone know?' I ask quietly.

Their silence is answer enough.

'Does *Peter* know?'

I dare a glance up and see Flora and Rachel looking very sorry for me.

'Oh God.' I look up to the ceiling which has large bits of paint peeling off it. 'What do I do? Do I just leave?'

'No, definitely don't leave,' says Jean, who has gone very flushed on my behalf. 'You've got nothing to be embarrassed about *really*.'

'Then why does it feel *so* embarrassing?' I reply.

The whispers have started up again. Jean, Flora and

Rachel quickly become my own personal PR team.

'OK,' says Jean leading the team, 'we need to think about damage control. What can we do?'

They all huddle tighter so that I am out of view of the rest of the Drama Club.

'We could claim that it's just not true?' suggests Rachel.

'No, I think denial is a dangerous route, especially because of the speech last week,' says Jean.

'We have to bury the evidence,' says Flora sombrely.

'What evidence? Peter?!' says Jean ludicrously and Flora shrugs. 'We're not burying Peter.'

Several ideas are thrown around, including: pretending it doesn't bother me (Rachel), claiming insanity (Flora), loving *a* Peter but not this one (Jean), and finally, the suggestion that I can't be in love with Peter because I've been in a secret long-term relationship with a famous actor (Jean, again). I am actually tempted to go with the last one just to see if it would be believable.

'Guys,' I say over Rachel trying to convince Flora that it's feasible for me to have had a twin this whole time, 'I know what I need to do.'

I shakily stand up and look around for Peter. I see him sitting with Tessa and Sam in the opposite corner. I begin walking over with my head held high and can feel people's eyes trained on me seeing what I'm about to do. *It's only bloody cake,* I think to myself. It's when I'm right next to Peter that he clocks me and looks up, surprised. I purposefully don't look at Tessa who is doing the same thing with me, apparently completely engrossed in picking the purple varnish off her nails. In avoiding Tessa's gaze I accidentally catch eyes with Sam whose look I can't quite decipher.

'Can we have a quick chat?' I ask Peter in a surprisingly strong voice.

'Yeah, of course.' I see him looking around and noticing that every single person is staring at us. 'Outside?' he suggests.

Outside the community theatre isn't the most scenic spot to have a dramatic conversation, but there aren't a lot of options. We head over to the only bench and I bury my hands deep in my pockets because I have circulation matched only by the elderly and the deceased. In my pocket, my numb fingers fumble with the letter I wrote to myself in Ms Beckett's office, which gives me a little jolt of confidence. I can do this very embarrassing thing because I have done so many embarrassing things. Like when I tried to get out of a hockey match by faking appendicitis, but I was too convincing and was about to get rushed to hospital so I had to say it was actually trapped gas. Peter and I get to the bench which is very rarely used because the only view you have when you're sitting here is of the car park, which is lacklustre at best.

I zip up my puffer jacket, wrap my arms around myself and grimace as I lower myself onto the freezing metal.

'Ooh.' Peter jumps as he also sits down. 'Cold butt.'

We both sit facing forwards, our breath snaking in front of us. I don't really know how to start this conversation.

'You know there was once a Porsche parked out here?' I tell him.

'Really?'

'Well . . . I think it was a Porsche. It was definitely a fancy car because everyone waited around after Drama Club for *ages* to see whose it was.'

I breathe in through my nose and it feels like my nostril hairs have iced over.

'Whose car was it?' asks Peter.

'Oh . . . just some guy,' I reply.

There's another little pause.

'Not the *best* story I've ever heard, I'll be honest.'

I smile. 'No, fair enough.'

'So . . .' Peter says, 'did you ask me out here to talk about cars?'

'Shockingly, I did not.' I turn to face Peter and brace myself, scrunching my eyes closed and letting it spill out. Difficult things are meant to be quick – like ripping off a plaster or the trend of fingerless gloves.

'I know everyone is talking about how I . . . fancy you, or whatever, and I just wanted to clear the air . . . because

I did like you – do like you – and I might have even asked you out, but I didn't know that you had broken up with Maddison or that you're with Tessa now, which is great, and I just don't want to make anything weird between us because . . . yeah.'

I open my eyes and Peter smiles at me. 'Thank you, Patch.'

'Oh well . . . you know,' I mumble in response.

'And I really like you too, you're *great.* Really great. I just . . . yeah. It's been such a crazy week,' and he runs his hands through his hair. Even though I'm jealous of his hands because I would like them to be *my* hands, he suddenly looks very lost.

I realize I've been so *obsessed* with the idea of Peter being my boyfriend that I didn't really think about what he was going through. He's in a brand-new country, away from his friends and living with somebody else's family. Maybe Peter doesn't need someone repeatedly convincing him to fall in love with him, maybe he just needs . . . some more friends.

'I mean . . . everything with Maddison and now stuff with Tessa,' he continues while he shakes his head. 'I don't even know what's happening with that, to be honest. Sam reckons I should spend a bit of time on my own before going into another relationship.'

The word *relationship* stings me a bit, but I allow it.

'Well . . . maybe more than ten minutes?' I suggest.

'It was more than ten minutes!' he protests and spins around to face me.

'How many minutes was it?' I ask innocently.

'Thirty . . . I think. I mean definitely over twenty.'

I hold my hand over my mouth. 'Oh, see Peter, I did not know that it had been *over* twenty minutes,' I tease. 'If anything you should actually think about speeding things up a bit.'

'Shut up,' he grumbles, but smiles as well.

We let the silence sit there for a second, before I ask, 'So, we're OK?'

He pushes his side against me on the bench. 'Yeah, we're OK.'

Before last week, I would have thought about that push against me non-stop for upwards of five days, but I know it was a platonic push. It was the equivalent to when step-dads in TV shows playfully hit their son on the arm after an important talk. Thankfully, both our hands were shoved deep into our pockets because I don't think my heart could survive a playful punch.

'Right, we should probably head back inside before we freeze to death,' I say.

'Agreed,' and we make our way back and walk into a chaotic warm-up game of Wink Murder (which was never going to work because Flora was the murderer and can't wink).

Chapter 17

Although I have lost the love of my life, or perhaps more accurately I have lost what *might* have been my first boyfriend, I am determined not to let it ruin my year. To quote a woman who wrote a self-help book after being axed from her reality TV show for throwing an ornamental shell at a co-star, 'If you let every obstacle knock you back, then you aren't doing this thing called "life" right.'

I still haven't worked out whether she was talking *literally* about the woman she threw the shell at and that was the obstacle knocking you back or metaphorically, but either way, I think it was good advice. This wasn't a wall, it was a hurdle. And even though I'm historically not amazing at hurdles I can just about get over them, and therefore I can get over this.

It's the same thing as me once saying I would *never ever* own a denim jacket, but now I have a whole mood board devoted to them! Things can change so fast. What isn't helping with my 'getting over it' plan is that Jean has been acting strangely towards me (and even possibly avoiding me?) ever since my humiliating chat with Peter. First, she claimed she couldn't FaceTime because her hands were too 'soapy', and then at school I tried to engage her in ways we could get back at Tessa for spilling about my liking Peter, but she avoided eye contact with me. I know for a fact that eye contact is one of her favourite things, so I knew something was up. I decide to finally get her on board properly at lunch because I know she'll be in a good mood after seeing fish fingers on the menu.

'So I was thinking we could start referring to Tessa as SC in front of her and she would go *mad* trying to figure out what it stood for, but the genius of it is . . . it won't stand for anything! So she'll be going through all the options in her head like maybe thinking it stands for . . . "Sordid Cow" or something like that! Genius, right?'

Jean says nothing and instead deposits a large pump of ketchup on her plate and scurries to the table. What is going on with her? If fish fingers aren't going to break her out of this mood nothing will. I need to confront the issue.

'Tell me what's going on,' I say as soon as my tray hits the table, nearly toppling my glass of what the school deems as orange juice. Mum's right, I *can* be a snob.

'What do you mean?' she asks, staring intently down at her plate.

'I'm trying to move on and stand in my light and . . . fine, punish Tessa a *bit*, but you are being so weird with me. Tell me what's going on!'

She only stares even harder at her fish fingers which have started to lose their structural integrity already and now their breadcrumb coat is peeling off. I rack my brain for what she could be annoyed about.

'Are you annoyed that I started using hair pomade without telling you? Because, Jean, I only didn't say anything because it's still in the trial period!'

She shakes her head. I exhale loudly.

'Are you annoyed that I said you wouldn't make a good Viking, because that was in the context of the discussion. I think you would make an excellent Viking *if* there wasn't the siege component!'

'I'm not annoyed at you!' she finally bursts out.

'Well, what is it then?' I demand.

Jean sucks in her bottom lip and then, still looking down, she says in the smallest voice I have ever heard her use, 'It wasn't Tessa.'

'What? What wasn't Tessa?'

She puts her hands in her lap and fiddles with the hem of her jumper.

'That told Peter about you liking him. It wasn't Tessa.'

'Of course it was!' I reply. 'Jean, nobody else knew apart from Flora and Rachel, and I made them swear on their rabbit's life.'

She finally looks up at me with giant glassy eyes and whimpers, 'It was me,' before burying her head in her arm and sobbing. 'It's all my fault!'

'What do you mean? How can it be *your* fault? It was Tessa who told everyone!'

Jean shakes her head, her chin dimpling as she holds back tears, 'But I told *her*.'

I can't believe it. Jean?! Jean was the one who ratted me out! Before I can demand a reason as to why she's committed this momentous act of betrayal she takes a huge gulp of breath and provides one herself.

'It was that day when you nearly told Peter you liked him on stage. I was so upset for you because, well, you deserve love more than anyone. And Peter being with *Tessa* of all people just felt so unfair. Anyway, that, combined with losing Zip, Zap, Boing meant that I was in one of my "volatile states". You know how I am when I get like that,' she says gravely.

I do. Usually I'm the one with the flair for dramatics, but when Jean gets into one of her 'volatile states' it can be much more . . . unpredictable. One year on a school trip she released a cage of goats from a petting zoo because she thought they were signalling to her that they were being mistreated.

She sniffs and continues, 'So when I saw Tessa go to the toilets at the end of rehearsals, I followed her. To defend you! The plan was to say something vague and devastating, but I hadn't really thought of what that was going to be.

So halfway through a very impassioned speech where I may or may not have been throwing paper towels at her, which I *know* is terrible for the environment, I realized I had accidentally told her that . . . you liked Peter.'

Jean holds her hand up to signal there's more to say, tears spilling over at the pressure of having kept this colossal secret in. 'I'm an idiot, I know, and I shouldn't have been blaming Tessa at all and I definitely shouldn't have said anything, but I was just so *furious.* Then afterwards I just panicked and left and . . . I'm *so* sorry, Patch. It's my fault!'

I'm speechless. Which is a new sensation. Part of me wants to tell Jean that it's fine because she's crying very loudly and people are looking at us, but a much bigger part of me is petty and somehow that part always ends up winning in these sorts of situations. I snatch my hand away from Jean and storm out of the cafeteria. It's only as I hear the door swing behind me that I realize I didn't get a chance to have *any* of my fish fingers.

Ten minutes later, after getting an emergency vending machine lunch (salt and vinegar crisps, a protein milkshake because I did some press-ups last week and a chocolate bar that I'm pretty sure they stopped making in the nineties), I'm pacing around Ms Beckett's classroom after cornering her for an emergency meeting.

'The *gall* of it!' I exclaim while shoving a crisp in my mouth. I spin around to face her. 'Did I use gall correctly?'

She nods and I continue, 'The *gall*! I mean, what did she think was going to happen?! Would you ever EVER follow your arch-nemesis into the loos after rehearsals and tell them that your best friend likes their new boyfriend?!'

Ms Beckett takes her glasses off her head and rubs the bridge of her nose. 'That's quite a specific situation there, Patch.'

'Well? Would you?' I press, raising my eyebrows.

'Well . . . I suppose . . . technically *no*, but I've—'

'Exactly! You never would because you have sense! I just can't believe that Jean would do something like that! And then Tessa immediately tells everyone. I mean, *come on*!' I continue pacing and ripping my chocolate bar open with my teeth.

'What do you want me to say here, Patch? Also, please don't eat that chocolate bar, they stopped making those before I was born.'

I put the chocolate in my pocket in the full knowledge that I would be eating it later. What do I want Ms Beckett to say? Obviously I *want* her to say something along the lines of:

You, Patch, are the peerless victim in all this and you have been wronged by someone you trusted! Even looking at Jean again would show a tremendous amount of strength and forgiveness. Also, and I probably shouldn't say this, but all of us teachers were discussing in the staffroom the other day and we all agreed that out of all the students at school, it's you that we really think is going places.

Ms Beckett continued, 'I'm just saying it seems like Jean had your best interest at heart. She was trying to help.'

'But she didn't help.'

'But she was *trying* to.'

'Well, just because I *try* to sing a high E note doesn't mean I'm doing it!' I reply, certain that I've made an amazing point, but Ms Beckett's confused expression tells me otherwise. Annoyingly, I do understand what she's saying, but even though things are fine with Peter now, they aren't *perfect* and part of that is Jean's fault. I avoid Jean for the rest of the day, trying to figure out how I feel and whether I'm angry at her or the situation. I reluctantly come to the conclusion that I am more angry at the situation. However, I still want to leave her grovelling for a little bit. The weekend comes around just in time because I can't deal with another day of Jean shooting me meaningful looks and sending me collages of our friendship, both of which I dutifully ignore.

Chapter 18

By Saturday, I've decided that I'm going to do something *crazy.* Something so spontaneous that when Jean hears about it, she'll be fizzing with jealousy. I just can't decide what that thing should be.

I think about maybe getting a piercing or a tattoo, but that feels a bit too big. Then I think about putting some temporary dye in one of the back sections of my hair, but that feels too small. Fate intervenes when I find out that Kath is going bowling with some of her friends and I beg – not threaten – to go along because next to the bowling alley is a cinema and I think that the mildly crazy thing that I'm going to do is watch a film on my own which apparently is one of the most 'cherished things you can do for yourself'.

'So you're going out with yourself?' asks Jen, one of Kath's friends, who's also being driven to the cinema by my mum. Kath scoffs, which is annoying because it wasn't a good joke.

'No,' I reply derisively. 'I'm taking myself out on a *date,* which is very different, it's about loving yourself.'

'I don't see it lasting,' says Kath. 'I *know* you and there's no way you're going to want to spend that much time with you, trust me.'

It's then Jen's turn to scoff, which is fair because at least Kath's joke was funny, even if I'll never admit it.

After reassuring my mum for the *third* time that I'm not meeting a stranger from the internet, I enter the cinema ready to take myself on my first-ever date. It definitely isn't the date that I was hoping to go on at the beginning of the year, but beggars can't be choosers. On the plus side, at least there won't be any awkward silences. I enter with the lofty ambition to watch a very sophisticated film with subtitles and shot in black and white. This is partly because I want my date with myself to be an *occasion*, but mainly so I can tell people that I have watched a black-and-white film with subtitles. *It's so much more interesting and heartbreaking than regular films, I could never go back to English-speaking films shot in colour!* I would say and toss my velvet scarf over my shoulder and people would nod as I sauntered away because they would see that I am truly *living*. As it happens, when I eventually get to the ticket counter, I bail and decide to opt for an animated film about a boy and his pet rabbit. My snacks of choice for this slightly less artistic film are a slushie (blue flavoured), buttered popcorn (small, because I'm not made of money) and a packet of chocolate raisins from home that I have stuffed in my pocket to add a bit of excitement (and fibre) to the viewing experience. I settle myself into the deep purple seat, ready to have the best (and only) date of my life.

The issue with watching films by yourself, I quickly learn, is that if you have a 'hot take', which I often do, you don't have anyone to share it with. So I resort to writing them down on my phone. They are as follows:

My (very perceptive) thoughts on the film:

- Are 3D films still a thing?
- I think the rabbit is a metaphor for greed.
- I wish they would use more Kelly Clarkson songs in animated movies. Maybe I should start a petition.
- The man in front of me is either crying or laughing, neither of which is really appropriate for the scene that he's watching.
- Good lord, the man was choking! His girlfriend just had to give him some water.
- I no longer think the rabbit is a metaphor for greed, but I *do* think I recognize the voice of the rabbit?
- I got distracted trying to find out who voiced the rabbit and I'm a bit lost plot-wise because they are now hurtling through space (?)
- It actually takes SO many people to make a movie.

Overall I would have given the film a solid 6.5 out of 10. I don't think I've grown as a person by watching it, but you can't be constantly growing. I've got about twenty minutes to kill before Mum is scheduled to pick us up, so I go to see if I can play any of the arcade games in the bowling alley.

Unsurprisingly, I can't see Kath and her friends as I walk in, most likely because they got bored bowling and are loitering somewhere and grunting about something. I cross the sticky floor, managing to swerve around several children who are chasing each other, and head straight for my favourite game, the claw game. I usually get quite stressed playing it while other people are watching so I think it will be a good time to practise. I set my sights on a toy that is either a cat or a chipmunk (or it could truly be *any* animal) and get to work. I only have three pounds which means I only have three chances to get Caleb (I have decided at this point I would call him Caleb). On the first go, I barely brush by Caleb. On the second go, I get hold of him but as soon as I motion up, the claw drops him. But on the third and final go, I get a proper grip on Caleb. I lift him into the air and just as I'm about to deposit him into the shoot and claim my victory, I get distracted by people whooping at the bowling alley and my finger slips. Just like that, Caleb is gone. Lamenting my loss, I peer through the Perspex glass to see the source of the whooping and spot two girls on the alley at the far end. They both have their backs turned, but the one closest to me has something glinting in her hair. A big, bright green cactus clip. I lean in to get a clearer look, my nose pressed against the glass, and yes, it's *Jean*! I'm just about to go up to her, partly because I'm bored with being annoyed at her and partly to see if I can borrow a pound, when the girl she's talking to turns around to check the bowling score and she swishes her blonde hair with her. I can't *believe* it. Jean is bowling with . . . *Tessa*!

I check the scoreboard to make sure my eyes aren't playing tricks on me and there, clear as day, are both of their names listed.

I sprint away from the bowling alley before they see me and run straight to the car park, where I take to pacing up and down, trying to digest it all.

Tessa and Jean . . . together?

I'm so preoccupied, I don't even notice when Mum arrives. She toots her horn twice to get my attention. I get in the back and strap myself in without saying a word.

'You OK, Patch?' asks Mum, peering at me in the rear-view mirror.

'Fine,' I stammer. 'Just a very moving film. I think I need to sit quietly and think about it for a bit.'

'OK, great, because I want to listen to the end of my audiobook.'

Mum presses play on her phone and a very raspy, sonorous American man continues telling her about the mystery of a missing girl while inside my head I try to solve my own personal mystery.

How could Jean do this to me? I mean, she was already in my bad books after what happened with Peter, but I was ready to forgive her on Monday, but now . . . I'm not sure I can ever forgive her for this. It's unforgivable! I can almost taste the metal of the blade she's stabbed in my back. Also, since when did Tessa and Jean start hanging out or even talk?! A cold dread creeps in. What if . . . what if this secret friendship has been going on for ages and I've been too stupid to realize? Oh my *God*! What if they are in cahoots? What if Jean and Tessa planned to tell Peter about my crush together to humiliate me? What if Jean told Tessa about me fancying Peter even *before* that point and that's why Tessa made her moves on Peter while I was away? My mind is whirring in a montage of all the ways that Jean might have been secretly deceiving me. Was she lying when she said that my colouring was 'cool autumn'?! Well, I'm onto their little tryst now and one thing is for sure . . .

Congratulations, Jean, you are now public enemy number one.

Chapter 19

It's surprisingly difficult to fill a weekend when you have been betrayed by your best friend. I thought being furious would kill a lot more time than it did, but by breakfast on Sunday I was desperate to get a 'coffee' with Jean and talk for hours about whether or not we thought boot-cut jeans were just flared jeans for people who were scared to make brave choices, denim-wise. But I remind myself that from this day forward I will never give Jean my enlightening insights on denim.

I even spent a large part of Saturday evening focusing on my professional life and updating my mood board for the after-play Prom. As head of the aesthetics department, I haven't been totally on top of the planning, but if my mood board is anything to go by, I think the Prom is going to be *unbelievable.* Despite going against my better judgement and compromising that Prom could be held in the theatre due to 'severe budget constraints', I think that means that Ms Jenkins will have no choice but to approve the custom flower-wall and the trapeze artists I've highlighted as 'necessities'. I also manage to find what I think is the email address for Helena

Bonham-Carter's agents, just to see if she happened to be available to make a guest appearance at the Prom (she plays Mrs Lovett in the film version of *Sweeney Todd*). I may have stressed the fact we have an 'ill cast member' a bit hard to pull at Helena's heartstrings when really it was just Charlie in the chorus who had a bit of a sore throat last week. But even with all my impeccable planning, I still need more distraction so I decide to tag along to Mum's Pilates class in town. I'm not technically invited but Mum's friends love me because I compliment their clothes (even when I really really don't mean it).

'Sensational jeggings, Pam!' I say upon entering the town hall, which from 10.30 to 11.15 on a Sunday is occupied by 'Bums and Tums . . . for Mums! Pilates'.

'Thank you, sweetheart, they're new!' replies Pam.

'*Such* a good transitional item!' I nod.

'Are you joining us today then?'

'I am indeed, Pam! I mean I have so many friends my own age that I could hang out with . . . *throngs* of them actually! But I thought, why not spend time with the older generation, you know? People who have really lived!'

Pam looks over to my mum, confused. Mum just shrugs her shoulders.

'I'm sure you'll find it far too easy going along with all of us *older generation*!' She smiles as she expertly whips out her Pilates mat in front of her which has a beach sunset scene on it with the phrase, 'Find Your Peace'.

I did *not* find it too easy. In fact, five minutes in and I was wheezing and 90 per cent sure I was about to pop a blood vessel after doing an endless number of 'little pulses'. Our instructor, a very bendy woman named Lauren who has the look of someone who doesn't believe in deodorant, was telling us to 'lean into the shakes' which, I'm sorry, feels like ludicrous advice. If you are holding your finger over a flame and it burns you don't just put your fingers further into the flame, do you, Lauren? Also, my 'shakes' had now become full body convulsions. I look to my left and Pam is somehow managing to do these little pulses at the same time as having a conversation with my mum about the celebrity chef they're both obsessed with. There's no way I can survive another forty minutes of this, so I do what any self-respecting sixteen-year-old would do in the face of the knowledge he was markedly less fit than his mum and her friends. I pretend to sprain my ankle.

'Ah!' I gasp sharply and clutch my left ankle.

'Everything OK?' asks Lauren in between her little exhales.

'Yeah, I think I just pulled something, I'm fine! I'm just going to walk it off! You carry on!' I explain, getting up before performatively limping out of the room.

As soon as I'm out, I decide to wait out the rest of the class in Costa because there's no way on earth I'm going back in there. For a second, I feel bad going into Costa without Jean and briefly think about turning around, but then I remember that I am furious at her and I march even faster. The bell chimes as I enter. What if the barista, who knows us as a pair, comments on my being alone? I'm not sure I'm ready to talk about the squalid details of our friendship's demise.

But when I order my coffee the barista, as usual, pretends he has no idea who I am. I'd like to think it's because I ordered a hot hazelnut latte rather than my usual frappe because I don't want my drink to remind me of Jean.

Because it's Sunday morning, Costa is pretty heaving with groups of friends, tired shoppers and people pretending to work very hard on their laptops. I look for a spot to sit and my stomach drops when I see Sam sitting on his own in the corner with his trademark hot chocolate. Oh God. I don't want to be stuck in a conversation with him where I'll end up feeling like an idiot and he'll look at me like one. My ego can't handle that right now. I crouch down behind a table where two women in their forties are discussing whether a man named Colin is able to commit, and hunch over as I try to leave the cafe without Sam noticing. When I'm about halfway out of the cafe, a man suddenly stands up from his table, shouting, 'It's over!'

I yell involuntarily as the man knocks into me, making me spill hot coffee all over my hand.

'Ow, bugger, bugger!' I hiss, trying to fan my hand while the woman left at the table stands up to chase after the man and jeer at him, 'Oh, real mature, Paul, just run away like you always do!'

With the unhappy couple both having left the table and everyone in the cafe having turned to watch the commotion, I'm left hunched over and very much exposed.

'Patch?'

I look up to see Sam looking at me from over his book.

'Sam! Hey! Fancy seeing you here!' I reply manically.

'Do you . . . Are you . . .' he begins and shakes his head slightly. 'Do you want to join me?'

Crap.

'Sure!' I smile through gritted teeth.

Sam moves his book so I have a place to put my coffee. It's definitely a table meant for one person because our knees touch under the table. For perhaps the first time in my life, I think about my knees and try to tense them so they aren't so knobbly. I stare at the little cup that has all the little sachets of salt, pepper, sugar and sweetener. I pick up one of the packets and rub it between my fingers for something to do, feeling the grains grind against each other in their paper home. I really don't want to humiliate myself in front of Sam again and I'm not positive how he feels about the whole Peter situation. As always, it's left to me to start the conversation.

'What book are you reading?' I ask.

'Oh,' he stammers, looking a bit embarrassed and staring down at the book he had slipped into his bag.

'You don't have to say!' I add quickly. 'Sometimes I read books that are very much just books for *me* and I would never admit to reading them. Like, this summer I was reading a book about a warlock who had to find gems or this evil overlord would take over his country of *Glaeydivir*, and that's not something you necessarily want to *say* that you're reading.' I nod, in a frenzied way, then realize I have somehow already humiliated myself. What if Sam was reading one of those books and is now too embarrassed to say? I lurch forwards trying to backtrack and in the process knock over the sachet container. 'Not that you should be embarrassed about reading those books!' I declare. 'I think as long as you're enjoying the book . . . what does it matter, you know? I think actually there's nothing wrong with *engaging* with different genres of books, I think it makes you more understanding of . . . yeah! The world, maybe?' To shut myself up because I am jibbering like a toy that's been wound too tight, I take a huge gulp of my hazelnut coffee which is, of course, piping hot – and immediately spit it out all over the table.

Spluttering and airing out my singed tongue by panting like a dog, I look at the social destruction I have managed to achieve completely by myself within seconds of sitting down. Sam is staring at me, his mouth slightly open.

'Oh my God, I'm so sorry. I don't know what the matter is with me,' I garble while trying to fan my mouth. 'I think the coffee must have gone straight to my head,' I reason.

Sam doesn't point out that I have yet to swallow a single drop of coffee, but instead pushes his glass of water towards me.

'Thank you,' I croak, and then down the entire glass. I grab one of the paper napkins from the table and dab the sides of my mouth delicately like some noblewoman in a Tudor court as if there's any point mustering up decorum after spitting all over the table. I then start dabbing down the table and Sam grabs some tissues and helps me.

'Really, don't worry, they make the drinks so hot. I always have to wait at least five minutes before having my first sip,' he says while doing the lion's share of the cleaning. 'And in answer to your question pre . . . tongue singeing. I'm reading *Sense and Sensibility*,' he mutters self-consciously.

'What?!' I reply incredulously, completely giving up any pretence of wiping. 'You let me yammer on about my silly magic gems book when you're reading the exact sort of book you *want* to be caught reading?'

'Well . . .' he starts while staring intently down at the table, before going silent again. It takes every ounce of self-control I have not to fill that silence with something which I would no doubt immediately regret.

Sam takes the book back out of his bag and places it carefully on the table. 'I saw you reading it when we were here last time and . . . I thought it looked good.'

I had somehow completely forgotten that *Sense and Sensibility* was my prop book when Jean and I came here to impress Peter. Partly because I had only read one page in the middle of the book over and over again while waiting for them and then never picked it up again.

'Oh.' I uncross my arms and pick it up. 'Is it good?'

Sam looks up at me confused. 'Haven't you read it?'

Crap.

'Have *you* found it good, is what I meant . . . Have you?' I correct, hoping he doesn't clock my panic.

Sam smiles tightly and nods. 'Yeah, I have actually. I mean I'm not sure I totally understand *all* of it, but I watched the film as well, which helped,' he admits.

'Completely fair,' I nod.

'So, which Dashwood sister do you think you're most like?' asks Sam.

I feel like I'm in a test for something I haven't revised for. I look pensive while I decide what to do, acting like I'm taking the question *very* seriously. I didn't even know there were sisters in the book. Or that their names were Dashwood. OK. One option is I could just come clean and admit that I haven't read the book. However, if I do that then I have to explain why I was pretending to read a book which would be far too humiliating. Vague answer it is, and logic dictates that if there are *sisters* in plural then there has to be more than one.

'The youngest one,' I say confidently and try to work out from Sam's expression whether I've got away with it.

'You mean Marianne?' he checks.

'Yes, definitely Marianne. A hundred times over Marianne. For sure.' I double down, hoping she isn't a psychopathic murderer or anything.

'How come?' he asks.

My *God*, let it go, Sam! Why does it feel like I'm in a police interrogation?!

'Good question,' I say slowly. 'Gooooood question. I guess my answer to that very good question would just be . . .'

I wave my hand in the air like I'm trying to find the most eloquent words to express myself (but actually any words will do), 'for the sort of obvious reasons, I guess. I mean I myself am a younger sibling, so there's *that*.'

Sam takes a sip of his hot chocolate, and I notice that there's a little sachet of salt open beside him so he's clearly been won over by Jean's trick.

'Ah, see, I'm the older sibling so maybe I'm more of an Elinor,' he replies mindfully. 'Also, I'm probably too logical, whereas Marianne is more emotional, you know?' while swirling his spoon in his hot chocolate.

'I do know. I *do.* But actually, I didn't know you had a younger sibling?' I ask.

'Oh, yeah,' he says and shows me a picture of him and a grinning, largely toothless, girl. 'That's Phoebe, she's five,' and he grins down at the picture. 'Which means she is of course a complete menace. The other day she found a frog and put it in my bed as a "present".'

'Oh my God,' I laugh. 'Well, she looks very sweet, frogs excluded. I've just got one older sister—'

'Kath, right?' Sam interrupts. 'You said something about her in Drama Club.'

'Yeah, exactly.' I smile. It dawns on me that I really don't know that much about Sam.

'Kath definitely *isn't* sweet, but I can believe that she would also leave a frog in my bed,' I admit.

Sam chuckles and I carefully bring my coffee to my lips. It's cooled down enough to drink, but I take a hesitant sip just in case.

I shift in my seat. I still don't think we can have a normal discussion until we discuss . . . The Peter Situation. And, as one of my mum's more brutal books says, '*if you don't address the elephant in the room, it will stamp you to death*'.

'So . . . the Peter thing?' I begin, while my fingers tap on the side of the mug.

Sam looks a bit taken aback and I see the tips of his ears go pink.

'I just, I know it's embarrassing, but I don't want it to be weird. And I read recently that "if you don't air your dirty laundry you'll eventually have to burn your closet".' That was a line from the same book.

Sam's eyebrows crinkle in puzzlement but he shakes his head. 'It won't be weird.'

'So it's not completely embarrassing?' I ask him.

'Well, I didn't say *that*,' Sam says seriously before smiling. 'Only joking.' He stares intently down at his hot chocolate and continues, 'I think it's good actually, that you said how you were feeling. People who don't do that? They're the *worst*,' he laughs awkwardly, then picks up a little pinch of salt and adds it to his hot chocolate with a furtive glance up at me. 'It's not embarrassing to fancy someone.'

I think about what Sam said. Maybe he's right. *Maybe.* Even though it feels completely deranged as it's happening, fancying someone is technically a completely normal thing that just means your heart is working. Sure, in this case I definitely let the fancying run away from me and decided that Peter was the love of my life simply because he was there, handsome, confident and American. But I didn't really *know* him yet, which with a pang I remember is the one thing Jean had warned me about at the beginning of the term; I had to make sure I *properly* fancied the person rather than just having a person be available.

'It might not be embarrassing but it's certainly not

fun unless it's mutual,' I reply to Sam. 'I once fancied my Geography supply teacher so much I kept on pretending to not understand where Canada was.'

Sam looks at me funnily.

'Sorry, probably too much information,' I admit. 'I always do that. Like one time in Year Five, I wrote an acrostic poem about the ins-and-outs of my parents' divorce and I had to have a chat with my mum about artistic boundaries.'

Sam shakes his head. 'No, it's not that, it's . . .' I can tell he wants to say something and is trying to find the right words. I remember what Peter said about Sam thinking too much and I think I'm the same, but Sam always thinks *before* he speaks which is a valuable skill and one I certainly don't possess, I think *as* I'm speaking and say everything even when I know I shouldn't.

'What?' I ask him and his shoulders slump. I can tell that I have frightened off whatever he was going to say. 'So . . . we're OK?' I ask.

'Of course,' he replies. 'And to be perfectly honest, I'm not really in a position to get rid of friends. Peter has been spending *a lot* of his time with Tessa recently.'

It takes everything in my power not to storm headfirst into a Tessa rant, but in the spirit of *rising above it* (something I've never done, what if I get altitude sickness?), I nod understandingly and decide it's very annoying to be a 'good person' if you can't tell people about it.

'Well, I'm also currently on the lookout to expand my friendship group,' I say tactfully. 'So how about hanging out? Next weekend?'

Sam smiles and extends his hand. 'Deal.'

We shake hands and I have to stop myself from saying that he has a very good handshake (which he does) because I would sound like the careers advice teacher at school who is constantly telling us that we should wear a suit for a phone interview. And from there, I am surprised by how quickly the time flies. So much so that I only realize the time when my now crimson-faced mother storms into the cafe looking for me.

Chapter 20

The conversation between Sam and me doesn't stop there, that week we text back and forth quite a bit. All the time, actually. He doesn't really text like other people our age; he writes very long, witty messages that feel more like letters than texts. We got into a particularly spirited debate about which cake was best where I explained the merits of a humble Victoria sponge while he attempted to defend a lemon drizzle.

In between crafting responses to these to seem like I am equally witty, I spend the rest of my time pointedly ignoring Jean which is basically a full-time job. On Monday she passed me a note in Biology (which feels quite vintage), which I later found out said *How long are you going to be mad at me for?* When she first gave it to me, I folded it up and kept glancing at it; torn between desperate to read it and wanting to tear it up. I ended up missing an explanation of how many chambers the heart has, so I raised my hand to ask our teacher to repeat it before turning pointedly to Jean and asking, 'and can the chambers work when they have been *broken*?'

Luckily it was only Sam and Tessa who had rehearsals this week so I didn't have to ignore Jean in Drama Club. She finally confronted me on Wednesday when I was on my way to Ms Beckett's classroom. I had spent most of my breaks there whether Ms Beckett was present or not. Increasingly she opted *not* to be there as she found my insistence on going over the step-by-step of what I saw at the bowling alley, and I quote, 'tediously detailed and quite draining'.

Jean is clearly hanging around because she pops out from an empty classroom like she's about to mug me.

'What is going on?' she barks incredibly loudly, shocking us both before clutching her chest. 'Sorry, I built up quite a lot of tension while I was waiting for you. I didn't mean it to be that loud.'

I hold my head high and attempt to storm past her, but she grabs me by the elbow and spins me around.

'OK, listen Patch, I know that I shouldn't have said anything about Peter, OK? I know that! But I was just trying to be a good friend, alright? And you, completely ignoring me and all my apologies, that is just plain mean!'

I purse my lips. 'A good friend?' I parrot.

'Yeah,' replies Jean.

'A *good friend*?' I repeat again, with even more venom and enunciating each word with such intensity that Ms Jenkins would be proud.

Jean looks at me, completely lost.

'That's interesting, Jean!' I continue, having riled myself up and increasing in volume. 'See, I didn't realize that *good friends* go behind each other's backs.'

Jean sighs emphatically. 'I didn't go behind your back—'

'So, I didn't see you?' I interrupt. 'At the bowling alley? This weekend?' I see Jean look puzzled and then a bolt of realization.

'How did you—' she tries to interject.

'With TESSA!' I cry, pointing my finger up in the air like I'm in some am-dram murder mystery announcing who the *real* killer was all along.

I see real panic in Jean's eyes which is very befitting of the situation considering she has committed the *ultimate* betrayal. 'Patch, it's not what you think, I promise, if you just let me explain! Basically—' begins Jean.

'No, Jean,' I say firmly.

She tries again, but I shake my head fervently. 'Jean, if you care about me *at all* as a friend then don't try and speak to me,' and I spin on my heel and march to Ms Beckett's office.

Jean clearly cares for me a tiny bit as a friend because she doesn't try to speak to me for the rest of the week. The only bit of correspondence I receive from her (aside from mournful looks) is a letter that is dropped off in my locker. I can tell it's from Jean because of the number of stick-on gems that surround my name, but I pledge to myself that I *will not* read it (which is incredibly difficult because I love getting letters and nearly never get them, especially after dumping Jean-Pierre) so I put it right at the bottom of my sock drawer (where I keep all my emotionally important things) and focus on my other, non-dead, friendships.

Sam and I agree to meet at one of Hiverhampton's *actual* parks. I say 'actual' park because Hiverhampton technically has several, but it's quite impressive what the council can label as a park these days. It's a bit like if I put a candle in a stale loaf of bread and call it a 'birthday cake'. Our plan is to meet in the only park that features both trees and a swing because we're spending the day with Phoebe who apparently loves both of those things. Peter is hanging out with Tessa (obviously) and Sam's parents are doing some sort of sailing course, so it will be just the three of us. I'm slightly stressed about spending time with Phoebe because I don't have the most natural rapport with children. Maybe because I say things like 'natural rapport'. Even as a child, if I was at a birthday party I would much rather wipe the sand off my shorts (sandpits were all the rage back then) and head inside where the parents were congregating and ask whoever brought the carrot cake how they had made it so moist. What do children even like? I'm slightly worried our coffee run-in was an anomaly of us getting on and we will go back to our usual relationship of me saying something silly and him looking at me as such. But I also want to see if I can get some information about Tessa's new friendship with Jean from him, because surely she must have said something if Tessa has been spending so much time at Sam's house.

I decide to get there a bit late so I can hopefully scout out Sam and see how he interacts with Phoebe and then replicate it, which I completely appreciate sounds quite psychopathic when heard in isolation. I decide to wear some colourful clothing so that if conversation runs dry between myself and Phoebe, I can at least point at the bright colours. I walk through the park, hugging the bushes so that I'm not clocked by them before I'm ready. I spot my targets, Sam and Phoebe, on the swings where he's pushing her dutifully. Sam, as always, is dressed like he might be 'called into the office' at any moment in a pristine sage green shirt, while Phoebe seems to have dressed as part-knight, part-fairy with a dash of vampire which I wholeheartedly approve of. I head over to them awkwardly and can't help feeling like I'm the new step-mum meeting the father's kids for the first time. A feeling not helped by the fact I'm wearing leopard print.

'Helloooo,' I say as I get in their eyeline and walk towards the swings. I'm a few steps in when everything goes dark and I hit the ground. Hard.

'Phoebe!' I hear Sam yelling and hear his feet running towards me. I think I'm incredibly winded but other than that I'm . . . OK? Nothing feels broken. I feel something wriggling on top of me followed by a squeal of laughter. I realize that, upon seeing me, Phoebe must have launched from the swings and onto her target. That target being me. I would have settled for a handshake, but I suppose this is a form of greeting too.

'Ugggh,' I groan and slowly lumber to my feet, clutching my stomach. I'm sure it must have the indent of a five-year-old on it.

'Are you OK?' says Sam, concern plastered on his face. He's clearly relieved that we are both somewhat standing.

Phoebe is still squealing with laughter as Sam tries to muster up a *very* serious expression while simultaneously wanting to laugh. 'Phoebe,' he says sternly, 'how many times do I have to tell you, some people don't like to be landed on. Say sorry to Patch.'

Phoebe, however, has already sprinted off and hurled herself back onto the swings stomach first.

'Phoebe!' Sam yells after her.

'Really, don't worry about it,' I say, having finally got my breath back but still sounding pained.

'We're trying to teach her the difference between different types of hello,' Sam explains apologetically. 'But it's not really taking. She basically thinks a handshake is the same thing as, well . . . being squished like a pancake.'

I look at my five-year-old assailant who is now doing what I think must be some sort of hopscotch. She looks like someone who is in a hurry but has completely forgotten how to walk.

'Please don't ask her to high-five me, I don't think my back could take it.'

Sam chuckles and, upon seeing Phoebe attempting to clamber into the bin, shouts, 'Phoebe, no!'

'Phoebe, no!' quickly becomes the catchphrase of the afternoon.

Things Phoebe does within the space of an hour:

- Runs up to a complete stranger, hugs their leg and calls him 'Mummy' . . . *Phoebe, no!*
- Manages to catch a squirrel (?!) who she names Daffy . . . *Phoebe, no!*
- Starts licking a lamppost . . . *Phoebe, no!*
- Pretends to be a dog and starts barking at an old lady . . . *Phoebe, no!*
- Ruins a young couple's romantic picnic by filling their plates with dirt . . . *Phoebe, no!*
- Went back to licking the lamppost . . . *Phoebe, no!*
- Tried to remove a child from a pram and clamber in herself . . . *Phoebe, no!*
- Lamppost, again . . . *Phoebe, no!*

'Honestly, looking after Phoebe is a full-contact sport,' says Sam as he tries to poke her shoes down from a tree with a stick after she deemed footwear unnecessary.

Despite her chaos, or maybe because of it, I find Phoebe completely fantastic. She is like a walking hurricane with no idea of the destruction she leaves in her wake.

'Pash! Pash!' comes an urgent call from the roundabout. 'Pash' is what Phoebe calls me, which I love because it's like a nickname (and one I hadn't been forced to give myself, for once).

'She really likes you,' says Sam, finally dislodging the muddy purple trainer which falls with a satisfying *thud* on the grass.

'Really?' I ask, even though I am pretty certain she likes me, if not only because she looked at my jumper for an uncomfortably long time, like an art critic appraising an item, before nodding decisively and galloping off to stick her head in a muddy puddle, like all great art critics.

'Oh yeah, she's actually very specific about who can push her on the roundabout. Tessa tried to do it the other day and Phoebe tugged a handful of hair out as she was going around,' Sam explains with a grimace.

'Oh no!' I cry in what I hope is a sympathetic way, but I'm glad that Sam is turned away because I am fully beaming at the image of Phoebe yanking out some of Tessa's shiny perfect hair.

We wander over to Phoebe who is impatiently trying to rock the roundabout forward herself. Together, we slowly begin pushing the roundabout while Phoebe clings on stamping her feet squealing, 'Faster, Pash! Faster, Pash!' It turns out that pushing a roundabout is exhausting and I'm soon clutching my heart and wheezing as the roundabout slows to a stop and Phoebe howls like a wolf.

We decide to end the afternoon with an ice cream even though it's a fairly cold day. There's an ice-cream truck in this park that I think must have broken down years ago because I've never seen it in any other spot and I'm pretty sure the ice-cream man runs in underground frozen dairy circles because none of his flavours seem that legitimate.

Sam went for 'Redberry', I went for 'Sweet Blue' and Phoebe requested three empty cones. The three of us sat on a bench. Sam and I deliberated on whether 'Redberry' was an actual type of berry and if 'Blue' counted as a flavour while Phoebe crushed the three cones in her hand and then ate out of it like a giant bird. It was, all in all, a great afternoon. Even if I managed to spill blue all down my jumper, but as it was already a powerfully colourful jumper, Sam made the good point that if anything it just enhanced it.

'How much longer until the next bus?' Sam asks gently, trying not to wake Phoebe. She fell asleep mid-sentence while we were waiting.

I peer at the bus timetable that's printed out on a stand and partly peeling away. Hiverhampton hasn't quite got to the avant-garde stage of an electric sign telling you exactly how many minutes away your bus is.

'I think . . . five-ish minutes? It depends if it's Helen driving because she likes to stop off near the BP garage for a Kinder Bueno so she's always a little bit late.'

'Right,' Sam replies, slightly bemused.

I look up at the sky which has turned an ominous shade of dark grey. This is always the worst time for chatting, when you're sort of ready to go so you can't get into anything properly and you end up in a conversational dead end. Sam and I were having such a great day I don't want to ruin it.

'You and Phoebe should head home or you'll get soaked.' As soon as I've said it, a fat splat of rain lands coldly on my forehead. I wipe it off with my finger and hold it up for Sam. 'See, I'm basically psychic,' and then it starts to spit down with rain, spattering the Perspex bus shelter with little marks like when you flick a fountain pen at someone.

'We'll wait with you,' says Sam cheerily. 'Besides, the rain might stop soon,' and as soon as he says that there is a perfectly timed angry rumble of thunder.

'And you,' I say gesturing smugly, 'are the opposite of psychic.'

Sam and I sit on either side of Phoebe and watch the rain and also the people who are doing the funny little run you do when you're caught out in the rain and want to properly run but are too embarrassed to.

'What are you up to tomorrow?' I ask, quietly very impressed that we had got through an entire afternoon without asking small-talk questions like that.

'Tessa is coming round to see Peter, I think, and we'll probably just watch a film. Or in other words, I'll watch a film while Peter and Tessa pretend to find *everything* the other one does absolutely hilarious.'

I am so grateful that Sam has finally said something a little bit mean. I also realize I had completely forgotten about my covert mission of finding out if Sam knew anything about Tessa and Jean's new friendship.

'So, has Tessa been around a lot then?'

'Yeah, she's around most evenings,' replies Sam.

'Wow, so her and Peter are pretty serious then?'

'I don't know if they're *serious,* I just think they're enjoying the beginnings of a relationship, you know?'

'But Peter likes her?' I ask somewhat incredulously, surely Peter can't genuinely like Tessa when she's so dreadful?

Sam is quiet for a bit and then murmurs, 'That's not why you came here, right? To find out about Peter and Tessa?'

'What? No, of course not,' I reply quickly, but from the look on Sam's face he clearly doesn't believe me.

'I just don't want to be the consolation prize,' Sam says quietly before going bright red. 'As someone to hang out with, I mean.'

'It's *nothing* to do with Peter, I just – it's . . . I'm having this weird fight with Jean at the moment and I didn't have anyone else to—'

'Ahh, so you're hanging out with me because you've got nobody else to hang out with?' he replies.

Although he's joking, I try to think of who else I could have feasibly asked to hang out with over the weekend that wasn't Jean or a relative. But Sam must have read something on my face because his face immediately drops. Maybe he wasn't joking? I immediately panic.

'Oh,' he says.

'No, no! It wasn't because of that!' I exclaim. 'I wanted to find out if Tessa had told everyone about me fancying Peter or if she'd said anything about why her and Jean are hanging out?' As soon as I've said it, I hear how it sounds like I had just been using Sam for information. I try to backtrack: 'No, that's not why I'm here, I just – I swear I'm having A LOVELY TIME!'

But it's too late; Sam picks up the sleeping Phoebe and balances her on his hip and tries to muster up a smile. 'Sure. See you, Patch. Hope you got what you came for.'

'Peter, wait— Sam, I mean! Sam! *Crap!*'

Sam turns back to me, hurt in his eyes, and heads into the rain. I'm not sure yelling 'I'm having a lovely time' was the most convincing argument and I'm just about to chase after him when I get splashed with a wave of cold water as the bus finally pulls up to the stop, drenching me in the process.

The doors open and Helen looks at me from the driver's seat with a semi-apologetic expression, a Kinder Bueno wrapper clutched in her hand.

By the time I look down the road for Sam, willing to miss this bus to explain myself, he must have turned a corner because I can't see him anywhere.

Chapter 21

'OK, everyone,' calls Ms Jenkins, clapping her hands officiously, 'let's go from the top of "Pirelli's Magical Elixir", and chorus, remember, it's a *magical* elixir not a *mundane* one so you need to look . . . bewitched!'

The fact that I thought I could be in a relationship by Prom now feels completely laughable (but not at all funny). Instead, it's the weekend of the tech and dress rehearsal for *Sweeney Todd* and I have become some sort of relationship grim reaper, swiping away at everyone close to me.

Sam won't reply to any of my texts, and continually pretends to be learning his lines when I try to talk to him. Peter is either with Sam or Tessa, making him a no-go zone, and things with Jean are worse than they've ever been.

She wrote me two more letters which I dutifully ignored and filed away with the other one in the sock drawer. Maybe I should have been slightly more forgiving (which would have been very saintly but not in my nature), but before I could, Jean decided it is *she* who has given up on our friendship and has now started ignoring me and publicly hanging out with Tessa! The audacity!

It's progressed from a cold war to an arctic war with both of us giving each other the cold shoulder. I refuse to be the first to yield. The only sliver of a silver lining I can think of is that my character of Judge Turpin wasn't meant to like anyone, apart from his daughter to a weird degree, so I'm hoping that my feud will make my performance more believable (impossible to say for certain, but if I had to guess I imagine the reviews will say something along the lines of, 'piercingly real, Simmons BECAME Turpin and set a new bar for youth theatre').

Because of all the friendships I've obliterated, rehearsals over the last few weeks have become somewhat of an emotional battlefield. And my side of the battle is basically just me (Flora and Rachel refuse to pick sides – I tried bribing them with friendship bracelets but Flora just argued that a blood pact would be more compelling).

If rehearsals have been a battlefield then I worry that tech rehearsal might be an absolute bloodbath. Officially, tech rehearsals are when you go through the lighting cues for the show, making sure the props work and that your costumes are all fine. They take ages and you're basically in the theatre all day which is why they always happen on a weekend. Unofficially, they are also where pressures reach boiling point within the cast and there is always a fight to be had. Or at least, I have historically always got into a fight with someone during a tech rehearsal. Like Dylan Johnstone, who wasn't making his foam axe seem believably heavy in *Little Red Riding Hood*, or Daisy Miller's mum whose sloppy needlework made me trip up in my *Cats* costume.

I think Rachel was worried about what might happen too, because she had brought what she called 'confidence cupcakes' for everyone else and 'conciliatory cupcakes' for me. We manage to sail fairly smoothly through the first half of tech, despite some unoriginal lighting choices from Ms Jenkins (a red floodlight for Sweeney's first murder, seriously?). But every time I see Jean and Tessa together I get a hot prickle all through my body that I quickly identify as rage – justified rage, but rage nonetheless. Previously, I've made . . . rash decisions when in a rage, so I need to somewhat quell it. But it's hard! Especially because tech rehearsals are some of mine and Jean's favourite times together. We usually set up base at the top left seats of the auditorium while we're not on stage and relay our personal thoughts on the performances. Our *real* thoughts, the things that Ms Jenkins is too cowardly to say. Granted, it might not be criticism that is constructive, but it didn't matter because it was just for us!

Luckily, I looked to one of my mum's books for advice on how to deal with today's tech rehearsal and one book recommended a breathing technique and some positive visualization. I had ripped one particularly poignant section to bring with me that read:

Listen Sister, you can completely control your environment! Sure, you might be sitting in your open-plan office with unflattering overhead lighting and your prawn-mayo sandwich in your top drawer that you're saving for lunch and don't want to put in the shared fridge in case Shelly from accounts steals it, but in your head anything is possible! Pick a happy place! My suggestion? Close your eyes and imagine you're in the Bahamas with an ice-cold margarita in your hands and maybe a handsome surfer in your eyeline. Hump-day indeed!

I had a few questions about the hypothesis. I didn't quite get the joke at the end (what is a hump-day? Is it a camel-related joke?) but I think that the spirit of the advice is truly brilliant. If I get annoyed or feel like I'm about to do something I might regret, I can simply close my eyes and imagine myself in a happy place where I'm not annoyed or upset.

I'm in the wings, waiting to go on when I glance up at Tessa and Jean who are sharing a packet of crisps. I feel that hot prickle of rage and so dutifully take a deep breath and scrunch my eyes shut and go to my happy place. My happy place is outside a hotel in London (unspecified which one); I'm leaving my hotel with my 'team' (except I keep forgetting to stop imagining Jean as my publicist) because I'm promoting a big film that I've done and outside my hotel are hundreds of my adoring fans screaming my name. *Hump-day indeed!*

It's my turn to do my 'big number' which is my (haunting) run-through of 'Johanna'. I practised the song so many times in my room that there was a brief moment when Mum thought I was straight and possibly in love with a woman called Johanna, while Kath has claimed that Johanna is now her top worst name in the universe.

I gave my technical ideas to Ms Jenkins at the beginning of the day, but she said we don't have the budget for a full choir to be unveiled halfway through and that 'flying' me in would be a health and safety nightmare. So instead, we have a silhouette of Johanna as I'm singing about her, which I suppose is Ms Jenkins' way of saying that too much going on on-stage would distract from my performance. I go through the song in sections as Ms Jenkins adjusts the lighting and even though it's only a technical rehearsal I plan on giving 110%. The problem is that every time Ms Jenkins switches the lights off before trying another option, I see Tessa and Jean sitting where *we* used to, in the top-left corner of the seats. They're whispering into each other's ears and, yes, they're giggling. *Giggling!* I try to quickly envision my happy place. *London hotel. Crowds.*

'Patch?'

I can't believe they're giggling at me. What a tactless thing to do. They're probably saying something like, 'Why is Patch wearing old leather boots under his tracksuits?' Well, I'm wearing them because these are my *costume* shoes and I need to know that they can grip the stage properly, for crying out loud! It's called being a professional storyteller! Dammit. I need to go to my happy place again. *Hotel. Crowds. People are screaming my name.*

'Patch!'

I bet Tessa and Jean are saying, 'Why is his voice doing that weird deep warbly thing?' And I'm sorry, but it's OK to try something during tech rehearsal, that's what it's *for*! And Judge Turpin is a lot older than I am and because my natural singing voice is clear as a whistle, I thought it might be good to try adding some gravity to the song! HAPPY PLACE! *London. Hotel. Crowds. Press Tour. Fans.*

'Patrick!'

And now they're just staring at me. The nerve of it all. Actually, as I pan around, nearly *everyone* is staring at me. Weird. Are they just completely entranced by my performance? Did I nail it in a way I can't even comprehend? I suck my cheeks in to stop myself from smiling, *Suck it*, Tessa and Jean! Maybe this could be my new happy place?

'Jesus Christ, PATRICK!'

I snap out of my reverie and see that Ms Jenkins is leaning out of her lighting box at the top of the theatre. Has she been calling me this entire time?

'Yes?' I answer hesitantly.

'Can you *please* get off stage, we've done your song.'

There's a little titter of laughter from everyone and I

see that Sam is awkwardly standing beside me, waiting to go through one of his songs. How embarrassing. 'Yeah, of course, no worries,' I say, trying to sound as casual as possible. 'Yeah, I think we got everything we need to,' I say nodding to myself. 'Great work, Ms Jenkins! Over to you, Sam!' and I quickly shuffle off stage. That is the last time I visualize.

Sam begins singing his song. He stumbles his way through most of it and really needs to work on his projection. Towards the end, it becomes very clear that he's completely forgotten how the rest of it goes, so his performance ends with an awkward pause, which Ms Jenkins thankfully interrupts.

'Right, I think it's time we take a break!' she calls, and everyone quickly hops down from the stage, careful to avoid the fake blood which is coating the floor. Sam hasn't quite figured out how to deploy the blood capsules and the opening number ended up being an unexpected bloodbath when he let them all off at once. Everyone sits in clusters in the auditorium and opens up their packed lunch. I'm sitting with Rachel and Flora while Jean sits with Tessa, Peter and Sam. I open my packed lunch which I have had planned since I found out we were doing *Sweeney Todd.* Because I've decided that Judge Turpin *isn't* vegetarian I've gone for a tuna and sweetcorn sandwich (for protein), some sticks of carrot (for fibre), some salt and vinegar crisps (for texture) and some Jaffa Cakes (for fun). But as I rootle through my bag, I can't find my Jaffa Cakes anywhere, and they were what the entire meal was leading up to. It's the finale, the *crescendo*, and I can't find them in my bag. I ask Rachel and Flora if they've seen them and they shake their heads, their mouths full with their gourmet ham and cheese baguettes. I get on my hands and knees to look under both my seat and under Rachel and Flora's, but I don't see a single sign of the orange and chocolate treat (but do find generations of gum). I'm about to make an announcement when I turn my head and spot a flash of orange and blue . . . and Jean is grasping a packet of Jaffa Cakes in her traitorous fist.

I know that I should employ a breathing technique. I know that, technically, Jaffa Cakes is a company and in order to remain financially stable, they need to sell more than one packet, but even though I do *know* this, the knowledge doesn't fully land as I'm marching up the aisle with the energy of a cinema usher about to tell someone off for filming on their phone.

'Are those my Jaffa Cakes?' I bark angrily, pointing at the packet.

Jean looks up at me, confusion across her face.

'Are. Those. My. Jaffa. Cakes?' I say, silently grateful that I did my vocal warm-up exercises so I can enunciate that question with such venom.

'Patch, why would I take your Jaffa Cakes?' she asks tiresomely.

'I don't know, Jean, why *did* you take them?' I reply, shaking my head. There is suddenly a hushed silence around us that tells me I'm not being as discreet as I thought I was.

'Are you being serious?' asks Tessa from beside Jean.

'Oh *please,*' I snap at Tessa. 'You are the last person I want to talk to about *my* Jaffa Cakes.'

'Those *aren't* your Jaffa Cakes!' Tessa retorts.

Jean holds the packet of Jaffa Cakes up. 'Look, Patch, I don't want to have a fight with you and I can tell by the way your nostrils have flared that you want to have a fight with me, but I'm not going to do it, OK? So just take the Jaffa Cakes and leave.'

I swat the Jaffa Cakes out of her hand, to which there is a gasp from the spectators. Spectators that, I suddenly realize with an icy shock, include both Sam and Peter who are looking at me from the row above, their mouths open.

What am I doing?

I look at Jean and Tessa sitting down in front of me, in the spot where I used to sit and it occurs to me . . . this might actually *not* be about the Jaffa Cakes after all.

I couldn't find my Jaffa Cakes, aka, my *friendship* (with Jean). Just as I'm about to explain this metaphor to Jean, loudly so that Sam and Peter don't think I'm a complete monster, I hear the sound of Ms Jenkins' kitten heels quickly clacking up the stairs.

'Patrick, Tessa, Jean,' she hisses with authority, 'with me . . . *now*.'

Tessa looks indignantly at Ms Jenkins and then at Jean who had already stood up with her head bowed as if she is about to be beheaded. 'But we weren't doing anything. Patch just came up to us and started shouting!' Tessa complains.

Ms Jenkins holds up her hands in the universal sign for *I don't want to hear it* and starts marching downstairs, leaving us with no choice but to follow.

Ms Jenkins takes us backstage and off into one of the 'dressing rooms'. By dressing room I mean a small room which has been painted somewhere between yellow, green and grey with no windows and one broken mirror. The faded carpet has held on to the smell of generations' worth of strong deodorant, including the most popular one with boys at our school at the moment, which is, revoltingly, 'cookie dough' flavour.

As soon as we are all in the room we launch into explanations at the same time:

'This has got *nothing* to do with us—' begins Tessa.

'I was only *pretending*—' I attempt.

'I am so sorry for disrupting—' apologizes Jean.

Ms Jenkins holds up her hand again, '*Enough!*' she stresses. I don't think Ms Jenkins has ever looked so disappointed, not even when I replied that perhaps everyone else should raise the bar when I was asked to sing quietly as a chorus member because my 'singing was drowning out everyone else'.

'Now there is clearly something going on between the three of you, and I want you to sort it out. *Now*. Drama is for on stage, not off.' She turns to leave.

'But what about the tech rehearsal?' I ask, desperate for an excuse to not have this conversation.

Ms Jenkins pivots round. 'We'll fill you in,' she says sharply and closes the door, leaving me completely alone with my two very worst enemies in the knowable universe.

Chapter 22

If anyone was listening in from outside they would have been very disappointed. Or thought that nobody was in the room. Or thought that the door was *very* thick and wouldn't let any sound out. This is because it's been nearly ten minutes since Ms Jenkins left and nobody has said a single word.

I am at the far end of the room with my arms crossed, staring fixedly at a spider in the corner who is absent-mindedly playing with its web, perhaps made uncomfortable by the frosty atmosphere we've brought into its room. Tessa has planted herself in the middle of the room on a little desk where people do their make-up before a show, swinging her legs. Jean is at the far end fiddling with her hair clip which is of a wrench which I suppose is as close as you can get to visually showing a tech rehearsal.

I don't really know what to say. I *know* that I should apologize for swatting the Jaffa Cakes out of Jean's hands because that wasn't overly necessary, but I don't want to apologize for anything else, which leaves me in a tricky position, because saying, 'I'm sorry for swatting your

Jaffa Cakes out of your hands *only,*' isn't really much of a sentiment. But I'm still in the right, I'm positive of it.

Jean blabbed about me liking Peter and then to make matters worse befriended our sworn enemy to spite me! And Tessa has historically been the devil incarnate. Also, it's basically two against one so I'm the victim. In a perfect world, Jean would loudly renounce Tessa and apologize to *me,* and I, being kind of heart, would forgive her trespasses and we would carry on being best friends, and Tessa could do whatever she wanted, I don't care, probably swish her hair or something.

I'm also aware that we're missing really crucial information about the technical runnings of the show and they are currently missing two *main* characters! And Jean.

A sudden intake of breath from Jean makes Tessa and me turn towards the source of the sound, hackles raised and ready to *fight* or *defend.* Jean's mouth is open and her eyes scrunched closed, her nostrils quivering. She does another intake of breath before letting out an almighty sneeze. The type of sneeze where you think somebody must be pretending to do a sneeze that loud. But I know for a fact that Jean isn't because she once revealed that she used her tenth-birthday wish to never have to sneeze again because it's too loud and embarrassing. Luckily, she only does about one sneeze a year, but it's always a year's worth of sneezes all at once.

'AAACHOOOOOO!!!!!'

Jean's head snaps back from the force of the sneeze. It's so powerful that I instinctively glance up at the web to check it hasn't blown away, and even the spider looks taken aback, clinging on for dear life. Jean recovers slightly and looks at me and Tessa, alarmed at the volume of the sound she has just created. Looking at Jean's startled face, the corners of my mouth twitch up into the beginnings of a smile. I suck in my lips to stop the smile from spreading and I can see Jean doing the exact same thing. We stare at each other silently, daring the other person to show their smile. Suddenly Tessa covers her mouth to smother the snort/laugh that tries to come out. I can't help it, I start roaring with laughter, clutching my stomach as thunderous rumbles rock through my body. I can hear that Jean and Tessa are in a similar state. I can feel the pressure of the day and of my fight with Jean all coming out in this frenzy of laughter. But just as I'm about to stop I look up and see Tessa's face scrunched up almost in pain and Jean panting like she's in the throes of labour and it starts all over again.

After what feels like a very long time, our wheezing and groaning slowly fades into the familiar silence.

'Bless you,' I say to Jean.

'Yeah, bless you,' Tessa repeats.

I can't help it, my impulse when Tessa says something is for me to roll my eyes and I do. Tessa spots this.

'What?' she snaps, her eyes narrowing again.

'Nothing,' I reply innocently.

'You rolled your eyes.'

'Did I?'

'Yes, why?'

'Well,' I start, 'I had already said bless you, you didn't need to say it again. If anything, that negates the bless you.' I know it's petty and I wish I hadn't said anything, but I *have* said it now so I have to stand my ground. 'Technically you actually just cursed Jean,' I add.

Tessa looks incredulous. 'Why on earth would I *curse* Jean?'

'Guys, don't—' Jean says, trying to stop us by standing up.

'Jean's my friend, I wouldn't curse her,' she says, gesturing to Jean as if I don't know who my *best friend* is.

'Jean is not your friend, Jean is my friend!' I snap back.

Tessa laughs theatrically. 'If she's your friend then why are you being so mean to her?'

'I'm not being so mean to her, I am being the appropriate amount of mean considering her betrayal!'

'You smacked a packet of Jaffa Cakes out of her hands.'

Yes. Fair point. I technically did do that.

'Well,' I falter, 'that's because I was worried that she might have developed a latent reaction to the orange filling! I was trying to save her!'

Terrible lie. Dreadful. Will it land? Judging from Tessa's face . . . nope. Tessa crosses her arms and we begin bickering in earnest. We step closer to one another as the rowing continues. I can't even fully work out who is making what point, but I know that it is fiery and intense and that I've called her 'conceited' at least three times because I learned that word the other day.

It looks as though our fight could honestly develop into a physical fight, but I think both of us are scared of that happening. *Thank God*, because Tessa would definitely win. I've developed quite an effective hair-pulling technique that I have had to use when getting into fights with Kath, but I don't know how effective it would be on Tessa, especially as her hair might be numb after all the highlighting. Just as I am about to throw 'conceited' into the argument for the fourth time, Jean shouts over both of us.

'Will you both BLOODY *STOP*!'

Jean crams herself in the narrowing gap between Tessa and myself and forces us apart, but we're both too shocked by the fact Jean said 'bloody' to put up a fight.

'Now, Patch—' she begins.

'I *knew* you were going to take her side!' I cry out.

'I'm not taking her side, I just want you to—'

'No!' I shout, a couple of octaves higher than I want to, so I repeat it again in a lower voice. 'No.' I can feel my eyes prickle and I know that if I don't get out of this room within the next thirty seconds then both Jean and Tessa are going to see me cry and I can't have that. Sometimes it's excellent for people to see you cry. If you want to get on student council, for example, and need to get the pity votes, then crying is the way to go.

But this is not one of those times.

Allowing Tessa and Jean to see me cry would be way too humiliating. They would know how much I care, how much I miss Jean. How much I miss both of them.

'Patch, please,' Jean tries as I turn to leave the room. She reaches out to my shoulder and I shake her off.

'Get off me, Jean,' I grunt, unable to face her because I know that my eyes are glassy.

'Please, just listen—' she tries again.

'I don't want *anything to do with you,*' I snap and I can hear her shocked little inhale of breath which makes my stomach twist in guilt. But I can't focus on that, so I just open the door and leave.

I make my way down the corridor and through another door which leads me to the stairs behind the stage. There's a bathroom there and I just need a few moments to myself to do some breathing and make sure my eyes aren't red or my face too blotchy. I'm staring down at the stairs, my vision going a bit blurry as tears threaten to spill over, so I don't notice when I bump into something solid.

'Patch,' comes Sam's surprised voice, 'is everything OK?'

Sam, of all people!

I feel like a pinball going between people who are mad at me, and I don't want him to see me cry either. The door to the bathroom is just behind him. I just need to get in there and everything will be fine. I work very hard to keep my voice level with my eyes still trained down on the floor. 'Everything's fine.'

'Are you sure, you look—'

'Everything's fine Sam, OK? So you can just stop pretending to care and go back to not liking me again. Just *leave me alone*.'

Sam looks at me, clearly hurt, before quickly passing something into my hands, clearing his throat and moving past me. I look down in my hands where I see a small paper box with a red ribbon wrapped around it.

I rush into the bathroom and as soon as I do, I go to the sink and look in the mirror and allow the tears to spill down my cheeks, like a cup that's finally too full. A tear splats on the paper box which is now blurry through my eyes.

I sniff and fiddle with the red bow until it comes loose and gently open up the box. After wiping my eyes on my sleeve, I am faced with the most perfectly presented slice of Victoria sponge cake I've ever seen. Fluffy sponge, a thick frosting of cream and jam which you can tell is made of actual strawberries and the whole thing is dusted with the perfect amount of icing sugar. I pick it up and it's surprisingly light considering its size. It's the type of cake that screams, 'I've come from a very expensive bakery'. Why has Sam given me a cake when he's made it very clear he doesn't want to talk to me? It's almost too beautiful to eat, but of course it's almost immediately entering my mouth at the same time I have that thought.

It's perfect.

I look back in the mirror where I now have cream all around my mouth and icing sugar on my nose. I would try to say 'it's only bloody cake' about this whole situation, but I've finished the cake now. The cake's all gone. And I've ruined my friendship with the person who gave it to me. I try and wipe some of the icing sugar off my face. Nice one, Patch, you've managed to upset your best friend, your worst enemy and the most thoughtful boy in the world within the space of an hour.

This year was meant to be the best year of my life, but I've completely ruined it instead.

Chapter 23

By the time I leave the bathroom, the tech rehearsal is wrapping up. I spent some time trying to think of ways I could blame my behaviour on my star sign or the cycle of the moon, but I couldn't get any phone signal in the bathroom. I also don't know what to say, I can't start apologizing now because *then* it would make it seem like I was the one completely in the wrong. I might not have handled myself like Julie Andrews, but I certainly wasn't the villain. Surely.

I sheepishly enter the theatre where everyone is grabbing their bags. Tessa and Jean must have told Ms Jenkins that we had sorted out our problems because when I come back out, Ms Jenkins gives me a nod as if to say, 'Well done for sorting things out'. Jean looks sadder than I've ever seen her, but I avoid her because I can't quite face it yet. I spot Sam on the front row stuffing his script into his leather messenger bag.

'Sam, that cake was just—'

'It's not a big deal,' he interrupts coldly, 'I just didn't want it.'

Before I can question whether the cake was in fact just a 'spare' piece of gourmet cake he just casually carries around, he slings the bag over his shoulder and walks out. I linger in the theatre so that I don't have to talk to anyone in the car park, but when Ms Jenkins finally kicks me out, Mum is, thankfully, already waiting there, mouthing along to 'Chiquitita' in the car.

Mum has learned by now that asking about why Jean and I weren't talking any more was a no-go zone, a zone which if she tried to cross, resulted in me calling her an 'emotional manipulator'. As I get into the car, I tell her that I'm not in a 'chatty mood', so we drive back in silence and I stare outside the window trying not to focus on how I'm feeling. When we finally pull up outside our house, I go to get out but Mum puts her hand on my arm.

'Listen, Patch, I know you don't want my opinion, and I *know* that I don't know the ins and outs of what's going on with you and Jean.' I go to interrupt but she presses on. 'Let me finish. Friendships like yours don't come around every day. Trust me, I had that kind of friendship once, and it's much easier to ruin things than work on them. So take my word for it and don't let the distance between you grow so much that you can't find your way back to each other.' And then she reaches behind her to get her overflowing bag from the back of the car.

I think for a second about what she said. *Don't let the*

distance between you grow so much that you can't find your way back to each other. It's the perfect mixture of poetic and true.

'What book did you get that from?' I ask quietly. 'And can I borrow it because that's quite good.'

Mum hauls her bag into the front seat and turns to me, beaming, but trying not to look too pleased with herself. 'Actually, that one was all me!'

I hope that, one day, I'll have absorbed enough advice from all of the books I read so that I can be as wise as her.

'You should write a book,' I say and quickly hop out of the car so I don't have to see her probably monstrously smug reaction.

I head straight up to my room and I'm pacing in front of my drawers where I know Jean's letters are. I think I always knew I was going to read them or I would have thrown them away as soon as I got them. Before I can second-guess myself for the twentieth time, I pull open my drawers, rootle through my socks and feel for the letters. I pull them out and open the first one.

Dear Patch,
I know you must have been really confused and FLIPPING annoyed about seeing me and Tessa at the bowling alley. I promise, promise, there is a good reason for it, but it's not really my place to say. Can you please talk to me?
Jean xxx

A 'good reason' for it? Seeing Jean's very round writing makes me miss her even more. I open the next letter and read.

Patch,
This is getting so silly now, why are you still so cross with me? You're putting me in a really hard position because you aren't talking to me. I just wish we could sort this all out. You are being so FLIPPING stubborn! But I love you and I miss you. I bet you aren't even reading these, I bet you're putting them in your sock drawer because we watched the same film where the main character put all the letters she got in her sock drawer.
Jean xxx

I had forgotten that was where the idea for the sock drawer came from. Dammit, she knows me too well. I open the last letter.

Dear Patch,
This is the last letter I'm going to write to you because it's not fair that you aren't replying to me. I'm not going to carry on begging to be your friend because good friends don't make people do that. You're being a bad friend. I miss you.
Jean

I spend ages looking at the empty space after Jean's name where there aren't any kisses. Has Jean's love for me run out? Has the distance already grown too big? Can we no longer find our way back to each other? I pace around my room and go back to the drawer. Now that I've pulled the letters out and the socks have been pushed to the side, I see the other things that I've left in there to remember, and I realize that this drawer isn't so much a sock drawer as it is a 'holding grudges' drawer. Inside the drawer is all sorts of memorabilia for things I don't want to forget that I'm annoyed or upset about, which includes:

<u>Memorabilia for things I don't want to forgive:</u>

- A sticky note saying 'DON'T FORGET ABOUT KATH BREAKING THE KARAOKE MACHINE' in big writing (and if I remember correctly, written with one of her favourite eyeliners).
- A parking ticket with '2HRS!!!' written on it to remember how long Mum left Kath and me in the car when she fell asleep testing mattresses.
- The letter that Jean-Pierre had addressed to someone called Felix with '*triste!*' written over it in red.
- An empty packet of gum from when Callum Taylor asked to borrow a piece of gum and then he handed the packet over to the rest of the Lodge Crew until they were all gone.

- A picture of Jean, Tessa and me at one of our sleepovers where we are all dressed up with feather boas and smoking fake cigarettes, but the picture has been ripped in half.

I get a funny knot in my stomach. I used to think that 'holding grudges' was one of my top skills, but looking at the evidence in front of me, it doesn't make me feel especially good and it definitely doesn't feel like a skill. I tentatively pick up the picture of Jean, Tessa and me and take it to my desk, trying to match up the ripped edges so it looks like a whole picture again. But the edges won't quite fit together.

I think about today from Jean and Tessa's perspective and the knot tightens even more in my stomach. Am . . . I the villain? The knot loosens slightly which tells me that it must be somewhat true.

I sit back in my chair. If I want to get Jean back, I need to make some serious changes. I need to prove to her that I really am sorry. And in order to do that, I need to somehow make amends with Tessa. In my mind, Tessa has been categorized under the *enemy* list for so long that even thinking of moving her into a different category goes against my every instinct. I stand up and go to my bookshelf and scan the titles looking for a pale blue book called *Love Kinder, Love Better* which I remember Jean reading out to me one time from my bed. I can't remember exactly what it said, but it was definitely something about forgiveness. I scan the bookcase again but can't see it anywhere. I must have lent it to Jean. Regardless, I'm sure that the book must have said *something* about forgiveness being a good thing (it's generally considered so, isn't it?) and I think it said something about it being a kind thing you can do for yourself and your children (it's worth noting this book was also specifically about forgiving your ex-husband to make life easier for your children, but *still*).

I need to make a plan. And I need to do the unimaginable . . . and so I text Tessa.

Chapter 24

I'm pacing nervously around in the theatre foyer for about ten minutes before I hear the door open and a wary, bleary-eyed Tessa enters. As she opens the door, I see that it's just starting to get light outside. Mum wasn't thrilled when I woke her up at seven on a Sunday morning demanding she drive me to the theatre for 'crucial relation reparations', but as I reminded her, 'That is what mothers are for, I'm afraid.'

'It's so early,' yawns Tessa, wrapping her arms around herself as the theatre still hasn't warmed up properly. I don't know if it's because she's tired or because I'm trying very hard not to look at Tessa as my nemesis, but she seems softer somehow, or at the very least looks like she's not about to say something mean and devastating.

'It is early, yes,' I admit, 'but the dress rehearsal starts at nine thirty and I really needed to speak to you before.'

Tessa looks concerned. 'For over two hours?'

'No. I've got something else I need to do as well, but I'll explain that later. Will you sit down with me?' and I gesture to the centre of the room where I've placed two chairs facing each other like we're about to do a very intense duologue.

Tessa sits down on one of the chairs, and crosses her legs and plays with the hem of her oversized green jumper. 'How did you even get in here so early?' she asks.

'Well, I texted Ms Jenkins last night saying that there was a Prom Planning emergency and she gave me the code to the lock box,' I admit, sitting down opposite her.

'So there's not a Prom Planning emergency?' she asks.

'Well, there is, insofar as I haven't *really* planned it.'

We both stare at each other's feet for a bit as I build up to say what I need to say. Tessa, I notice with a little pang, is wearing her clogs.

'Your text was so vague. Why am I here, Patch?' she asks.

'Well, if you give me a second, I'll tell you,' I snap.

'Why should I give you a second, you've been *dreadful* to me!' she snaps back.

'I've been dreadful to *you*? Wait—' I begin, but stop myself and take a deep breath. 'I didn't ask you here to argue. We need to work out a way of speaking to each other without it always turning into . . . bickering – and I started it that time, *I know*,' I add before she can call me out.

Tessa looks at me with pursed lips.

'For Jean's sake, at least,' I say and her expression softens a little. 'I think the only way we can make *her* happy at all is if we find a way to at least talk to each other.'

Tessa stares at me for a second, and nods for me to continue.

First, I lay out the ground rules of this conversation which I learned from Jean ages ago because she is basically a professional at conflict resolution ever since her family went to family therapy following arguments about whether or not to get a dog.

Jean's rules for conflict resolution:

1. No speaking over one another.
2. No hurtful names.
3. No shouting.
4. No rolling eyes.
5. Listen to one another.
6. Only the person with the speaking stick is allowed to be talking.

Tessa agrees to all the rules, but we both admit we probably won't be able to stick to number four, but will try our best. We also don't technically have a speaking stick, but I found the Baby Jesus doll from the nativity play a few years ago in a cupboard near the dressing rooms so we use that instead. The very same Baby Jesus I tore the arm off when I didn't get the part I wanted. I hold the Baby Jesus on my lap and start bouncing it on my knee as if it's a real baby. I see Tessa stifle a smile.

'I want to start with saying sorry for yesterday, I shouldn't have called you a conceited cow so many times—'

'I don't think you mentioned the cow bit yesterday,' Tessa interrupts stonily.

I hold up the Baby Jesus to mark that it's still my turn and continue: 'Regardless, I think I was just jealous that you and Jean are friends now and . . . I felt left out and so lashed out.'

Tessa reaches for the Baby Jesus and I hand it over to her.

'What I don't understand is why me and Jean being friends means you two *can't* be friends or . . . you know . . . why we . . .' but she trails off.

'What?'

'Well, I guess it's completely impossible that the three of us could be friends?' she asks quietly and a bit self-consciously, pulling the sleeve of her jumper over her hands.

'But is that what you . . . Sorry, can you pass me Jesus,' and I extend my hand and accept Baby Jesus. 'Thanks. What I was saying is, is that what you even *want*? I mean, you don't like me?'

Tessa extends her hand for the Baby Jesus, but I think this passing back and forth of the son of God is getting in the way of real conflict resolution.

'Shall we just put Baby Jesus down?' I suggest.

'Don't let God know, but yes, alright,' she replies, making me smile despite myself.

'I do like you, Patch. Don't get me wrong you're *impossible* and to be honest recently I *haven't* liked you, but I do like you in general.' She takes a deep breath and carries on. 'And believe it or not . . . I'm actually the one who's been trying to make up with you all term.' She shrugs and adds, 'You don't need to look so shocked,' and I close my agape mouth.

Tessa has been trying to be friends *all term*? In what *world*?! This reparation just won't work if Tessa continues to lie throughout it!

'The *first* thing you did on our first day back at school was make fun of my necklace!' I argue.

'I wasn't making fun! OK, my tone might have been a bit off, but we hadn't spoken normally to each other in ages and I was genuinely trying to talk to you both, but the Lodge Crew were there so . . .'

'Right,' I say sarcastically, 'because heaven forbid the *Lodge Crew* think you could be friends with us. The facts are, you ditched us for them!'

'It's not that simple,' Tessa stresses. 'Right, I'm going to tell you what happened . . . but you have to promise not to interrupt, OK?'

I reluctantly mime zipping my mouth closed and nod in agreement and then, after a year and a half of speculation, Tessa finally tells me her version of *The Tessa Situation*.

She explains that although she *had* rejected us for the Lodge Crew, it wasn't for the reasons we thought, and a lot of it had to do with her mum.

Jean and I both knew that Tessa's mum could be a bit tricky. Tessa was always vague about how, but we did know that she would have much rather stayed with her dad after the divorce, but couldn't for various reasons which we knew not to press too much about. Turns out, Tessa's mum had been very popular at school, the Slough version of head cheerleader, she said, and was seemingly annoyed that Tessa wasn't popular. Moving to Hiverhampton was meant to be a fresh start and Tessa's mum gave her a hard time about not immediately making friends. So when Jean and I came up to Tessa and complimented her clogs, she had felt like she was fitting in for the first time since moving. We hung out for nearly a year without ever properly meeting Tessa's mum, but when we finally did it was a disaster. I remember that day, it was one of the few days we hung out at Tessa's because her mum was meant to be at work all day. We had been trying to finesse a dance routine (which had both historical and contemporary influences) when her mum had come home early and caught us mid-routine. It had been . . . awkward, to say the least. Apparently Tessa and her mum had got in a huge fight afterwards, which I didn't know about. Tessa got a bit uncomfortable telling me that the fight had been about her mum thinking that she should spend her time with a more 'selective crowd' (aka, a 'cooler crowd'). I had never really put the timeline together before, but that was the summer that everything changed. Tessa told me that her mum had got her some gradual tan and booked her to get her hair highlighted without even asking if that's what she wanted (I knew that Tessa *really* wanted to dye her hair blue and cut it short like a detective from a cartoon she watched when she was younger).

Classically, when Tessa got back to school, the cool kids *did* start treating her differently and they invited her to hang out. She told her mum, because she knew how proud she would be and apparently it was the best day they had had together in *for ever*. She wanted to carry on having those good days so Tessa distanced herself from us and began hanging out with the Lodge Crew. Her mum even suggested that she should give up Drama Club, which she did. At first it was exciting, she admitted sheepishly. It felt amazing to be part of something that other people wanted to be a part of, it felt powerful. But even after a few weeks that wore off and she realized that she had made a mistake. She wasn't having fun. She only ever *pretended* to vape because she hated the feel of it and she also knew deep down that she still wanted to be an actor and had to protect her throat. By the time she realized the mistake she had made, she thought it was too late as Jean and I had now been giving *her* the cold shoulder in return (which is putting it nicely). She felt like she had burnt her only real friendship, so had no choice but to stick with the Lodge Crew or she would be left with no friends. Again. So she immersed herself in the popular crew and thinks she became *so* snarky to us because she was jealous that not only were we not friends with her any more, but worse, we didn't seem to miss her at all. But this year she had promised herself she was going to try again. Obviously it didn't go perfectly, she admitted, but it's hard. That's why she rejoined Drama Club, she tells me, so she could try and make friends away from the judgemental gaze of the Lodge Crew. She finished her story with a very quiet (audibly) but very loud (metaphorically) 'Sorry'.

I take a beat to think. Huh. So there really *are* two sides to every story. I always thought that was more of an expression. The first thing that comes to mind is a list of the meanest things that Tessa has done over the last year and a half that I want explanations for.

<u>Mean Things Tessa has Done to Me:</u>

1. I heard her calling my political poem about nuclear families that was published in the school newspaper, 'childish and obvious'.
2. She laughed and called me a 'suck-up-trip-up' when I fell over myself as I was running to open the door for the very attractive substitute teacher.
3. She gave me a disparaging look when I opted out of the bleep test for vague 'political reasons'.

But as I was creating the list in my head, another list popped up alongside it.

Mean Things I Have Done to Tessa:

1. Said that her highlighted hair reminded me of cheap spaghetti.
2. Told our teacher that Tessa had cheated on a history test by writing important dates on the inside of her glasses case.
3. Called her rendition of 'Driver's Licence' at the school talent show 'vapid and flat'.

I look back at Tessa, who is biting her lip nervously.

'I didn't know things with your mum were so bad, I'm sorry,' I say, and she shrugs. 'And I'm sorry for all the things I've done too, like when I tried to spread the rumour about you having had a nose job—'

'You did what?' she interjects.

'*Anyway,*' I say, moving swiftly on, 'I've recently learned that I have a bad habit of holding grudges. I thought it was something I was good at, but actually it's something I'm really bad at.'

'*No,*' says Tessa sarcastically.

I smile, 'I know, I know. But I want to say . . .' I take a deep breath to punctuate the moment, 'I forgive you and I'm sorry.'

'Well, I forgive you and I'm sorry too,' replies Tessa, grinning. I grin back.

'And it doesn't matter who has done *more* wrong things,'

I add, 'because if we were tallying them up it wouldn't even be *close*—'

'Patch,' Tessa says warningly.

'Sorry, yes, not the point. I genuinely thought this chat was going to be more about forgiving and then moving on and somehow both being friends with Jean, but, I mean, if you're up for it, I think we could give *this*,' I gesture between us, 'another go too?'

Tessa looks at me for a second and launches across the space between us and towards me.

Now, I've played this scenario in my head *many* times before – what would happen if the snarky comments between Tessa and me became a fully-fledged fight and she launches herself at me to attack – like I was worried she was going to do yesterday. I had already pre-planned that if she did do that, I would have let her land one blow and then I would basically play dead. Because of this, she would be terrified she had hit me too hard and take a step back, at which point I would quickly get up, run away, and tell an authority figure that Tessa launched herself at me and needs to be sent to a very strict military boarding school overseas. But I had never really played out the scenario of Tessa launching herself at me to *hug*. But remarkably that is exactly what's happening.

It takes me a second for my arms, which are stiff by my side, to tentatively reach up and hug her. Tessa squeezes me tightly and I squeeze her back, like we're making up for all the hugs we've missed. But there's still something on my mind.

'I do have one question,' I mumble into her shoulder.

'Oh, I just use a conditioning mask and hair oil, doesn't need to be a fancy brand,' she replies without a beat.

I lean back and laugh. 'I *was not* going to ask how you get your hair so shiny!'

Tessa grins back. 'I'm *kidding*! What?'

I disentangle myself from the hug and look at her.

'Why did you go to Jean? Why not come to me?'

'I did want to talk with both of you, but every time I tried it would go wrong. Anyway, I could tell that you and Jean were fighting and I kept seeing Jean eating alone at lunch while you were with Ms Beckett and I was with the Lodge Crew and . . . anyway, one time I saw her go into the bathroom to wash her hands before eating—'

'Was it a sandwich day?' I interject.

'Yes.'

'That adds up, continue,' I nod.

'So I followed her in there and went to talk to her. At first I think she thought I was asking for a tampon or something because before I could speak she whipped out her little stripy bag and started offering me pads and painkillers and everything.'

I know this bag that Tessa's talking about. Jean always

carries around a bag with 'Viva La Vulva' sequinned onto it and inside is a perfectly arranged selection of tampons, pads, painkillers, spare pants, baby wipes, hand sanitizer and little 'power to the period' stickers.

Tessa continues, 'Then I told her everything that I just told you and after that . . . yeah, she said she understood and I asked if we could maybe hang out. She warned me you would be furious about it if you didn't understand the reasons and so that's why we met up at the bowling alley so we could talk through a gameplan of how to tell you. Also because the Lodge Crew would never go to the bowling alley as they think activities are childish so . . . yeah. That's why I went to Jean first.'

I sucked my lip. 'And then I was an absolute monster to Jean and punished her for ultimately being a good person,' and new waves of guilt wash over me.

'Well, yeah,' agreed Tessa tentatively, 'but she didn't give up on you, even when I thought you were being unforgivably dreadful. Although, I do think she was really upset yesterday.'

I nod, reliving the horrid experience of me saying that I wanted nothing to do with Jean which was obviously not true.

'She really is the best of us, isn't she?' I say to Tessa, who nods in agreement.

'Will you help me win her back?' I ask her seriously.

Tessa grins and nods. 'I was hoping you would say that.'

'We've got approximately ninety-four minutes before everyone gets here and I have a plan. Operation "Get Jean Back" is on!'

Chapter 25

It took about ninety-two minutes all in all, and I had to text Rachel and Flora to see if they could come in early to help with some of the final touches.

'It looks AMAZING,' whispers Rachel in awe.

'It really does,' pants Tessa, who has been running back and forth to the foyer to make sure nobody comes in early.

'I still think some cobwebs would look good added in,' says Flora, 'but I have to admit, it looks pretty good.' For Flora, this is a *huge* compliment.

I stand back and look at what I spent most of last night and all this morning doing and I have to say . . . I'm pretty impressed. I actually don't think I've worked on anything so hard in my entire life.

Hanging up across the theatre on strings of ribbon are about a hundred photos of me and Jean from across the years. The first photo is us from when we started nursery and our parents found it funny that we wouldn't stop holding hands and the most recent photo is of us on the bus on the way to meet Peter and Sam at Costa. Photos of us at birthday parties, sports days, holidays, sunny days, rainy days, Tuesdays, important days and unimportant days. All the days that we've been in each other's lives, which have made all the ordinary days a bit more extraordinary. Alongside the photos are copies of all the recipes and letters we've written each other (like the letter Jean wrote to me when she had her first kiss on holiday in Spain even though she had already called me to tell me the same evening it happened – I've blacked out the salacious details). And on big sheets of paper hanging up along the pictures are huge, glittered letters spelling out: I'M SORRY, JEN.

Annoyingly, I must have left the 'A' for 'JEAN' in Mum's car and I couldn't find the supplies to recreate it at the theatre, but I'm sure she'll know it's for her.

I am aware that Ms Jenkins might be slightly annoyed that I have done this before our dress rehearsal and we'll have to spend time getting everything down, but Big Gestures are necessary for the people you love the most.

Tessa comes and puts her arm around me and I turn to Rachel and Flora who are attaching some coloured lanterns that they had at home to what I'm calling 'the tapestry of apology', and go over the plan again.

I'm waiting backstage as I hear people file in. It feels weird that the last time I did this, I was *with* Jean and felt a hundred times braver. It also felt like there was less on the line that time. That was for a silly crush, but this . . . If Jean decides that too much has happened and she no longer wants to be friends, I don't know what I'll do.

I've sent Ms Jenkins a long text begging for her patience and explaining that I had to do an announcement at the start of the dress rehearsal and promised her it wasn't me coming out for a fourth time, but instead was me laying my heart on the line for platonic love. She replied with a thumbs up emoji. I also sent Sam a text apologizing for snapping at him, but he left it on read.

I see the curtain shake as Tessa moves it. The signal that it's time.

Over the speakers, the sounds of 'Forgive Me' by Leona Lewis start playing. I take my spot in the centre of the stage and I feel the purple and red lights turn on as the curtain is raised.

As the apology tapestry is revealed, there is a collective gasp which I think is completely deserved. I hear a few people whisper to each other asking who 'Jen' is but luckily most people get it. As my eyes adjust to the blaring lights I look out for Jean, all of a sudden a bit worried about how she'll respond to this. Will she be annoyed that I've made it a theatrical ordeal instead of just apologizing? But it's *me*, of course she would know I would make it a theatrical ordeal.

I scan the crowds, passing over Sam and Peter who are looking up, awestruck, and seeing Tessa's eyes glint as she spots the photograph of us that I've (quite badly) taped together. But I don't spot Jean. I scan the crowd again, looking for a hair clip glinting in the crowd but she's definitely not there.

'Where's Jean?' I ask, but realize nobody can hear me over their excited whispers on the display.

'Excuse me, hi!' I wave before loudly asking, 'WHERE'S JEAN?'

Rachel and Flora push themselves to the front of the crowd. 'She popped to the loo the second we gave you the signal, sorry!'

'Ah,' I say, feeling somewhat deflated and embarrassed. 'Right.'

I look out at everyone's faces and just as I'm about to launch into some gentle crowd work, asking people how they were feeling about the play, the doors open and Jean enters, squeezing some hand sanitizer on her hands. However, when she looks up to see everyone staring at her and then looks up at the stage and me in the middle of it, the hand sanitizer misses her hand and squirts onto the floor.

Flora runs up and restarts the song as Jean takes in everything that's happening on stage. However, Flora obviously hits the wrong button and instead of 'Forgive Me', 'Bad Romance' by Lady Gaga plays which is completely the wrong vibe.

'Damn, sorry!' calls Flora from the speaker and starts playing the right song.

I look back to Jean who is covering her mouth, her eyes huge and glassy.

Feeling a bit light-headed, I reach behind me and take out the final big sign and hold it up high above my head.

On it is written in big letters: I LOVE YOU. WILL YOU GO TO THE PROM WITH ME?

Jean's face splits into a grin and she nods and climbs on stage.

She stands opposite me on the stage (balancing the space beautifully) and puts her hands on her hips. 'Patrick Simmons, you are the worst person in the world,' before running and giving me a giant hug and whispering into my ear, 'I love you.'

'Woo!' shouts Peter loudly and starts clapping, and then everyone joins in, even Ms Jenkins. And before we know it, we've just got our first standing ovation.

Chapter 26

It takes Jean a good fifteen minutes to stop crying once she found out that Tessa and I had resolved things. But after that, it's funny how quickly things slip back into being normal. Like puzzle pieces that have been pretending not to be part of the same puzzle, but then they go 'OK, fine!' and all slot into place. That's what it was like with Jean, Tessa and me. We were weird magnets that sprang back together again the moment we stopped pulling away. I vocalized both of those metaphors to Jean and Tessa, but Jean, who has always been a stickler for Physics, reminded me that magnets only work as a two. But they both appreciated the sentiment and especially liked the puzzle one. We went for a walk around the park on our lunch break (we invited Flora and Rachel, but they said they needed to make some calls after I last-minute enlisted them as 'co-creative chairs' for the Prom and they swiftly found out there was quite a lot of work left to do). It felt like our mouths couldn't move fast enough, we had so many unspoken conversations that needed to be unearthed, unpacked and unpicked. I told Tessa about the weird things my mum had been doing and the idiotic things Kath had been doing and Tessa told us about all the embarrassing and uncool things that the Lodge Crew did.

We had tenderly avoided the topic of Peter for the whole walk to the theatre, but then Tessa said, 'Oh, and then Peter did this thing—' before clamming up.

We were now in the car park of the theatre and Jean, sensing the one untouched conversation that needed to happen, turns to us and says, 'I'm just going to run inside and grab some . . . extra blood capsules,' and hurries away.

We're still early for the end of our lunch break, so Tessa and I sit on the bench outside so that we won't be interrupted by people coming in. The very same bench that Peter and I sat on a few weeks earlier. Tessa speaks the moment our bums touch the metal.

'I want to start by saying I shouldn't have told anyone about you liking Peter. I'm really sorry. It's my fault, not Jean's. But before she told me, I really had no idea you liked him. Well, OK, I could tell you wanted to talk to him lots, but to be honest, I didn't know *I* liked him.'

Tessa turns to me and puts her hands on top of mine. This was something that I had really missed about Tessa, she was *tactile.* Some friendships aren't hug friendships. Jean and I, despite being *insanely* close, don't hug that much. But Tessa absolutely loved hugging. She couldn't talk to you without holding your hands or having an arm around you or rubbing your back and I had missed it.

'I mean, I thought he was *fit*,' she continues. 'OhmyGod, undeniably good-looking. Seriously, though, so gorgeous in a—'

'Tessa,' I interject.

'Right, sorry, I got off track there. But I didn't really think that much more about him until his party. He had a girlfriend and everything so I just thought he would be a good-looking guy I know. I only really went to the party because I thought that you and Jean would be there, but neither of you were. We got to chatting and went for a walk and he's so easy to talk to, you know?' she implores, and I nod in agreement. 'So, I basically just spilled all the stuff that was going on with my mum and then he told me about the things that were going on with *his* parents . . .' She bites her lip for a second and then says in a quiet voice, 'They're having a seriously messy divorce, you know? That's why he's staying with Sam's family, but don't say I told you. Anyway, he was upset, we were both lonely and it just sort of . . . happened,' Tessa finished.

I understood what she meant, in theory, but I think things like that tend to only 'happen' to incredibly good-looking people. Like, if I went to a party and was upset and lonely and met another upset and lonely person we wouldn't end up kissing, the other lonely person would likely suggest

I help clear up to distract myself.

'When I found out you liked him, I genuinely nearly broke up with him.'

'But you didn't,' I remind her.

'No, sorry. He is *so* fit. Also I didn't know if we were ever going to be friends and I had already started distancing myself from the Lodge Crew and didn't want to burn *every* bridge.'

'Well, I hope you're happy,' I say and Tessa gives me a quizzical look. 'I meant that genuinely,' I quickly clarify. 'It's quite hard to say it earnestly. *I hope you're happy with Peter.* Is that . . . better?'

Tessa throws back her head and laughs, clearly relieved that I'm not going to give her a hard time about Peter. She shakes her head. 'Terrible. Really sounds so, so sarcastic.'

My feelings about Peter were still a bit . . . swampy. By which I mean that some bits were clear, some murky, some still underwater. And much like a swamp, I'm not going to spend too much time there. What wasn't swampy is the lightness I feel having Tessa next to me and talking to me and, let's be honest, doubling my friend count. I am, I'm discovering, quite a lot of work, but sitting next to me is someone that is willing to put the work in . . . and be very forgiving, which is *crucial.* I never thought when I did this Big Gesture, it would end up being two friends for the price of one.

I smile, looking at my ex-worst enemy, savouring the

moment before standing up with a theatrical groan. 'Right, we better head inside or else Ms Jenkins will send out a search party.'

We're just about to go inside when she turns to me. 'Before we go in, what's going on with you and Sam?'

I blink at her, confused at what she means. 'Sam? Oh, well he's next on my apology tour, I sort of made it seem like I was using him to get information on you and Jean,' I say, before adding guiltily, 'which I suppose I sort of was, originally.'

'Oh,' says Tessa.

'Why?' I ask, as clearly that wasn't the answer that Tessa was expecting.

'No, it's just, I thought you guys were maybe . . . a thing?'

'Me and *Sam*?' I say incredulously. 'Why would you think that?'

'Just the way he would talk about you when I was round at Peter's. I thought maybe he was into you and something had happened?'

'Noooo,' I say firmly, 'I only recently found out he doesn't *dislike* me. Although he probably actually *does* dislike me now.' I feel a twist in my stomach. I really hope that's not true. 'God,' I groan emphatically, 'why is it that I always end up having to apologize to people so much?'

'No idea.' Tessa smiles and rubs my back as we head into the theatre. 'Not a *clue*.'

Chapter 27

I burst into Ms Beckett's classroom first thing on Monday morning to give her the updates which I can only assume she has been anxiously awaiting.

'You won't *believe* what happened this weekend!' I roar, only to discover Ms Beckett not so much on the edge of her seat but slouched in her chair, sunglasses on and a huge Lucozade in her hand.

She lifts her head groggily and mumbles, 'Can we *please* use inside voices?' before slouching back over.

'This *is* my inside voice,' I explain excitedly. '*This* is my outside voice,' and as I breathe in to show her how much my projection has improved over the course of rehearsals, she quickly raises her finger to stop me.

'I'm feeling a bit . . . *delicate* today, Patch, so can we use our *even* gentler inside voices?'

'How come?' I ask even though I'm pretty sure I know the answer. She looks remarkably similar to my mum when she was feeling 'delicate' after her school reunion.

'It was the wedding on Saturday, but I'm still feeling the repercussions,' she explains before tenderly unscrewing the lid of her drink and taking a medicinal glug.

'Of course! Your ex's wedding! I can't believe I forgot, tell me *everything*!' I reply excitedly, before catching Ms Beckett wincing at my increasingly loud voice.

'Sorry,' I whisper. 'Inside voice,' and *quietly* pull one of the classroom chairs closer to her desk to sit down.

Ms Beckett pushes up her sunglasses to reveal puffy eyes. I decide not to tell her that she still has the remnants of a wing on one eye because it seems like she has enough going on.

'It was going fine,' she begins. 'Normal wedding things; boring church bit, speeches that left too long a gap for laughter and too-small sharing plates, but *then* they started serving espresso Martinis. And after . . .' I see her trying to count in her head before giving up, '*many* glasses, I decided I had something to say to the bride.' She puts her head in her hands at the memory.

'Oh dear.'

'Yeah,' she continues, pulling what looks like a piece of confetti out of her hair, 'so after a fairly lengthy rant about how this could have been *my* wedding and that she was the reason I didn't have a plus-one, I realized I was actually talking not to Sophie but a poor twenty-two-year-old called Katie who was wearing a pale pink dress that was sort of similar.'

'Oh dear,' I repeat.

'They both had capped sleeves!' she tries to explain before shaking her head. 'I don't remember too much after that, but I was told by a friend I gave a "haunting" rendition of "You're Still the One" by Shania Twain.'

'Oh dear,' I repeat for a third time.

'And there wasn't even a karaoke machine,' she finishes, before quickly adding, 'Oh dear. I know. I shouldn't have told you any of that, please forget it immediately.'

I shift in my seat and try to conjure up some advice. I think back to the day after my mum's school reunion. 'Whenever my mum is feeling . . . delicate, she makes a tea with five sugars and then makes a salad but orders a pizza. That might help?'

Ms Beckett looks at me, unconvinced, but takes a deep breath and visibly tries to compose herself. 'I'll try that, thanks Patch. Now what was it that you were going to tell me?'

'Oh nothing, I'll tell you another time,' I mutter as I stand up to leave her office, wanting to give Ms Beckett the few minutes she probably needs before she has to start explaining to her Year 9s that *To Kill a Mockingbird* isn't actually one of the *Hunger Games* films.

'No, I need the distraction, what is it?'

'OK, fine!' and I spin on my heel, too excited to restrain myself any longer. I tell Ms Beckett about not only Jean and me becoming friends again but also me and *Tessa.* Ms

Beckett was visibly shaken to the core by this (by which I mean she slightly raised her eyebrows), but this isn't surprising considering I have often referred to Tessa as a 'reprehensible menace to society' in this very room. I tell her how the three of us had spent the rest of the weekend joined at the hip, and how we even let Tessa into our culinary business! In fact, on Sunday night we created a recipe that we unanimously decided was going to get us a cooking show by the end of the year, if not the month. This was just before discovering that we had unwittingly made a Greek salad.

I was right in the middle of debating whether you can call it a Greek salad if you used Tesco own-brand 'salad cheese' instead of feta when she asks, 'And what about . . . what's his name? The American one.'

'Oh, Peter! Well . . . he's with Tessa, isn't he? And there's no way I can get in between Peter and Tessa *now*. Also, oh my God, Tessa told me that she thinks that Sam might like me!'

Ms Beckett looks sceptical, which I'm about to take offence to, but then says, 'Maybe now would be a good time to focus on your friendships rather than your love life,' before adding almost to herself, 'That's what tore Sophie and me apart.'

I think about this for a second. 'Maybe. But I think I'm only agreeing to that through lack of choice.'

'I've got to stop getting so invested in the love lives of teenagers,' Ms Beckett says, taking another gulp.

'Aha!' I cry, raising my finger. 'I knew you were invested!'

Ms Beckett rolls her eyes, but I can tell her mind is back on her behaviour at the wedding as she does a little wince as if she's just remembered something else. I'm unsure as to how I would give the wisest woman in the world advice, but I tentatively begin, 'I'm sure you don't need my advice, but have you thought about maybe just . . . talking to Sophie? Without espresso Martinis, I mean.'

Ms Beckett smiles at me. 'It's not as simple as that, Patch, there's too much history. You're young, it's easier.'

I nod, but press on, 'I'm sure that you're right, but *have* you ever thought about sitting down with Sophie, a neutral third party, and most importantly, using a talking stick or talking Baby Jesus if a stick isn't available?'

Ms Beckett looks very confused, then chuckles.

'I'll think about it,' she says gently, but I can tell that I shouldn't push the issue any further.

Ms Beckett lifts up her drink to get the final dregs and puts it down on the table. She looks at me quizzically. 'Right, you should get off to your next class, Patch, but I'm glad you've made up with Tessa.' Then she adds, 'It's very easy to get swept up in the looking for boyfriends and girlfriends and all that when you're your age – what am I saying, even when you're *my* age – and it's very easy to forget the people who already love you while you're doing all the looking.'

I do a mime of my head exploding because, once again, Ms Beckett has knocked it out of the park. I hurry to leave so that my morning isn't ruined by being told off for being late to French, but as I close the door behind me, I see Ms Beckett get out her phone. Maybe to text Sophie? Probably to order a pizza to the staffroom.

Chapter 28

'OK, everyone! Huddle round!' calls Ms Jenkins as we form our last huddle before the actual show. The *opening night*. Holy smokes . . .

It feels strange that after *so much* rehearsal our production of *Sweeney Todd* is only on for two nights. Two nights! So much time and energy. Blood, sweat and tears (literally all three in this case; I stubbed my toe during a quick transition) and it's over in the blink of an eye! I have repeatedly campaigned for a three-month run with the promise of a London transfer, or at least a five-day run, but apparently the theatre is booked after Saturday for an alcohol awareness seminar, which is annoying because you can't argue too strongly against alcohol awareness at the risk of being labelled 'insensitive' and I pride myself on being incredibly sensitive.

I'm trying very hard to 'be present' and focus on what Ms Jenkins is saying in our last-ever huddle, but my mind is occupied by other things. Having friends is obviously taking up a huge amount of headspace, especially trying to think of witty comebacks to defend Tessa when the Lodge Crew give her side-eye now she's ditched them for us; Callum Taylor even threw a croissant at her on Thursday, but I don't know what a witty comeback would be to that . . . ? Throwing a pain-aux-raisin at him?

Then there's the fact that I have completely forgotten yet again that I'm meant to be in charge of planning the Prom tomorrow; thankfully I've enlisted Flora and Rachel as co-chairs so we can share the blame and told Ms Jenkins that it's BYOD (bring your own decorations) which I framed as an 'exercise in community where, much like the play, we all bring things in to create something beautiful.'

And then, as always, there's the section of my mind reserved for 'boy drama'. At least now it's real boys rather than wondering if Fred from *Scooby-Doo* would leave Mystery Inc. for me. Sam is definitely still being off-ish with me, but across the huddle I see him staring into the middle-distance genuinely looking like he might throw up, so I'm boiling that down to nerves rather than just holding a grudge and I'm going to try and break the ice again after the first show. My eyes wander to Peter who is standing next to him. He's clearly not listening to Ms Jenkins either because our eyes meet. I smile, but he then quickly averts his gaze and looks at Ms Jenkins with complete concentration as if he didn't see me at all. That is my second sign that Peter is also being off-ish with me. I had said to Tessa when we became friends again that I thought it was important for us to all hang out with Peter as soon as possible so it wouldn't be weird. So we organized to see him very briefly yesterday after school and I can't put my finger on what exactly he's doing, but he's definitely acting a bit . . . strange. I asked Tessa about it and she told me not to worry because apparently he's being a bit weird with her too, but Jean sagely told us that long-term relationships often go through these ups and downs and she had lots with her ex Joe, which I thought was impressive considering they only dated for five weeks.

I thought I knew where I stood with Peter (he liked me but didn't fancy me) and Sam (didn't like me, then did like me but doesn't fancy me) but now I'm more confused than ever.

Clapping and whooping tell me that the speech has ended and I join in, perhaps whooping a bit too loudly to make up for the fact that I definitely wasn't listening. I take a deep breath. I am an actor, a professional, and I shan't let anything get in the way of my career. It's showtime.

My pre-show routine is pretty straightforward. It goes like this:

My Pre-Show Routine:

1. I do vocal warm-ups (tongue-twisters mostly, my favourite is '*she sat upon the balustraded balcony, inexplicably mimicking him hiccupping while amicably welcoming him in*').
2. I do body warm-ups (touch my toes for ten to twenty seconds then get a bit bored).

3. I look in the mirror and say 'hello' to my character (always a bit awkward because everyone shares a dressing room).
4. I wipe away my old self (clean my face).
5. I put on my character's face (concealer I stole from my mum and a bit of face paint applied with a sponge to make it look like I have stubble).
6. I make a sacrifice to the God of theatre, Apollo (usually a bourbon left outside the theatre doors even though I know I'm contributing to the theatre's mouse problem).
7. I have a quiet moment to myself (which mostly involves me telling everyone I'm going to take a quiet moment and then running out of time).
8. I check I don't have anything in my teeth (can you imagine?!).

'Nope, nothing there, just dazzling pearly whites,' says Tessa confidently while she artfully applies some flour to her costume.

Just then, Ms Jenkins knocks on the door and pokes her head through.

'It's time,' she tells us theatrically. 'And it's a full house!'

My stomach twists and there's a flurry of movement as everyone does final checks for the opening number. I'm pleased that it's a full house, but considering there are just fifty seats in the whole theatre (forty-seven if you discount the broken ones), and over twenty-five cast members it would have been actively bad if we hadn't reached full capacity. Jean, who had been helping Flora with her costume, runs up to Tessa and me and we clutch one another and put our heads together.

'This is it,' I say, squeezing their hands.

'I know I don't have much to do,' begins Jean, despite us telling her time and time again that her voice cuts through the chorus like a knife through easy-spread butter, 'but you two are going to absolutely *slaughter it*.'

Tessa smiles and looks down. 'Even if we don't . . . *slaughter* it, doing this play has been the best thing I've done because – I mean, look,' she gestures to the three of us all huddled together, 'we're back!'

Everyone else has headed out of the dressing room, but we take one last look in the mirror and I push the sides of my fake sideburns down for the millionth time to make sure they don't slip. Suddenly, Peter comes running in looking panicked. 'Has anyone seen Sam?' he asks breathlessly, his eyes darting around the room clearly looking for him.

'Sam. Has anyone seen him?' he repeats urgently and we all shake our heads. This can't be good. Peter grimaces, which just confirms it. 'I thought he went to the loo, but I can't find him anywhere.'

It takes a moment for what's happening to sink in. Peter finally looks me in the eyes. 'I think he's gone.'

Chapter 29

We split up like a SWAT team; Tessa and Jean research the bathrooms, Peter checks that Sam's not already backstage, and I go out into the main foyer to see if he's out there. I poke my head in, not wanting to be seen by anyone. The last of the audience members are filing in, clutching their thin plastic cups of questionably coloured wine. In the corner chatting to Jean's parents are Mum and Kath. They're coming both nights; one time to enjoy, one time to film, as per my request. Ms Jenkins usually makes a speech before the opening night, so I think we've got about five to ten minutes before the show starts. I dart out, quickly moving across the foyer and rushing outside. I do a quick scan of the theatre's entrance and am about to head back inside when I spot a pair of feet sticking out behind one of the cars. And the boots are unmistakably Victorian.

'What are you *doing*?' I hiss urgently as I rush up to him. Sam is sitting behind a Ford Focus with his head in his hands like he's drunk too much of the questionably coloured wine. 'Firstly, it's incredibly dangerous to sit behind a parked car, but also the show is starting *now*. As in, *now*, now! Come on!'

I try to put aside the weirdness between us since our day at the park and stick out my hand for him to grab onto, but he shakes his head. 'Patch, I can't. I can't do it.'

'Of course you can, come on!' and wiggle my hand in front of his field of view, hoping he'll take the bait, but instead his face crumples and his head retreats back into his hands. I knew that the nerves were getting to Sam, but I hadn't realized the extent of them, perhaps because I always claim that I get *very severe* stage-fright, but more so it looks like I've overcome an emotional hurdle rather than actually being nervous. Looking at Sam's face now, I can tell he is suffering from the real thing, I just have to make sure it's not terminal.

I decide to go for a different tack. I tentatively sit down next to Sam, not wanting to crumple my trousers, and wait for a second until I can hear his breathing start to calm down again.

'Sam,' I begin gently, 'what do you think it is? That makes you so nervous, I mean.'

'It's everything,' he mumbles into his sleeve.

'OK,' I say reassuringly. 'But what is it *specifically* about everything?'

I realize I am copying the exact tone that my mum uses on me when I fly into one of my more melodramatic episodes, like when I threatened to put myself up for adoption because I wasn't allowed a second choice of ice-cream on holiday because I didn't like the first. I tried to blame that specific episode on jet-lag despite being in Devon.

'It's the first line,' Sam says miserably and I patiently wait for him to continue even though we are rapidly running out of time. 'I just go over and over it in my head and I'm thinking so much about it that I'm worried I won't be able to remember it.'

He's staring down at his fingernails that I can see have been chewed to an inch of their lives.

'We could do that breathing thing I showed you before your audition?' I suggest. 'That might help?'

'You mean the time you nearly made me faint because you didn't tell me to breathe out?'

I was hoping he'd forgotten that little detail. I am so used to being the one having a breakdown, I've not been in this position before.

'I'm the main part,' whispers Sam. 'What if I mess the whole thing up?'

Sam finally properly lifts up his head and looks up at me with his long cow eyelashes.

'It's only bloody cake,' I say quietly, almost to myself.

'What?' he asks, looking at me as if I've lost my mind.

I try to explain, 'One time I was getting myself all worked up because I had made the wrong cake – for Jean actually – for this bake sale she was doing. I had made this cake and it was honestly disgusting and I . . . completely freaked out and lost perspective on the fact that it was just a cake. I think sometimes our heads trick us into thinking these things are the most important things in the world, when they're not! They're just cake. And this play. This Drama Club production of *Sweeney Todd*, where the part of Judge Turpin is played by a sixteen-year-old with a sponge face-paint beard,' I say and turn my head slowly from left and right to help illustrate the point, 'you need to remember that really, it's . . .'

'Only bloody cake,' finishes Sam, smiling slightly. I nod to him, smiling back.

'What is your first line anyway?' I ask.

Without hesitation, Sam delivers his first line of the play.

'See! You know it!' I tease him. 'And if you forget it, then you scream "What's my bloody line?!"'

Sam laughs and nods to himself and suddenly pushes himself up to his feet and extends his arm to me. 'Come on.'

'Really?' I say, forgetting to take the surprise out of my voice because I really didn't think that would work.

'Unless you don't want the chance to steal the show with your song?'

I grab his hand and Sam pulls me up. 'Well, I couldn't do that to a paying audience, could I?'

We make it back just in time. I see the visible relief on Peter, Jean and Tessa's faces as Sam and I crash through the backstage door, apologizing. Jean admits that they had to tell Ms Jenkins that Sam had a dodgy tummy. Luckily for Sam, there's no time to explain that he was actually outside having a major crisis of confidence. Ms Jenkins pokes her head around desperately and upon seeing Sam screams, 'Sam! There you are. OK, places everyone!' before trotting over to him and pressing a packet of Imodium into his hand.

'Thank you?' says Sam awkwardly.

Ms Jenkins nods and heads to the lighting booth. She must have been taking the stairs three at a time because within a minute the lights have gone down and the murmur from the audience quickly stifles into a heavy silence. The silence that means *showtime.*

Suddenly, my heart starts racing. I've been thinking so much about Sam that I haven't had the chance to get even a *little* panicked myself. And that little bit of panic, I think, is crucial to a good performance.

I take myself off and start pacing behind the heavy maroon curtain so I can centre myself undisturbed. I see Jean and Peter go on stage for the opening chorus number. I feel a hand on my shoulder and spin around to see Sam. 'Are you alright?' he whispers, adjusting his coat.

I nod. 'Yeah, fine, I just need to try and calm myself before I go on. My turn to be nervous,' I joke. 'Also, I know we don't have time now, but I just want to say, what happened at the park and then me snapping at you at the tech rehearsal, it really wasn't—'

'It's OK,' Sam says gently.

'No, it's not OK. And I really did want to hang out and it wasn't about finding out about Jean and Tessa.'

Sam gives me an incredulous look.

'OK, it was a *tiny* bit about that, *but* as soon as I started properly spending time with you, I completely forgot about all that. And then I snapped at you just before you gave me that cake which made me feel twice as guilty.'

'So sorry about that,' Sam chimes in, sarcastically.

'That's not what I meant,' I smile.

'I know, the whole park thing. I think I overreacted and so the cake was my very indirect way of apologizing,' he mutters.

'Ah, see I wouldn't know anything about overreacting,' I reply, which earns me a laugh. 'The cake was delicious, by the way. Victoria sponge is my favourite.'

'Yeah, I know,' Sam says smiling.

'How do you know?' I ask incredulously. 'I think it's quite off-brand for me to have a simple cake as my favourite.'

'It is,' agrees Sam, 'but remember we had that very heated text argument about how my favourite was lemon drizzle and yours was the humble—'

'Victoria sponge,' I finish quietly. 'I forgot I told you that.'

There's a beat where we both smile at each other clumsily. How is it that Sam can be so thoughtful and I can be so thoughtless? I mean, of course Sam has one of those very rare skills that I certainly don't possess of actually listening.

'Sam, that's . . . I don't know what to say.'

'It's only bloody cake,' Sam smiles, shrugging.

'No,' I say firmly. 'Not this time. Thank you.'

Sam looks down at the floor awkwardly before gazing back up at me and seems to look at me in a very proper way that heats my cheeks slightly. Though that could also be an allergic reaction to the face-paint beard.

'Anyway,' I say, breaking the silence, 'I've been on a bit of an apologizing spree recently and I definitely owe you one.'

'You are forgiven,' nods Sam ceremoniously. 'Shall I try your breathing thing on you? To help with the nerves?' he asks. 'I promise I won't let you faint.'

'Sure,' I say breathlessly.

'OK,' he says, shuffling a bit closer. 'So, breathe through your nose.'

I do.

'Hold it for a second.'

I do.

'And out through your mouth.'

I do, closing my eyes.

'In through your nose,' he repeats.

I do.

'And out.'

I exhale slowly and open my eyes to find Sam staring at me with a peculiar look on his face. Like he's about to say something but isn't quite sure what. His eyes scan my face.

In that moment, I notice a lot of small things happening all at once. I notice the smell of the stage smoke. I notice the sound of the opening chord for the first number. I notice the dust dancing through the gaps in the curtains where the light is shining through. I notice the rustle of clothes as Sam leans closer and I notice my eyes close and lean closer in response. Then I notice the fact that there are lips on my lips.

Well . . . almost. Technically, I notice that there are lips *somewhere* between my nose and top lip. I notice all those things and the one opening chord that seems to go on for ever. And just like that, his lips aren't near my lips any more. And that opening note now seems like the shortest note in the world.

I open my eyes, groggily, like I'm just waking up from a hundred-year slumber.

Sam is looking straight at me, trying to gauge my reaction. I have no idea what to say, my mouth isn't working and my head is fuzzy like it's gone into standby mode.

'Sorry,' says Sam quietly. 'Couldn't help it.'

Before I can reply, Sam has spun around and headed on

stage and I'm left reeling and slowly realizing that . . . YES. Well . . . maybe? Definitely, maybe.

Have I just had my first kiss?

I'VE JUST HAD MY FIRST KISS!

Chapter 30

The show goes remarkably well considering everything in my life has just been turned on its head. There was only one small hiccup when Tessa's costume got stuck on Sweeney's barber chair, but she managed to make it work by doing her entire song in one spot. I had to do my very best to stay in character and not scream to the audience, I JUST HAD MY FIRST KISS. SAM KISSED ME! I KISSED SAM! SORT OF! But I am a professional through and through and didn't let this huge life event (maybe the biggest life event in my, or anyone's, life so far) detract from my performance, and to be perfectly honest: I am sensational. The show must go on! It simply must!

After our bow, Sam comes up to me and I embarrassingly purse my lips, anticipating that he is about to declare his love for me in front of the audience and kiss me again, but instead he leans in close to my ear and whispers, 'Let's talk at Prom. Tomorrow.' In the most mysteriously romantic way, which almost has me swooning. Until he finishes by asking if we could keep *this* between us for now. I nod, slightly disappointed that I haven't been dipped and kissed in front of an applauding audience, but completely giddy that there's *this* to talk about. It takes every fibre of inner strength I have not to immediately run up and tell Tessa and Jean, analysing every tiny little detail to an exhaustive degree . . . but it's not my place to tell Tessa and Jean that Sam is queer, so I somehow stop myself, which is partly growth, but mainly because Jean would tell me off.

As I'm in the dressing room packing up my vocal steamer and my carnelian crystal (which is either meant to promote creativity or fertility, I can never remember), my mind occupied with trying to decide if I should exfoliate my lips tonight or tomorrow morning for my upcoming kiss, I feel a gentle tap on my back. I turn around to see Peter looking somewhat sheepish.

'Can we talk?' he asks awkwardly, which is very un-Peter.

Oh God. What if Sam's got cold feet and Peter is delivering a message from him saying the entire thing was a mistake and to pretend it never happened?

I quickly stuff my crystal in my backpack. 'Sorry, would love to,' I say frantically, 'but Mum's waiting for me in the car and I need to see her before she forgets any specific compliments from the show, but . . . chat tomorrow, yeah?' and bolt, leaving a confused-looking Peter in the dressing room. It's only as I'm pacing to Mum's car that I realize I don't know if Peter even knows about me and Sam. *Me and Sam.* Can't believe I can say that.

I have to tell *someone.* I pace around my bedroom, repeatedly staring at myself in the moon mirror to see if anything has changed now that I've been kissed. Do I have rosier cheeks or have I just not taken my stage make-up off properly? I go to my desk and put my phone in front of me and tap it anxiously.

I want to text Sam and say something completely casual but also interesting and romantic, but not *too much*, something like:

Possible texts I could send Sam:

- '*It's a five-star review from me for opening night and I say encore!*'
- '*Your lips have scorched themselves in my memory for eternity.*'
- '*hey hows you?x*'.

I want to text Peter and ask if he knows about Sam and if Sam has said anything to him. I want to text Jean and Tessa desperately. I can't keep this all bottled up! My mind is reeling and I need to make sense of everything that's happened. But who can I tell? Someone who doesn't know Sam or anybody else that I know . . . I quickly go to my desk and get out a piece of paper and a badly chewed pen. Welcome back into the fold, Jean-Pierre.

Dear Jean-Pierre,

I realize that in my last letter I was fairly strict in telling you not to send me any more letters, however I can't help but feel a BIT resentful that you didn't reply to:

- *Beg me to continue writing to you.*
- *Thank me for the good times (e.g. that time I thought we had an ongoing inside joke but it was actually just a grammatical error).*
- *Return* Going the Long-Distance*, that self-help book I lent you.*

Luckily for you, I've turned over a new leaf (not sure if that's an expression that translates well) and I've learned to be much more forgiving. So I forgive you Jean-Pierre! Gosh, that feels good to write down. I can't recommend becoming the best version of yourself enough! But you could still send the book back if you wanted to. And if you're sending the book then you might as well send some Milka bars with it. Partly as a peace offering, but mainly because they really are impossible to find in Hiverhampton.

Anyway, the reason for this letter other than showing how much I've grown is to give you an update. I realize it was completely unfair (cruel, even!) to tell you of my mission to get a boyfriend and then not give you any updates. You must be on the edge of your chair! Your chaise!

Well, here it is, Jean-Pierre.

While I might not have a boyfriend (yet), I have had my first kiss with a boy! Sam! I know you don't know who Sam is, but that's huge, a classic enemies-to-lovers tale that I'll tell you about another time. We've agreed to speak at a party tomorrow, but I have no idea what I'll say. I wasn't even sure that Sam liked boys let alone liked me! Needless to say, I'm very excited about the whole venture.

Jean-Pierre, I must go to bed because it's the final show tomorrow and I also want to look amazing before the party, so beauty sleep is a must.

Do let me know if you want me to update you about what happens at the party, but I'll assume that you do unless you tell me you don't explicitly.

Yours,
Formerly-single/still currently-single-ish/soon to be COMMITTED,
Patch x

Chapter 31

I'm still on cloud nine when I go to the theatre that afternoon. Cloud ten, maybe! No, cloud nine because I'm still worried that Sam will say that he wants to be just friends and I'm not being dramatic when I say that if he says that I'll have to run away. Although, when you're sixteen is it still running away or is it just leaving home?

Regardless, I've decided that because I did *such* a good job of not telling anyone about what happened with Sam last night (apart from ex-pen pals, but he won't get the letter for a few days, so *technically* I still haven't told anyone) that I can congratulate myself by telling Tessa and Jean and they in turn can reassure me that Sam *isn't* about to friend-zone me. I spot them sitting in the corner of the room, but the issue is Rachel and Flora (wearing pale green and emerald respectively) are sitting with them . . . Oh well! They can find out too! I'll just make them swear to secrecy. I rush over loudly declaring, 'Guys, I have something huge to tell you!'

But Tessa looks up at me and it takes me a moment to realize that her eyes are red and Jean has her arm around her.

'Oh no, what's wrong?' I ask, my life-shattering sentence evaporating as I sit down and join them.

Tessa goes to say something, but her eyes begin filling up with tears and instead of answering she makes a strange sort of whimpering sound, not unlike a dog that's accidentally been stepped on. Although I don't say that to her, of course.

Jean rubs her shoulder and leans towards me and says in a hushed tone, 'Peter broke up with her last night.'

What?! Peter broke up with Tessa? I can't believe it. Is that the rules of the universe? As soon as one romance starts to blossom another has to die? Is that what our Biology teacher meant when she said that all energy is transferable . . . ? Probably not, but still! I turn to Tessa to confirm that this is true and she nods glumly. I see her try and get all of her sadness out with an annoyed exhale. 'Ugh! It's just, I *knew* something was wrong. I *knew* it, I told you!'

'Did he say why?' I ask, not really knowing what else to say. In movies, often when someone breaks up with someone, the friends then start ripping apart the boyfriend, but I don't know what I would even say in that case because annoyingly Peter is so great, I would probably end up saying something like, 'Well, his teeth are *too* straight, it's sinister!' which wouldn't help things. Oh God, was that what he wanted to talk about with me after the play last night? What I thought about him breaking up with Tessa? Could I have stopped this from happening?

'He was really vague about it,' Tessa says, shaking her head. 'He just kept on saying that it was a combo of things, but that he still really wanted to be *friends*,' she says, rolling her eyes.

I put my arm around Tessa and the five of us form a tight little huddle.

Jean, as our group's resident break-up expert, says, 'When I broke up with Joe I thought my life was over. Patch can attest to the fact that I very seriously considered moving away and starting all over.'

'It's true.' I nod in agreement. 'She bought a one-way train ticket to Brighton.'

Rachel, Flora and Tessa all look a bit confused.

'I needed to be by the sea,' Jean says solemnly. 'But the point is that it feels like the worst thing in the world being broken up with, and then eventually it's not and it's just . . . a thing that happened.'

Tessa pulls away slightly and tries to dab her eyes on the sleeve of her jumper. 'It's OK, I just . . . ugh. Let's talk about something else, I don't want this to ruin the final show.'

We look at Tessa cautiously, unsure if she actually does want us to talk about something else or is just saying that because she needs more words of comfort.

'I'm serious,' she repeats sniffing. 'Can we please talk about literally anything else?'

Jean, Rachel, Flora and I look at each other trying to

think of something to say.

'Patch, what was the big news you wanted to tell us?' asks Rachel, excited that she had thought of a topic of conversation to detract from Tessa's sorrow, even if she had unwittingly picked the worst possible one. I mean, I definitely can't tell Tessa that Sam (sort of) kissed me *now*, that would be incredibly cruel timing. And I only want my timing to be impeccable, never cruel.

'Well, I . . .' I begin frantically thinking of what I can say. It's annoying because I'm usually fantastic at thinking on my feet. All great actors have a capability for improvisation, but at this moment I can't think of a single thing.

'What?' asks Jean, who's squinting at me. She can definitely tell something is a bit off.

'I found my green jumper that I thought I had lost, which is cool!' I blurt out, trying to nod enthusiastically to one of the most anti-climactic lies ever told.

Tessa, God bless her heart, tries to muster up encouragement. 'That's amazing, Patch, where was it?'

'Just in . . . my cupboard, actually,' I say and do a little fake chuckle. 'It's a funny one, isn't it? It's always in the most obvious place.'

There's a bit of a pause before Jean says, 'Patch, I think we need to find some sort of scale for what we count as "huge news" from this point on, you know?'

I nod. 'Yes, fair enough.'

Jean, Flora, Rachel and I take turns distracting Tessa by telling increasingly mundane stories about our evenings (apart from Flora who tells a harrowing story about how someone once lost their arm in a boating accident). Rachel is right in the middle of telling a particularly riveting story about how she opened a green banana that she thought wouldn't be ripe enough, but (and you won't believe this) it was, when Sam and Peter walk in. Sam does a quick scan of the room and catches my eye. I know my first instinct should be feeling bad for Tessa, but I can't help but notice that I, Patch Simmons, am now *finally* someone who catches eyes with someone! I'm an eye-catcher! He gives me a little smile which I, graciously, return. I like to think of it as a *knowing* smile; a smile that is only possible when there's something *known* that neither person is saying.

Peter follows Sam's eyeline and sees Tessa, takes a breath, and begins to walk up to her. Behind me, however, I hear Jean mutter, 'Right,' before briskly walking over to Peter. They exchange a few words, which I don't hear, and Sam and Peter walk off to sit somewhere else.

Jean returns, sits down, and says, 'Now, Rachel, back to the banana story. How did you feel when you found out it *was* ripe?'

Jean really would be excellent in a crisis management position. I look back at Sam who has taken Peter off to the opposite side of the room. Peter has dark circles under his eyes that make it seem like this break-up wasn't an easy decision for him either. I turn back to Tessa and decide that until the party, I am only focusing on Tessa and her bruised heart.

Throughout the play, I'm trying very hard to make sure Tessa is alright by giving her little arm-squeezes and sympathetic looks. What I love about Tessa is that she's a professional, much like me. She doesn't let matters of the heart get in the way of her overarching love: the love of theatre. Because of that, I do let my focus shift slightly onto Sam. And he is completely nailing it.

I'm not sure if it's because it's the last night of the play or if I'm just focusing more on him this evening because we are official love interests, but he is an unbelievably good actor. He's doing a better Sweeney Todd than I ever could (which is the highest possible compliment!). At one point, I'm so mesmerized with the inner turmoil of his song that I nearly forget my entrance.

I begin planning for our future as we get to the final number (I'm dead, of course, but had insisted to Ms Jenkins that I come on as a ghost) and I start thinking about what Sam and I will do when we're both West End actors and both auditioning for the same role.

I think what will happen is this:

I'll be at the console table, the light shining through my hair and nonchalantly arranging the flowers gifted to us by our adoring fans, when Sam will come in from his jog and after planting a kiss on my cheek would say: 'Listen, Patch. I've had some time to think, and . . . I'm dropping out of the audition, I want you to have it,' and I'll of course put up a big fight, I'll say things like 'I couldn't possibly!' or 'Over my dead body!' but ultimately he'll be so convincing that I will, reluctantly, give in. But it's fine because then he'll get a part in a different play the next week and people will call us 'London Theatre's power couple', but of course, we roll our eyes at that, even if it is actually pretty accurate. And then before I know it . . .

I can hear Mum whooping in the crowd and we're taking our bows. The play might be over, but the show is only just beginning . . .

To clarify, by 'show' I mean that later on Sam and I will kiss on the lips.

Chapter 32

The end of a show is always bittersweet. The excited chats in the dressing room detailing how brilliant everyone is as we get into our own clothes; Rachel handing out some sort of congratulatory baked treat, this evening's being a rocky road; the way everyone only pretends to wipe off their stage make-up because they actually like the way it looks. And soon we're shimmying into the foyer where all our friends and families are waiting to clap and we pretend to be embarrassed. This time, I'm desperate to get the chats with family members over so we can get to Prom and I can finally find out what's happening with Sam (we haven't said anything to each other apart from 'good show' in very sultry tones, I think) but I'm also terrified of getting to Prom because what if Sam doesn't say what I want him to say?

When I get downstairs, I'm shocked to spot Sam talking to Mum and Kath. This could either be disastrous or he's asking permission to propose – which might be a bit hasty, even for me . . . although very dramatic, which I do like.

'Hi!' I say loudly to stop them saying whatever it is

they're saying. Mum turns around, beams at me and plants a huge kiss on my cheek.

'You were brilliant, darling. Completely brilliant!' she gushes.

I look self-consciously at Sam, worried that now he'll only see me as a child instead of the sophisticated soon-to-be adult who is capable of long kisses and long relationships.

'Thanks, Caroline,' I say in the deepest voice I can muster.

'Why are you calling her Caroline, weirdo?' grunts Kath and I stare daggers at her before forcing myself to laugh, trying to convince Sam this is a 'bit' we do.

Sam turns to me, grinning mischievously. 'Your mum was just telling me about how you used to bring signed headshots after your nativities?'

I glare at her. 'Was she, now?'

'Shame you didn't bring any tonight,' he says, before touching my back. 'I have to go see my parents now, but lovely to meet you both,' he says to Mum and Kath.

His fingers graze my back as he leaves and I stare into the middle distance feeling the ghost of where his fingers just were.

'What a charming boy,' says Mum, looking after him.

'I – yeah – I know – completely,' I falter, still not over the back graze.

Kath gives me a scrutinizing look through her heavily

eye-lined eyes. 'Your voice warble has actually got quite good,' she says begrudgingly.

'My *vibrato,*' I correct her. 'And thank you. Yeah, I completely agree. Mum, what are you looking around for?'

Mum is craning her head and looking around at everyone mingling, 'Who is it then?' she says under her breath.

'Who's who?'

She turns back to me and tuts, 'The *boy*. The one you liked whose party you wanted to go to instead of going to Gran's.'

'*Mother!*' I stare at her furiously with my jaw clenched and my cheeks getting hot. Peter is, of course, standing right behind her as she says this. I look at him talking to Rachel, and even though he pretends not to hear I know he has because I see him twitch his head towards us and smile slightly. The only thing I can do is ignore this and continue to accept the lashings of praise from friends and family members before we all need to leave.

We have about an hour until Prom starts. Because Jean lives closest, Tessa and I go to hers to get 'glammed up'. We're allowed to have a sleepover there after, which is perfect because I think momentous occasions always need to be marked with a sleepover. Luckily, we had decided last week that we would all go to Prom together in celebration of our friendship. I love Jean's room, partly because I know it so well, but also because it's just very *her*. It's like walking through a pride parade; her room is every colour under the sun. The walls are lime green and she's painted swirly orange stars onto them. Her bed is one of those old iron beds with black metal bars which she's wrapped multi-coloured fairy lights around. The wall opposite the bed is completely covered with pictures, mementos, stickers, train tickets and completed Costa stamp cards, so you can't even see any of the green paint underneath. There's also, naturally, several pride flags up on the wall as well as a poster, handmade, on how to be a better ally. Which reads:

Advocate for others, make your voice heard!
Listen to the community!
Learn if you make a mistake and try to do better!
Yearly cake sale for charity (or more)

Jean admits that the 'Y' was a bit forced, but she's stuck to her word and hosted two cake sales earning about £32.79 for Mosaic Trust. She says she could have raised more but her oven is quite small.

The room, while usually tidy, is currently covered in outfit options. Tessa is sitting cross-legged on the floor in front of the long mirror that Jean's borrowed from her parents' room and is heating up her curler. Jean's rummaging through her cupboard while I'm trying to quickly finish the cards that I'm giving to everyone at the Prom. Giving gifts at the end of a play is a time-honoured tradition and one that I take incredibly seriously. I made all my cards from scratch, but did slightly run out of time towards the end so some of them are more elaborately decorated than others. My final card has just a single star sticker on it and a hastily drawn smiley face which makes it look like a card from a distracted four-year-old. Throughout the years, I have developed a formula to writing my cards which always works. I start with an inside joke, then I say something about how brilliant they were in the play and then I say something incredibly sentimental. For example:

Dear Alexa,
Firstly, can I borrow that mop?! Hahahahah honestly will never forget that!

I thought you brought so much nuance to Bird Seller, I genuinely forgot they were fake birds, you really brought them to life (and your singing range is one in a million, jealous much!).

I really think you are one of the most special people that I've ever met and know I'm very lucky to get to call you a friend.
Patch xxx

Or,

Dear Caitlin,

Is there room on that plate for one more tomato?! Hahahahah honestly still makes me cry with laughter!

I think ensemble is one of the trickiest parts in any play, but somehow you brought so much truth to your role, and also you had to move the heaviest box which is no small feat!

I really think you are such an amazing person, with a smile that can light up a room (if not a house!) and I'm so glad I met you.
Patch xxx

But I'm spending ages deliberating on Sam's card, which I left until last (I've also used all my best stickers on him, including a very cool plant sticker that I was planning on saving for myself). I can't think of the right tone to go for: playful, romantic or sincere? In some ways I want to lean into the romance, and inspired by Jean's poster, I even drafted an acrostic poem that spelt out 'soulmate', but quickly realized that was a bit much considering I don't even know his middle name or his favourite flavour of Skittle. The version I've got now is, I believe, the perfectly toed line between jokey, flirty and heartfelt.

Dear Sam,

Turns out the Demon Barber of Fleet Street isn't so bad after all.

In fact, I would love to book in a shave with him soon.

If you could check his availability and get back to me that would be great.
Patch

PS As I played a judge in the show; I can confidently rule that you have very soft lips.

I was second-guessing the PS when Jean loudly proclaimed, 'Right!' having clearly finalized her options. Before I can question myself too much, I lick the envelope and seal both the letter and my risqué little joke inside.

I turn to Jean who is holding up two denim jumpsuits. 'Which one?' she asks.

'Jean,' I reply smartly, 'they didn't have denim in Victorian times.'

Jean raises her eyebrow. 'They didn't have brow gel either, but that certainly hasn't stopped you.'

I quickly look in the mirror and check my eyebrows. I accidentally used Jean's eyebrow gel instead of mine which is a lot darker and it's given me quite a severe result. Not great, but certainly noticeable and I've decided that 'noticeable' is a good enough adjective for me this evening.

I turn back to Jean and appraise the two jumpsuits she's still waving in front of us.

'I think the darker denim is definitely the way to go, more sophisticated and more of an evening denim,' I answer assuredly, confident in my choice. Jean nods in agreement and goes to the bathroom to put it on.

I turn to Tessa who is staring absentmindedly at one of Jean's photographs stuck on the mirror. 'I think the curling iron's hot enough,' I say gently.

'Yes, right!' blurts Tessa, shaking out of her reverie. She picks up the curling iron and teases out a strand of her hair. She's painted her nails what she's called 'London Smog Grey'. Her attention to detail is inspiring. But I can tell she's still preoccupied with something.

I get up to sit down next to her and we catch eyes in the mirror. Tessa does a sad little smile.

'You OK?' I ask.

She nods, and a small amount of steam comes out of the tongs. She drops her newly coiled strand. 'I am. I really am.' Her jaw clenches in resolve, steeling herself against crying again.

'I don't think it's even about Peter or Callum and the rest of the Lodge Crew,' she continues. 'Not really. It's just I think I spent all of last year feeling like I wasn't quite good enough for the *cool* crew, or, you know, enough for . . . my mum and now Peter.' I can hear her voice get cloudy with tears. 'I am just so sick of feeling like I'm never quite enough.'

I always thought of Tessa as the most confident person in the world, so I'm surprised to hear that she doesn't feel like she's enough. I try to think how I can put into words how brilliant she is. It's like if you were in a vintage shop and you found the perfect jumper that you know you could never find again and just as you're ready to spend the rest of your life with that jumper it goes, 'actually I think I'll fit this person better' and flies off into someone's bag. Tessa is a one-of-a-kind jumper from a vintage shop and she doesn't even realize it.

'Do you want me to help with the back bits?' I ask her and Tessa nods. I carefully take the curling iron from her and begin working on the back sections of her hair. I think about using the vintage jumper metaphor on Tessa, but actually she's (bizarrely) more interested in Maths than fashion, so I try and gear it towards her.

'You know in Maths when Mr Clarke talks about fractions?' I begin, and I see Tessa's eyebrows furrow, but I carry on. 'So two quarters is a half, and four quarters is a whole. Or three thirds is a whole?'

'Yeah,' she says, still unsure where I'm going with this.

I release her hair from the curling iron, which is now warm and shiny, and pick up another piece.

'Tessa, you're like fifteen quarters. You're like fifty thirds all on your own! You are absolutely more than enough, it's crazy. It doesn't make mathematical sense how enough you are.'

I have to quickly hold the curling iron up in the air so I don't burn Tessa as she swings around to give me a giant hug.

'Thank you,' she mutters.

'It's the truth, and you don't need to thank your friends for the truth,' I shrug.

'Thanks anyway,' she replies, her head on my shoulder.

'Oh no!' cries Jean from the doorway, having got into her dark denim jumpsuit. 'Am I missing a moment?! Wait, wait, wait,' and she totters across her room, avoiding great piles of clothes, and joins in on the hug, 'I don't know what this is about but, *me too,*' and she squeezes her arms even tighter, forcing Tessa and me to make squished noises.

In that moment I think how impossible it would be to find a tighter-knit group of friends, literally. I also can't believe I *finally* understand fractions!

Chapter 33

I think we were all secretly expecting a hushed silence as the three of us entered the Prom holding hands. I'm not ashamed to say that I also envisioned a little round of applause as we strode in as emblems of the power of *friendship*. But we weren't emblems; we were three sixteen-year-olds with too much hairspray and clammy hands and our entrance goes by largely unnoticed. Regardless, the place looked *amazing*. I'd go as far as to say magical! I would love to accept full credit for this (and likely will) but I hired Rachel and Flora as my two assistants in the full knowledge that their aunt owns a party shop that they would have access to.

We've managed to remove the first two rows of seats from the audience area, which aren't proper theatre seats but seats that you can stack up, so that the party is split over two levels: the area for chit-chat and photographs is where the seats used to be, and the stage is taken up by the dance floor and the crisp table, and I think that's all you need for a good party. There's a real mixture of both Flora and Rachel in the decorations; while Flora clearly delved into the Halloween section of the shop via the cobwebs, spiders and skeletons on display, Rachel opted for Christmas decorations with hanging stars, tinsel and a slightly too realistic life-sized Virgin Mary with a party hat on. The overall effect is quite chaotic but mesmerizing.

On stage, there are balloons with actual helium, fairy lights and even a disco ball that scatters light over the whole theatre, making even the crisp and dips table look impossibly glamorous. Sure, it wasn't strictly Victorian-themed, but I'm positive that if the Victorians had access to a disco ball they would have used it.

What else made the crisp table more glorious? Sam and Peter were leaning up against it talking to one another. Sam had opted for what I recognize even at this distance to be a fancy crisp, yet another sign we are perfectly matched. We steer Tessa in the opposite direction and go to get our photographs taken. We've all put a lot of effort and volume into our hair and that needs to be documented before it loses height. Because what's a Prom without a Prom picture? An abomination, that's what! I managed to convince one of Kath's friends who is a budding photographer to do it for free for his portfolio. Largely he prefers to photograph quite dreary car parks or pieces of rubbish in the park, but the brief I gave him was 'glitzy and glamorous' which I'm sure was a tough pill to swallow for someone who voluntarily calls himself 'Spider'. There isn't much of a queue, but it gives the three of us enough time to agree on our classic four poses: arms around each other, pretty-silly, actually-silly, and Charlie's Angels.

After we've had our photographs taken and I've firmly reminded Spider that part of our deal was that I get a final say on which ones are put online, we turn to the dance floor. What's great about having Prom in the theatre is that we have access to the stage lights for dancing and there were already coloured lights flashing on and off and spotlights whizzing around like we were at an old-school Hollywood premiere. One of the things I'm proud of (and there are many) is *never* being embarrassed to dance. It might be because my mum is always dancing around the kitchen or because I've learned it's much more embarrassing to be embarrassed than it is to just go for it. But mostly it's because I'm a *great dancer*. Those combined reasons mean that Tessa, Jean and I are the first ones onto the dance floor.

Everyone else is milling around nervously, unwilling to transition from bobbing from foot to foot to full-on dancing. As committed drama kids, we know the importance of 'balancing the space', so we make sure to take up the whole dance floor by throwing ourselves around in a combination of 'interpretive dance' and 'recently possessed by a maleficent ghost'. Of course, the floor quickly fills up. Rachel twirls in a sparkly cornflower-blue dress, while Flora sways slowly in a gothic velvet navy dress with lace gloves and a black veil. I'm halfway through a particularly jumpy song when I feel my phone vibrate on my leg. I take out my phone and my heart skips when I see it's a text from Sam.

Meet outside on the bench in 10?

I see Sam looking up at me from the crisp table. I smile at him and nod and he grins back. Jean and Tessa are spinning each other around when I grin and mime to them that I'm going to go to the loo.

I extract myself from the crowds of drama kids mouthing along to a song they collectively know about 30% of the lyrics to and move backstage to go to the bathroom. I need to look perfect for my reunion with Sam so I've brought a little bag of essentials with me for check-ups. Certainly no sideburns or fake dirt this time. I get to the bathroom and lay out my kit which includes a bit of powder in case I have an oily t-zone, the brow gel, hair wax, tinted lip balm, cream blush and the remnants of an aftershave that Mum's ex, Ralph, left in the bathroom. It doesn't smell particularly nice but certainly smells strong.

Once I'm finally happy with the artful strand of hair that I have falling in front of my face (encouraging Sam to push it back like people often do in films before they kiss), I pack up my bits and go to leave the bathroom. My heart is hammering against my chest. The last time with Sam caught me off guard so I didn't have time to think about anything, but this time I'm going into a situation where I'm 99% sure we're going to kiss. I wonder what we'll talk about before we kiss or whether we'll get straight down to it. I imagine there will be some sort of preamble. Maybe I can ask him what sort of crisps he was eating as I arrive? Is that erotic? I'm right in the middle of deciding whether I should lead with 'Hey' or 'Hello you' when I open the bathroom door and bump into someone waiting outside. When I look up, it's Peter.

'Oh, hey,' I say.

'Hi,' Peter replies, looking a bit strange. Nervous, even.

'Were you waiting to go in? Because I was only in there for such a long time because I was doing check-ups,' I quickly explain, worried he thinks I have stomach problems.

'No, it's not that,' he says, looking around to see if there is anybody else coming. 'I wanted to talk to you.'

'Oh, OK.' I reply.

Oh no. This is it. Sam did tell Peter about our kiss after all and must have thought it was a huge mistake! Or maybe Sam's given him a message for me? A riddle? That would be quite weird, but perhaps it's a prerequisite for Sam that he'll only date people who can solve this riddle. I'm terrible at riddles!

Thankfully, Peter interrupts my deranged thought process.

'I just, you know . . . well obviously Tessa and I broke

up,' he starts, and I nod sympathetically. 'How is she doing, by the way?'

'Oh, you know, not *great*, but I think she's OK. I think she's maybe a bit confused as to . . . why?'

Peter looks pained and nods, shifting his feet. 'Yeah, I get that. Well, I told her it was a combination of things, and it was, but there was sort of one main reason I didn't tell her about, which is why . . . I . . . did that.'

He pauses and looks at me. I don't have time to think about what the reason could be before he takes a step forward and says:

'It's you, Patch,' he says, so quickly I think I've made it up. 'You're the reason.'

My head goes into overdrive and in the process completely malfunctions. I'm the reason Peter broke up with Tessa? Me? As in Patch? Formerly Patrick?

What?

He continues, 'Ever since I found out you liked me, I haven't really been able to get you out of my mind. Eventually I realized I was thinking about you way more than I was about Tessa or anyone else, in fact, and that wasn't fair. And then when Sam went to hang out with you at the park, I realized that *I* wanted to be the person hanging out with you instead.' He pauses and swallows. 'I like you, Patch. *Like* you, like you.'

For some reason the first thing that pops into my head

is that I really need to buy the actual bottle of this perfume because evidently it drives men wild. I can't even fully comprehend that, somehow, I have two boys, two amazing boys, and they both like me?

'But . . . what about Sam?' I ask without thinking.

Peter's eyebrows furrow in confusion. 'What *about* Sam?'

Sam obviously hasn't told Peter about his crush (aka, me) for some reason, and although ideally Sam would be telling everyone, especially all my old crushes, how much he fancies me, he clearly isn't quite there yet.

'Oh, it's nothing, I just—'

'—Listen,' says Peter, his hand reaching out to touch my arm and then retreating back, 'I know it's a lot of information that I've just given you and I know you've just made up with Tessa again and I really don't want to get in the way of that, *really*, but I also just felt like I had to say something because . . . well, I don't know . . . I just needed to say it. Had to.'

Peter shrugs helplessly and smiles at me and my heart melts a little bit. Then he leans forward and kisses me on the cheek. I always thought a kiss on the cheek was formal – it's what adults do to each other and what I once, unaware that it was not the norm, did to my Year 1 teacher on my first day of school. But this cheek kiss is anything but formal and Peter certainly isn't my Year 1 teacher. It's a slightly longer kiss on the cheek than is traditionally done and I can feel it there even after his lips leave . . . Before I have time to say anything else, Peter smiles, turns, and goes back to the party.

It takes a second to get my brain into gear and sort out what's just happened. I try and say it out loud, as a fact to myself, so that I believe it. 'Somehow, inexplicably, Sam and Peter both fancy me. Peter and Sam both fancy me. They *both like ME.*'

Now I will fully admit I can be somewhat of a fantasist, but never in my wildest dreams did I imagine when I first saw Tracksuits and Trousers that I would actually be in a position where I would have to decide between them. My powers of manifestation are *too powerful* and—

Oh my God. I have to decide between them.

Emotionally, I'm swinging like a pendulum between being very excited and being very overwhelmed.

Getting a boyfriend was a much more fun thing to do when it was a theoretical gameplan. I think the stress is already giving me a stomach ache. Also, I thought beggars couldn't be choosers! And let's face it I was certainly willing to beg. I mean, before this conversation with Peter, if I had gone outside and Sam had said he wanted to just be friends, I would have fully begged, definitely. *Oh God.* Sam! He's outside now. What should I do? Do I really have to decide the entire destiny of my romantic life in the next two minutes? Can't I apply for extra time or extenuating circumstances?

I follow my feet back into the auditorium in some sort of trance, where people are still dancing. I find it almost rude that people are still enjoying themselves when I am going through such emotional turmoil. I spot Tessa and Jean in the centre of things, who are now wearing prop moustaches and waltzing around. I hear Jean squeal as Tessa tries to lift her up. My silly wonderful friends. I want nothing more than to go up to them and explain the whole situation, but that would mean telling Tessa that Peter liked me. And although that technically isn't my fault (apparently, I'm irresistible now) I don't think it would do amazing things for our friendship.

I take a calming breath just to see if it unlocks any clarity of thought. No luck. Instead, I hear the squeak of the door as Sam pokes his head back into the auditorium. How long has he been waiting outside for me? How long have I stood frozen in this spot? Two seconds? Ten minutes? Eight hundred thousand years? Who knows? He sees me and gives me a quizzical look before making his way over to me. *Crap.* I look around for something to save me from this impending car crash of a conversation that I am definitely not ready to have, desperately trying to catch eyes with Jean, but instead I catch eyes with Peter who is stood behind her (when did I become someone who can't stop catching eyes, I don't have the stamina for this!). Peter smiles nervously and also starts heading over to me. *Double crap.*

I'm literally in between a rock and a hard place, except the rock is an American that I really fancy and the hard place is an English person that I really fancy.

I'm going to make America and England fight over me. I'm just like the British violations of US maritime rights in 1812! Why is that fact in my head?

I tear through my mental rolodex of advice from my mum's books as the two boys of my dreams head over to me in some sort of living nightmare. I can't think of anything?! The Battle of Hastings was 1066. The Great Fire of London was 1666. There's nothing beyond historical facts! I can't giggle my way out of this in a way that seems both mysterious and enticing!

Time, being the weird thing that it is, moves very slowly and when they are about three metres away from me, I pull my Last Resort. This is a resort I have only resorted to twice before in my life and only when there is no possible option left. The first time I used it was when I wanted to get out of the end-of-year swimming gala (I was given butterfly, the most humiliating of strokes) and once when I was asked to help Kath de-weed all of my gran's garden. Now, I'm not proud of this, but sometimes difficult situations call for difficult choices. So I decide to shut my eyes and fall.

Bang.

Luckily, I'm trained in pretend fainting from various school productions, so I know how to do it without injuring myself badly, but I do think I'll get a bruise on my knee. As my shoulder hits the ground I hear both Peter and Sam yell my name and come over to me. I keep my eyes firmly shut as I hear lots of people notice that I've fainted. The music is suddenly turned off and the overhead lights get turned on. I hear lots of people saying my name, as they crowd around me; their fallen star.

'Patch, are you OK?'

'Oh my God, is Patch dead?'

'He's not breathing! Patch isn't *breathing*!!!'

'He is breathing, look.'

'Oh, yes, he is.'

'Don't go towards the light!'

'Patch, open your eyes!'

But I don't open my eyes, I keep my eyes firmly closed. As I hear people fawn over me, I can't help but feel glad that part of my 'new year, new me' has worked. People are finally calling me Patch! Then I hear Jean's voice very close to my right ear.

'Patch,' she whispers very quietly, 'I can spot one of your fake faints from a mile off, what are you *doing*?'

How do I explain to her that somehow over the course of a single evening, I've got everything I have ever wanted for this year, and now I have no idea what to do about it. I quickly lick my lips which have gone bone dry and numb; perhaps due to the turbulent emotional situation or because

I applied a liberal amount of expired plumping lip gloss.

'Look, he's licking his lips!' someone calls excitedly. Damn, didn't think that one through.

'Is he waking up?'

'Oh my God, is he having a sex dream?!'

In order to stop this from spiralling out of my control and rumours spreading of me having a sex dream in the middle of Prom, I flutter my eyes open and do my best dazed expression. Ms Jenkins has been alerted of the situation by now and I hear the frantic clack of her heels as she rushes up to me.

'Patch, are you alright?' she asks breathlessly.

I slowly sit up while Ms Jenkins motions everyone to give me space. I make sure not to catch eyes with Sam or Peter and make a big deal out of blinking as if slowly regaining consciousness.

'Can someone get me a drink?' I croak, as if I've been wandering the desert for many days.

'Here, Patch,' someone says as they hand me a plastic cup.

'Drink some water, Patch,' says Ms Jenkins gently.

I look down at the glass of water. 'Do you have anything else?' I ask, handing the cup back to Ms Jenkins. 'Maybe a decaf frappuccino, ideally hazelnut-flavoured?'

The look of concern that was on Ms Jenkins' face quickly disappears and is replaced with scepticism. 'Right,' she says, standing back up, 'I *think* Patch is just about going to survive. Everyone carry on! Jean, why don't you take Patch to sit down for a bit?'

'Yes, of course!' says Jean quickly and, ever the ally, she makes a show of helping me up to my feet. Tessa, who had been warning people, including Sam and Peter, not to crowd me like she's my own personal security guard, comes up to Jean and me.

'Are you OK?' she asks, clearly unsure whether she should be genuinely concerned, and helps Jean take me to one of the seats in the auditorium.

Once we've sat down, Tessa leans into me. 'That was a fake faint, wasn't it?'

'How did you know?' I ask, annoyed that both Tessa *and* Jean saw through my performance so easily.

'I recognized it from when you were asked to do your Physics presentation,' replies Tessa matter-of-factly. I nod, having forgotten that I had *also* pretended to faint when I forgot to do my Physics homework at the end of last year . . . I might need to be more selective when I use my Last Resort.

'What's going on?' asks Jean.

I look first at Jean and then at Tessa and nod to myself. Right, I have to tell them. Not *everything*, obviously. I think I have to opt for a 'partial truth'. Partial truths are very annoying when anyone else does them. For example, partial truths are dreadful when Mum says we're going to pick up a treat from the petrol station when we are actually picking up a treat *en route* to a swimming lesson, despite me repeatedly telling her that the chlorine is too harsh for my sensitive skin and, if push comes to shove, I would rather drown. But partial truths are gracious when I do it, *very* Julie Andrews. Plus, I don't really have a choice. I just can't bring myself to tell Tessa about Peter, no way. His crush on me would crush her, which is lovely in a wordplay sense, but awful in a friendship sense. But I at least need to *sort* of tell them what's been going on, so I decide to tell them about Sam.

Looking out at the party where everyone has formed some sort of half-hearted mosh-pit, I finally tell Tessa and Jean about how Sam and I kissed. Because I haven't been able to tell them about the kiss for what has felt like years, I have really finessed the storytelling element of it and even managed to secure a gasp as I build to Sam taking a step closer to me. I might have embellished some of the facts, such as fairy lights flickering on as I closed my eyes, but once I have brought them up to speed there is a little pause.

'You have no idea how hard it's been having had my first kiss and not being able to tell you guys!' I say, shaking my head. I'm expecting more whoops or at least a squeal, so I look to Jean and Tessa who are instead looking at one another. Jean opens her mouth to say something, but then shuts it.

'What?' I ask.

'So,' says Jean carefully, 'did you have your first kiss after that?'

'What?' I say, confused as to where she got lost in the story. 'No, that was it! Have you not been listening?'

Jean and Tessa look at each other again. 'What is it?!' I hiss. 'Stop looking at each other!'

'Sorry,' Jean says quickly, making her seat squeak as she moves closer to me. 'It's just you didn't *really* have your first kiss, did you?'

'Of course I did!' I protest.

'But didn't you say that he kissed you just under your nose?'

'So?'

'Well,' she says, carefully looking to Tessa for support, 'I'm just not sure that counts as a first kiss. I mean, your lips didn't touch.'

'But the *intention* was to kiss, he just . . . missed! Surely that counts?!'

'If you want it to count, it definitely counts,' says Tessa, 'but I think it's a grey area.'

'A grey area, exactly,' parrots Jean. 'What I would say is that *emotionally* you've had your first kiss but just not . . . physically.'

I look back out to the party where a small crowd has formed around Miles who is boldly attempting to do the worm.

'Dammit,' I mutter, 'I still haven't had my first kiss, have I?'

'Afraid not,' says Jean, patting my thigh.

Tessa loops her arm through mine and puts her head on my shoulder. 'Very close though! As close to getting a first kiss as it is possible to get, a centimetre away!' she says and then gives me a nudge in my side with her elbow. 'And don't ever not tell me things. Even if I'm sad I always want to know.'

'What? Even to tell you that I *almost* had a kiss?' I say, feeling slightly deflated.

'Even then,' and she squeezes my arm and I can hear the smile on her lips.

'Wait a minute!' Jean says excitedly, sitting upright like she's just been stung by a wasp. 'What does this mean now? You and Sam?! Oh my goodness. I mean, Patch, you could get your first kiss *right now* if you wanted?! You could technically get a boyfriend in time for Prom!'

Tessa bolts upright too, the metaphorical wasp having moved onto her. 'Yes! He clearly *wants* to kiss you, do you want to kiss him?'

I look up and over to Sam, who is comforting Miles who looks like he might have bitten his tongue in the process of 'the worm'.

'I . . . do,' I say hesitantly. Jean and Tessa squeal as my eyes cross over to Peter who is jumping animatedly to the song that's just come on. 'But it's complicated,' I add.

'No, it's not,' says Jean in her relationship-advice voice. 'Everything can be complicated when it comes to *matters of the heart*, but it's not. It's a simple question, do you fancy him?'

'It's not that simple!' I complain.

'It *is*,' both Tessa and Jean say in unison.

'Do you fancy him?' Jean repeats, leaning forward in her dating-show host way.

Do I fancy him? Clearly I've been watching too many rom-coms and they've actually rewired my brain because a little montage plays in my head, helped along with the musical backdrop of the song that's now playing on the speakers. It's a montage of Sam. The shy way he introduced himself on that first day, the slightly embarrassed joy on his face when he tried a bit of salt in his hot chocolate, his long eyelashes, reading in the cafe with his eyebrows furrowed, singing the opening number, sweeping to pick Phoebe off the ground when she was trying to make 'mud-angels' and then later using his arm to cover her from the rain.

The way he looked at me before he, very nearly, kissed me.

I smile to myself. 'So much. I actually think I fancy him so much.'

Jean whoops and Tessa stamps her feet in excitement.

'Well, there we go then!' Jean trills. 'Now you have to *tell him*!'

'Oh my God, *tell him*!' screams Tessa.

I nod. 'You're right, I need to tell him,' I say to them, but in my head I say *I need to tell both of them.*

Chapter 34

I instruct Tessa and Jean, firmly, to rejoin the party because there's nothing worse than your overly supportive friends watching you try and secure your first kiss. They reluctantly agree and I follow them down the stairs. Tessa goes up to Flora who is having an animated discussion with Spider. He's showing her pictures of what looks like roadkill. Jean hesitates at the bottom of the steps before turning back to me and grinning.

'Right,' I say, looking out for Sam. 'Showtime.'

'Good luck,' says Jean and squeezes my hand.

'I just need to speak to Peter first,' I say quietly.

Jean looks at me quizzically, but instead of questioning me she nods slowly. 'OK, but be quick, Ms Jenkins is shutting this thing down in half an hour.'

Jean turns and joins Tessa and Flora who are posing in front of the now sheepish photographer. I look towards Sam and Peter who are chatting, which is not ideal, but then fate intervenes (thanks, fate!) and I see Sam mime that he's going to the loo and take my chance to go speak to Peter.

I push through the crowd. He's at the far end, nodding

along to the song, hands deep in his pockets.

'Hey,' I say over the music.

Peter looks over to me and grins slightly and for the first time *ever* I see him look a bit self-conscious.

'Can we talk?' I say, trying to keep my voice as casual as possible. I can't believe I'm now the type of person who says 'Can we talk?' about a romantic issue rather than me saying it to someone who I think has been copying my pencil case for three years straight (Holly Jones). He nods and we walk off the stage to the side of the theatre where it's quieter and slightly hidden from prying (aka, Jean's) eyes.

'It's a good party, isn't it?' I say, for some reason resorting to small talk in a bid to put off saying what I have to say. One side of Peter's mouth rises in amusement, but I continue, 'I was wondering if you had any feedback on the Prom thus far . . . considering I'm head of the planning committee?'

'Hmmm,' says Peter as he puts on an exaggerated thoughtful expression. 'Well, I suppose the one bit of feedback is there might be too many fairy lights?'

'No such thing,' I reply.

'And,' he continues, leaning in slightly and lowering his voice, 'I would also suggest that the head of the planning committee actually say what he brought me over to say.'

I nod. 'Right, good feedback. Excellent feedback, in fact. Right to the point.'

I take in a steadying breath. 'So,' I begin confidently, but then Peter, with his hands still in his pockets, looks at me and my resolve melts slightly, 'I just, I um—'

Before I can figure out how I'm going to phrase what I want to say, I see Peter's shoulders drop slightly and he nods sadly. 'Right,' he says.

'But I haven't said anything yet?' I say, confused.

'I've had enough of these conversations to tell pretty early on which way it's going.'

'You've had loads of *these* conversations? God, you're so lucky,' I say before I can stop myself. 'Sorry, I just mean, this is my first romantic conversation *ever* and—'

'It's OK, I know what you mean,' he interrupts before I dig myself even further into the hole I've created. I gear myself up to tell him what I have to say next. 'I do really like you, *really*, but I've . . . I've realized that there's someone else I like, too.'

Peter is visibly quite surprised by this, but quickly covers it up. 'Oh,' is all he says.

There's a moment where we both just look at each other, unsure of what the next step in this conversational tango is.

'Am I allowed to ask who?' he says quietly, but before I can respond he quickly adds. 'Actually, no. I'm not sure I want to know yet.'

I nod, quietly grateful because firstly it's definitely not my place to tell and secondly I don't want to. I can only imagine the thoughts running through Peter's head, but he doesn't voice them, instead his eyes are trained on the wall behind me like he's reading something very interesting, when I know for a fact that the only thing on that wall is a very outdated fire-safety poster.

'Are you OK? I'm so sorry, I just . . .' and I let the sentence trail off, unsure of where it was heading.

'Don't be sorry, it's my fault,' he says firmly. 'I took too long to . . . and I'm . . . pleased for you, as weird as that sounds,' and he tucks a loose bit of hair behind his ear.

There's an awkward pause where we both sort of nod at each other, but thankfully, Peter breaks the silence.

'Listen, I think I might head off—'

'No!' I interrupt. 'Please, I don't want to ruin your whole evening!'

'You're not ruining it, I just – I think I want to walk home, you know? Clear my head.'

I look at him, unconvinced.

'Really,' he smiles, 'I'm fine,' and he turns to go. 'Will you tell Sam that I've . . .'

I nod. 'Of course, yeah.'

'Great show by the way, Quill,' he says quietly and opens the door.

'Thanks, Spoon,' I say, but he's already gone.

Chapter 35

God, romance is the *worst.* I haven't even had a first kiss and I feel like a world-weary romance veteran. I watch the door Peter's just left through and I can't decide if I should follow him . . . I don't really know what I would say if I did. Beg him to be completely fine? Feels like an unlikely result. If I was Peter I would probably want a little bit of time alone to play sad songs, feel a bit sorry for myself and watch *Titanic* at least twice.

I turn so my back is pressed against the cold wall and watch the cast and crew of *Sweeney Todd* swaying to Taylor Swift, just like they would have done in the Victorian times. Sam, who has now returned from the loo, is swaying too, but clearly doesn't know any of the words so is instead making very vague mouth shapes in the hopes this will pass as 'singing along'. I once asked Sam what his favourite song was (not my most original question) and he looked immediately flustered before replying that it was 'that one by that singer'. Upon further interrogation it turned out that Sam's musical knowledge was limited to an almost prehistoric level and that he basically only listens to what his mum calls 'crooner songs'. These are songs sung by people like Frank Sinatra and Nat King Cole. I think I've worked out what makes a crooner song:

<u>What makes a crooner song:</u>

1. They use less autotune.
2. They have less catchy songs or at least songs that are harder to dance to.
3. They are much cooler to listen to than my personal choice of music which is 'whatever the internet tells me to like'.

The song ends and everyone claps. I take a step towards him, but at that exact moment Ms Jenkins gets up on stage and claps her hands, smiling broadly at us.

'Right, I'm afraid that is all we have time for tonight!'

There's a chorus of groans that are more in harmony than some of the songs in the show, but my groan (as always) rises above the masses.

Prom is the perfect location to have a first kiss and now I'm too late!

Unaware she is ruining my love life, Ms Jenkins continues to look around the room. 'I know, I know, but we have to leave before ten p.m. because that's when the exterminators are coming back in for round two,' and she does a big fingers-crossed gesture to us all, despite none of us knowing that there had been a round one of extermination. Before we can think too much about what exactly needs to be exterminated, Ms Jenkins continues.

'But I just wanted to say thank you so much for all your hard work. I've seen this play in the West End,' and she leaves a big pause and looks around proudly. 'It's true! And I've also seen it on tour and I really mean it when I say I think Hiverhampton's production could give them a run for their money!' Everyone looks very pleased at this before she adds, 'If not in terms of talent then *certainly* for enthusiasm, so everyone give yourselves a round of applause!'

While everyone is giving themselves a lacklustre round of applause I stare at the back of Sam's head willing him to turn around and look at me, but he remains looking ahead at Ms Jenkins. I change tack and stare at the back of Jean's head, willing her to turn around. No sooner have I willed it does Jean spin around on her heel and look at me, her scissor hair clip glinting. Our psychic connection is completely unparalleled.

'What is it?' she mouths.

Our conversation is entirely mimed, but because we both have excellent articulation it's pretty easy to understand one another.

'*Sam!*' I mouth urgently.

'*What about him? Oh my God—*' before unhelpfully covering her mouth in excitement and mouthing something else. On seeing my bewildered expression she quickly moves her hands away from her mouth.

'*Sorry, did you kiss?*' she excitedly mimes.

'*No, I need to speak to him?*'

'*Speak to Kim? Who's Kim?*'

'*No, HIM. I need to speak to HIM!*'

'*OH! OK!*' and I see her think for a second before deciding on something and mouthing, '*On it!*' to me before whispering something into Tessa's ear who looks back at me and nods eagerly.

Not entirely sure what I've just unleashed, I look back to Ms Jenkins who is now looking down at her watch. 'Right, the exterminators will be here soon and trust me when I say you do not want to be here when they start spraying.'

'Wait!' calls Jean and hurriedly joins Ms Jenkins. 'We've got some things that we want to say too! Some thank-yous!'

Ms Jenkins looks concerned. 'Jean, they're going for a stronger chemical concentration this time, as apparently the infestation has become resistant to the last batch.'

'*But* part of that thanks is for *you*, Ms Jenkins,' says Tessa earnestly as she joins Jean.

Ms Jenkins' cheeks flush and she pats down her skirt awkwardly. 'Well, if you must, quickly though!' and she joins the rest of the crowd facing towards Jean and Tessa where I spot her subtly put her bag down by her feet as if ready to accept a giant bouquet of flowers with both hands.

'Well, yes,' stutters Jean, clearly trying to think of

something on the spot. She glances at me briefly, her eyes wide. 'Big thank you to Ms Jenkins who was the captain of our, um, ship! There were some days that felt as though the waves were going to get a bit too turbulent to weather, but overall it was a pretty good, yeah, *voyage.* Everyone was pulling their oars nicely and the sails were in the right direction for it to be a successful trip and nobody drowned!'

Everyone looks sceptically at Jean who clearly has a pretty basic understanding of sailing.

'Let's give Ms Jenkins a round of applause!' whoops Tessa, which gets the crowd going and everyone claps while Ms Jenkins does a self-conscious little bow.

'We did have a gift for you, Ms Jenkins,' says Jean and Ms Jenkins takes an excited step forward, 'but I can't find it, so we'll have to give it to you later.'

Jean pulls a face at me. Hopefully Ms Jenkins won't follow up on this fictitious gift. I try to hold Jean's gaze to get an idea of what she's doing, but before I can ask she continues.

'And now, I think Patch had something to . . . add!'

I ferociously shake my head, desperate to signal that this is not what I had in mind *at all.* I don't know exactly what I did have in mind, but definitely not this. My track record for making public announcements thus far has been catastrophic. But it's too late, people are already turning to look at me expectantly.

'Let's welcome Patch to the stage!' trills Jean, clapping

enthusiastically like I'm the newest contestant on *Who Wants to Be a Millionaire?*, but I don't want to be a millionaire, I want to be a million miles *away*. My legs are suddenly made of lead and I reluctantly lumber towards the stage, eyes fixed ahead. I never thought there would be a time where I would be reluctant to go on stage.

I glare pointedly at Jean as I join her and she pulls a grimace, whispering, 'Sorry, panicked! Big gesture?'

I turn Jean slightly away so nobody can hear or see what we're saying.

'Jean, I don't know if Sam is even properly out yet, I can't *do* a big gesture,' I explain quickly.

Jean looks immediately concerned and shakes her head. 'I didn't think of that! You absolutely can't, it's a very personal journey coming to terms with your sexuality and how and when you tell people is that person's choice *alone*.'

I stare blankly at Jean. 'Yes I'm aware of that, Jean, so what am I supposed to do?!' I hiss, gesturing to everyone behind us who has begun to get restless and start chatting.

Jean not so subtly rushes away from the stage, dragging Tessa with her, who throws me an apologetic look.

My mouth is dryer than the shrivelled contact lenses that Kath leaves on our bathroom sink.

'I just wanted to say,' I croak, before seeing Jean gesture to speak up. I throw her a look that tells her that she is already on *wafer* thin ice and she quickly drops her hands.

'I just wanted to say . . .' I repeat a bit louder and I finally let my eyes drift to the spot where I know Sam is and see him watching me slightly quizzically. When he notices me looking he smiles and my head gets fuzzy. I look back to everyone.

'I just wanted to say . . . how proud I am of *everyone.* And thank you so much to Rachel and Flora who basically pulled this whole thing together.' There's a round of applause and Rachel and Flora beam at me. The applause goes on for longer than I thought, so I add, 'I mean, a lot of the creative inspiration was provided by *me,* but could not be executed without them, so actually I think I deserve a little bit of applause too . . . ?' To which there is a slightly less enthusiastic and notably shorter smatter of applause.

'But mostly I wanted to say,' and I look back to Sam and take a little intake of breath, just enough breath to say the thing I want to say next. 'I just wanted to say how much I like *Sweeney Todd.*' I let the moment hang there for a moment so Sam understands what I mean, so he knows I'm saying how much I like *him.* He tries to swallow his smile, but quickly loses this fight and his whole face lights up, the best lighting cue of the whole production by far.

'And I hope that Sweeney Todd likes me,' I add, raising my eyebrows at Sam.

He pretends to think for a second then nods, his eyes twinkling. When he nods, it's like putting on sunglasses that have nice lenses and everything suddenly looks a bit better, the whole world turns up a bit in volume and you feel like you could inexplicably do a backflip despite never being formally trained in gymnastics. I hear a small gasp and see Jean clutching her chest, her eyes brimming with tears while Tessa is doing a silent excited scream and running on the spot. Everyone else, however, looks . . . uneasy. And actually, this is understandable, because for everyone else, including Ms Jenkins, who looks like she's considering tackling me to the floor, I didn't just lay my heart out in a sweet but playful sort of way, instead I just admitted how much I like a fictitious serial killer and hope that feeling is reciprocated, which I think is a pretty universal red flag.

'Obviously, I don't like that Sweeney murdered people, I just meant, well, obviously murder is *very wrong*,' I blurt out and I hear Sam snort in laughter. I need to wrap this up before I end up coming out again.

'So I guess, the point I'm trying to say is that . . . murdering is wrong,' nodding confidently. I can't tell who, but one person starts clapping but quickly stops. Usually this type of humiliation would leave me in a steep downwards spiral, but not today. Sam likes me! I like Sam! And also, murdering people *is* wrong and I don't see the harm in making that super super clear through a public speech!

As everyone slowly begins chatting again, Jean and Tessa rush up to me. 'That was the single most beautiful thing I have ever heard in my entire life,' says Jean, her eyes huge and her voice warbling with emotion.

'Just perfect, Patch, *perfect*,' says Tessa reverently.

'Really?' I ask. 'It wasn't too . . .' but I don't actually have a word to finish it because I can't help agreeing with them. I completely nailed it.

'OK! That really has to be it for speeches,' calls Ms Jenkins, clapping her bejewelled hands above everyone's heads. 'Everyone out!'

Jean and Tessa and I are immediately caught in the sea of people leaving and I realize I need to actually speak to Sam. I turn around to see that he's already making his way towards me, pushing past Rachel and Flora who are trying to wrap up the fairy lights around their arms as quickly as possible. I realize there's no way that I can have a proper conversation with him now, not least because getting sprayed by strong chemicals isn't the romantic setting I had in mind, so I mime to him that I'll meet him outside. He nods and I follow the crowd out of the theatre.

Chapter 36

The road home, for all of its faults, has a certain beauty to it tonight. To be fair, all ugly things are a bit more beautiful when you can't see them very well, but this road could almost look like a dark still river (but a cement one and with more Ford Fiestas than rivers typically have).

Everyone said their goodbyes and exchanged their farewell cards as they left the theatre, but a small yet rebellious group (including Flora and Rachel, riding high from an organizational success) have gone to a pub in the hopes they will be served, but considering they're all wearing backpacks and two of them still have braces, I think it's going to be a round of Appletisers and cheese and onion crisps for them.

Although we're meant to be heading to Jean's house for our sleepover together, as soon as we leave the theatre, Tessa and Jean stumble their way through several reasons for why they have to leave ahead of me right this minute, even though we all know exactly the reason they are leaving. I can't tell you the number of times I've had to make myself scarce so other people can kiss, so it really is refreshing to see things from the other side. Jean whispers, 'Go get it,' in my ear as she hugs me goodbye before adding, 'Sorry, no idea why I said that, but remember if at any point you're not feeling it you can always say—'

'I think I'll be OK, thanks Jean,' I whisper back in her ear and she squeezes me tight one last time. Tessa goes for the much more conventional, 'Good luck, love you tonnes,' thank God.

So now it is just Sam and me and we're walking down the road, and because I'm feeling a bit nervous, I keep on pointing out landmarks except that there aren't really any landmarks in Hiverhampton, so I just keep on pointing out objects like a child learning to talk.

'That there's a lamppost,' I say clumsily. 'And it's a funny story actually, that lamppost has a sticker on it for an energy drink that simply doesn't exist, I've googled it.'

I begin to wonder if people can stop fancying other people when they tell boring stories about lampposts? Seems like I'm definitely going in the right direction to prove that theory.

'Interesting,' says Sam, kindly.

'It isn't, I'm just . . . nervous,' I say.

'Me too,' says Sam breathlessly.

Sam and I are both walking slowly with our arms crossed, which is definitely closed-off body language. I try to put my arms down by my side but am suddenly way too aware of my arms and feel like I'm not walking like a human so quickly cross them again. How is it that I find it so much harder to make private declarations than public declarations? I want to stop him right now in the street and say something cool like 'pucker up' . . . except definitely *definitely* not that.

I spot a turning. 'Let's go this way,' I say and I lead Sam off our current road and down the little street that I know leads into 'the fancy square', which is filled with all the houses that Jean and I love.

'In here?' he says nervously.

'Yeah, this is where the fanciest houses in the town are,' I explain to him. 'Jean and I used to walk around this square all the time and we would decide which house we would live in when we're older,' I say, gazing at the houses as we walk past. They're all very well-manicured and you can see little snapshots of the lives of some of the families as you walk past the windows, like flicking through channels on the television.

'Which house did you want?' asked Sam, as we walked past a house with ivy sprawling over one side in a fancy way.

'There was some friction with that,' I confess.

'Why is that not surprising?' replies Sam, grinning.

'I really liked the faded yellow one with the glossy black door on the other side of the square, but Jean likes this lilac one here,' I say, pointing to a house which is clearly empty because none of the lights are on.

'What was the issue?' asks Sam.

'Jean thinks that if we were going to live in the same square we might as well live next door to each other because then we can build a door between our houses and when the other one is on a weekend away, say in Italy, the other one could have two houses for one,' I explain as we carry on meandering around the square.

Sam contemplates this for a second. 'She makes a good point. What was your counter-argument?'

'Well,' I begin, but then our fingers brush past each other and my head goes all fuzzy again and I've never been so aware of my fingers and I have to really concentrate to grab hold of the sentence in my head. 'So, I thought . . . that if we lived on opposite sides of the square then, firstly, we could leave fun notes for each other on the top floor windows and also we could meet in the private communal garden in the mornings for a coffee as a halfway spot.'

Sam nods respectfully. 'Good counter-argument.'

'Thanks, I was pretty happy with it too. The only *issue* is I don't really know what it looks like in the garden because there are too many trees in the way,' I say as I cross the road to the black railing that goes all around the garden. 'So it might not be a good spot for coffee, but I can only assume it's very nice,' I call back to Sam, who is still standing on the other side of the road.

He quickly checks both sides of the road (safety conscious, check) before joining me as I try to peer through the railing.

'Haven't you ever tried to climb in?' he asks.

I turn around to face him. 'I think it's time to come clean to you,' I say in a very serious tone, dropping my head.

Sam's face blanks slightly. 'What?'

'The thing is, Sam,' and I take a dramatic pause, 'I'm not the daredevil you think I am.'

Sam bursts out laughing, relieved, but I continue. 'I know, *I know* it's shocking. I mean you've seen me wear cargo trousers for crying out loud and even though every single part of me screams "*adventurer*", I actually am quite a stickler for the rules.'

Sam manages to recover his composure, but he sucks his lips in to stop himself from smiling,

'I see,' he says gravely. 'While that is a huge and life-altering confession, I myself am not so much a stickler for the rules,' and he raises an eyebrow mischievously. 'Show me the entrance to the private garden, then.'

I lead Sam around to the other side of the square where there is an arched gate about seven feet high. Sam instructs me to turn around. 'I can't reveal all my tricks in one go,' he says mysteriously.

I turn away from Sam and the gate so that I'm facing a periwinkle-blue house, which has two perfectly round hedges on either side of the wooden door. I hear a fair amount of clanking and shaking but then Sam proudly exclaims, 'Tadah!' and I turn around to find him grinning by the open gate.

'How on earth did you do that?' I say, rushing up to him and poking my head through, afraid to go in in case alarms start blaring or something. I turn back to Sam and he zips his mouth closed and smiles.

'Are you sure we can go in?' I say cautiously, still on the pavement side of the gate.

'Only one way to find out!' he says confidently and marches into the garden where I quickly lose sight of him.

'Sam!' I whisper urgently. 'Sam!' but he doesn't reply, so I have no choice but to follow him in.

I can't make out everything in the garden because it's too dark but I can tell that it's beautiful, and not 'tarmac road at night' beautiful but properly beautiful. It's on a slight slope which I hadn't expected and is also smaller than I thought it would be. There are few patches of flowers running alongside the trees around the edge, but I can't tell what colour they are in this light, although I would guess a pale blue or lilac. In the middle of the garden there are two benches facing a beautiful tree which has long spindling arms and silvery leaves that almost rattle in the wind.

I can't see Sam, so I walk to one of the benches. It's made of a pale wood that almost gleams in the moonlight, there's an inscription on it that I have to lean in close to read.

Archie and Stan, who loved nothing more than to sit and talk about nothing and everything.

I get a little shiver and can't tell if it's the cold or not. I turn around and spot Sam, who is standing under the tree and looking up at it, and go to join him.

'Wow,' I say, looking up.

'Yeah,' he says.

But when I look down I realize that he's now looking at me.

'Oh, I haven't given you your card,' I say awkwardly and pull out the final card from my jacket pocket.

I hand it over to him and his thumb covers mine on the card, and we let our hands hang there for a moment.

'Thanks,' he says and pulls the envelope towards him. 'Shall I read it now?'

'Sure, or later, or whenever. I mean you don't need to read it *at all* if you don't want!' I chatter nervously, fiddling with the zip on my jacket and playing with the cold metal between my fingers.

Sam opens the envelope clumsily with cold fingers and shimmies the card out. He sucks his cheeks in slightly and his eyes (and cow eyelashes) flick up to me before opening the card and reading. He stares at it for a second but squints almost cartoonishly as he brings the card closer to him.

'Is there a spelling mistake?' I ask, wishing I had read

it over once more. 'Or grammar?! I *never* know how to use semicolons but just sort of wing it!'

'No, no, it's not that,' he says with the card still close to his face. 'I just – I can't read it in the dark.'

I relax slightly. 'Oh,' I say and he gives up trying to read it.

'Will you tell me what it says?' he asks, and takes a barely perceptible step towards me, but because I am so aware of *everything* at the moment that barely perceptible step looks like a giant leap.

I avoid his gaze and stare down at the card in his hand. 'I can't really remember what it says,' I say unconvincingly, grateful it's dark so he can't see how red I'm sure my cheeks have gone.

'Yes, you can,' Sam teases, and I look up to meet his stare. '*Please.*'

'Ugh,' I exhale. 'Fine.' Sam grins broadly at his victory and dutifully places his arms behind his back, ready to listen.

'OK. Basically there was sort of a joke about maybe booking a shave in with you . . . because you were playing Sweeney Todd,' I explain.

'No, I get it,' smiles Sam, nodding.

'And then I did a little PS at the end that I just can't repeat because it's too embarrassing, but you can look forward to that,' I quickly mutter.

'No, you *have* to tell me!' insists Sam, doing a little excited jump.

'Absolutely not,' I say firmly and shake my head. 'I draw the line!' and mime the line in between us.

'I'll *die* if I don't know what the PS said!' cries Sam, reaching out and grabbing my hand. 'You have to tell me.'

At Sam's touch, I'm worried my hand feels both clammy and freezing and force my skin to become a normal and casual temperature for him. My stomach is wriggling like you wouldn't believe, I can feel the blood roaring to my head and am surprised Sam can't hear my heart, which sounds like it's furious after being locked in my chest for so long.

Sam looks down at us holding hands, and his thumb presses gently into my knuckle. He looks back up to me, his smile gone and his breathing shallow. He closes his eyes, leans forward and I . . . of course, ruin it.

'I'm scared we're going to get told off!' I blurt out, just as Sam is centimetres away from my face. He pulls back, confused.

'What?'

'I'm sorry, I'm just scared we're about to get told off!' I repeat, anxiously looking around me. Both furious at myself for ruining the kiss and knowing that I can't kiss someone while my authority complex is kicking into overdrive.

'For being two boys kissing?' says Sam carefully.

'No! God, no, I'm not scared about being told off by like . . . God,' and I see Sam relax and do a sort of half-exhale, half-laugh. 'I just mean what if someone calls the police because we broke into the garden and maybe we'll be made an example of so people never do it again and I can't be made an example of, Sam! I won't survive in prison!'

I think the nerves that have been building up because of this expectant kiss all come out at once and I'm speaking at a million miles per hour, but Sam just looks slightly sheepish.

'We're not going to get told off,' he says matter-of-factly.

'How do you know?' I say, confused by his confidence in the rules of private-garden invasion.

Sam grimaces and looks slightly embarrassed. 'Because I live in one of the fancy houses,' he admits with his face scrunched up. 'I just wanted you to think I was cool and daring by breaking into the garden, but I didn't break in, I just put in the code.'

'Oh, thank God, Sam,' I say, my shoulders finally dropping, 'I've been trying so hard to be in the moment but I was just ready for floodlights to come on in the garden and a big voice to boom out yelling, "PUT YOUR HANDS WHERE WE CAN SEE THEM", or something.'

Sam chuckles, 'I really hope the police have bigger fish to fry. And there might not be floodlights but we do have this . . .' and he turns away from me and squats down by the bottom of the tree. I hear him rootling around at the base of the trunk and then makes a triumphant 'Aha!' As he flicks some sort of switch, the big sprawling tree above us lights up. I hadn't noticed in the dark, but there are tiny fairy lights wrapped around each of the branches twinkling in the night, and because everywhere else is so dark it's the only thing I can see and it's completely magical.

'Everyone always forgets the lights are there, but I like turning them on,' he says, pushing himself up and coming to stand next to me, his face now partly lit by the fairy lights.

'I can't *believe* you live in one of these houses,' I say. 'Wait, did I pick your house as my dream house?.'

Sam shakes his head quickly and looks over to the area that my dream house is, despite not being able to see it. 'No, but I would pick the yellow house with the glossy black door too. The problem is it's actually owned by the grumpiest woman in the world called Doris,' and the way he stresses the name *Doris* immediately makes me laugh. 'She once called me a "ne'er do well" for eating a sandwich with my hands.'

'How else are you supposed to eat a sandwich?' I ask, utterly perplexed by this piece of information.

'Ask Doris,' Sam replies seriously. 'Seems she has some pretty clear guidelines.'

I laugh and so does Sam, but then he looks nervous again, blinks and asks quietly, 'Is it embarrassing that I pretended to pick the locks on the gate to impress you?'

'Absolutely not. Is it embarrassing that I called these houses the "fancy houses"?'

Sam shakes his head. 'Is it embarrassing that I immediately bought *Sense and Sensibility* after seeing you read it so I would have something to talk to you about?'

A golden nugget glows in my belly, I smile and shake my head slowly. 'Is it embarrassing that my PS was me saying you had soft lips?'

Sam grins. 'Is it embarrassing that I missed when I tried to kiss you?'

I pretend to think for a second. 'Hmmm, it's all a *bit* embarrassing, isn't it?'

Sam smiles and looks up at me from his cow eyelashes.

'Mortifying,' he nods in agreement.

'Oh well,' I say, and without thinking, without giving myself another second to overthink my way out of it, I close my eyes and lean forward.

Epilogue

Dear Jean-Pierre,

It's me again, salut! I'm going to address the éléphant in the room and admit that I know you're receiving a lot of correspondence from someone who said you would <u>never</u> hear from them again, but I'm willing to forgive myself for that and encourage you to join me on that endeavour!

I'm staying at Jean's house (overly supportive friend with the hair clips). She and Tessa (we're friends again! I'll explain more in a future letter) have fallen asleep. I can't sleep because, and I can't believe I'm writing this, I HAVE A BOYFRIEND!!!!!!

OK, so technically I haven't got a boyfriend quite yet, but I wanted to reel you in and I'm also assuming that by the time this letter gets to you, Sam and I will have established our relationship and we will be boyfriends by then. What I can say with absolute certainty is that I've had my first kiss! I <u>know</u> what you're thinking, Jean-Pierre: 'Didn't you say you had your first kiss in your last letter?' And yes, but further information has led me to realize this was *not the case, but it's definitely the case now, I promise. I double-checked with Jean and Tessa AND an online forum and I definitely definitely just had my first kiss! Case closed! And I initiated it, if you can believe it!! Speaking of, don't be alarmed if you see little drops of red on the page; I initiated my first kiss with a little more gusto than I planned and accidentally headbutted Sam, causing my nose to start bleeding. But after we established that I was fine and he didn't need to call someone, we kissed properly and it was PERFECT!!!! To be honest with you (and I know I can be, Jean-Pierre) I didn't really know what to do kissing-wise, but luckily I had read in one of my mum's books called* Art-tractive: The Art of Enticing Your Way into His Heart, *that it's super important to keep your mouth relaxed. I'm worried I kept my mouth* <u>*too*</u> *relaxed and I looked dozy. Either way, Sam was gentleman enough not to ridicule me and although I don't have tonnes (or anything) to compare it to, Sam was a 10/10 amazing kisser. Ooh la-la!*

I wanted to kiss Sam until I died, but annoyingly I had to get back to Jean's parents' house because nothing ruins a romantic evening more than getting told off by your best friend's mum for being out too late. I still have to keep my relationship somewhat under wraps ATM (so please don't tell anyone in France) because Sam still isn't officially out yet and, to cut a long story short, his best friend is also in love with me (that's kind of my vibe now).

But obviously I had to tell Jean and Tessa everything, so we talked *about it for hours, but I made it super clear to them that I won't become someone who can <u>only</u> talk about their boyfriend. Neither of them believed me and that's fair because I'm 99% sure I will become one of those people, but sometimes life is about 'accepting who you are and standing in your power'.*

ANYWAY, I don't want to bore you with the details (unless you want them? Let me know! Very happy to send a follow-up with a detailed account!) but as someone who is newly committed, I also think it's important to give other relationships a chance in the same way Sam took a chance on me, so I'm thrilled to say, Jean-Pierre, that I am willing to rekindle our pen-pal relationship!!!

And I only have four rules!!!

- *You must write to me at least twice a month.*
- *<u>No</u> questions about my sister.*
- *Write at least one sentence in French.*
- *You come to me or I come to you ONCE in the next year (ideally me to you).*

I think that seems fair! You are of course allowed to have your own rules, but I'm pretty sure I've covered everything.

Can't wait to hear from you! Can you believe how much has changed in my life already? In the space of one term I've somehow managed to:

- *Come out as gay twice more (unplanned).*
- *Had one bitter friendship feud.*
- *Had two powerful friendship make-ups.*
- *Been unofficially banned from a local barbershop.*
- *Finally understood a 24-hour clock (unrelated, but still important!).*
- *Given an 'uncomfortably earnest' performance as Judge Turpin (I'll send a copy of the DVD).*
- *Had my first heartbreak.*
- *Broken my first heart.*
- *Had my first nearly kiss.*
- *Had my first actual kiss.*

I've got no idea what the rest of the year will bring, but I for one can't bloomin' wait and don't worry, I'll keep you VERY up to date with the journey.

Yours faithfully,
Patch Simmons, certified heartthrob (!!!!!)
xxx
PS Still waiting on that Milka bar.

Acknowledgements

I'd like to start by sincerely thanking my MacBook Pro 13-inch (2019). You've been there from the start and I'm sorry that I wore out your exclamation key because of how I am (!!!).

See, I can be playful! But now it's time to get serious. I mean this in the *most* literal way when I say that this book would not exist without my agent, Jessica Hare. Thank you for believing I had this book in me and thank you for coaxing it out of me over pasta and a train journey. For a long time, you were the only person who read this book; thank you for taking such excellent care of Patch, and of me.

My editors, Charlie Castelletti and Emma Jones. I've always dreamt of saying 'my editors' as I think it sounds impossibly chic but you two surpassed my wildest dreams. Thank you for your belief in Patch and your guidance with me. I'm sorry that I don't *really* know when to use a semicolon and I'm sorry that I continue to use them with reckless abandon. To the whole glorious team at Macmillan and Sara Goodman at Wednesday books, I can't thank you enough (but will endeavour to).

To Clementine Ahearne and Elizabeth Guess at ILA, thank you for letting this book be seen by as many people as possible and thank you to Rachel Vale for the cover design. I hope that people do judge this book by its cover because it's a wonderful one.

To my mum, you are the first person I ring when something is good or bad (or powerfully mundane). It is because of you that I can make brave decisions in my life. You believe in me too much sometimes, but that's alright because I love you too much sometimes. To Jack, I'll never forget that you took me to get lottery tickets on the day I came out to you because you thought a big day would equal a big win. We might not have won the scratch cards but I absolutely won the lottery with you.

To my family, I love you all so much I simply cannot deal with it! To my grandma who always believed I had a book in me, I miss you every day.

I could write a whole book of poetry about my friends but I'm still not positive what makes a poem a poem so it might take a while. You know who you are and I love you eternally. But a necessary shout-out to my Coffee Mornings WhatsApp Group (and the real friends it subsists of), you are the loves of my life. Until I get a boyfriend then you will be 'friends I was once close with'.

To my Row, thank you for making me laugh and for supporting and believing in me when I didn't believe in myself. I love you very much. And I know that you claim not to remember the fight we had about Ariana Grande but I just want to say right here . . . I forgive you.

There are so many people I've forgotten but I can hear the music playing so I must stop now.

But one last thank you (I promise). To you. Thank you for picking up this book and reading it, words can't express how much it means (because I used up all my words in this book). If, however, you've picked up this book and skipped straight to the acknowledgements, I do quite rate it?

And if you're someone who is reading this book who thought a big silly romance might not be for you, it is. It absolutely is. I wrote this book *because* of how much I believe that.

About the Author

©Patch Studios

Harry Trevaldwyn is an actor, comedian and writer born in Oxford.

His acting credits include *Ten Percent*, *The Outlaws* and *How To Train Your Dragon*, and he has multiple writing projects in development with leading production companies.

He is also the author of *The Romantic Tragedies of a Drama King*, which is surprising when you find out how long it took him to spell his last name.